TROUBLE ON THE TIDE

Eliza Kane Investigates
Book Three

Rosie Travers

Copyright © 2023 Rosie Travers
All rights reserved.

The characters and events portrayed in this book are fictitious. Any similarity to real persons, living or dead, is coincidental and not intended by the author.

No part of this book may be reproduced, or stored in a retrieval system, or transmitted in any form or by any means, electronic, mechanical, photocopying, recording or otherwise, without express written permission of the author.

Cover Design © Berni Stevens

ISBN: 9798853237612

For Neil

CHAPTER ONE

Eliza

VERY FEW MEN can pull off red velvet and Ian Kane wasn't one of them. Just as I was wondering how best to avoid the colourfully dressed character striding purposefully towards me along Cowes' cobbled high street, recognition dawned. He could have warned me he was back on the island.

'Hello there, Eliza.'

'Dad?'

'Got it in one, sweetheart.'

His cheeks were flushed crimson to match his jacket. As he leaned in to give me an awkward hug, I smelt whisky on his breath. Tucked under one arm was a flat parcel, wrapped loosely in brown paper. The other hand clenched a plastic carrier bag, concealing something bottle shaped.

'What on earth are you doing here?' I asked, untangling myself. As far as I was aware Dad hadn't stepped foot on the Isle of Wight for the last thirty years.

'I was coming to find you. Meg said you were temporarily based in Cowes.'

My sister knew he was here? Why hadn't she mentioned anything? After such a long absence Dad's return was a significant event, if not exactly a cause for celebration.

'You've seen Meg?' I asked, puzzled.

'I would like to,' he replied. 'But apparently she's too busy.' He mimicked a typical Meg eye roll. 'I spoke to her on the phone an hour or so ago. Anyway, my fault, I didn't let either of you know I was coming. Didn't know myself until a few days ago. I came to pay my respects to an old mate.'

It was a good three years since I'd last seen my father. We'd met for lunch when I was on my way to compete in a golfing tournament in Lancashire. He'd lost a little more hair from the top of his head since then and gained a beard which aged him a good decade. I'd certainly never seen him wearing anything so incongruous as his current choice of attire.

'What's with the fancy dress costume?' I asked.

'It was for the funeral service. It's what Stewie wanted, all mourners in red. I picked this up in a vintage shop in Harrogate. I'm rather fond of it, although I did get a few funny looks coming down on the train.'

He was getting a few funny looks now from a crowd of revellers sat outside the Anchor Inn enjoying their afternoon beers in the early spring sunshine. The dress code in Cowes was strictly nautical while Dad's costume was straight out of a 1970s sitcom. I was anxious to move on.

'Have you got a few minutes to spare?' he asked. 'I'm dying for a coffee.'

'I'm actually a bit tight for time. I'm helping a friend in his shop this afternoon.'

'Ah yes. I've heard about Charlie from Meg. No problem, I'll come with you. I'd like to meet this young man of yours. I understand he's quite an entrepreneur.'

Entrepreneur was not a term I personally associated with Charlie Harper's haphazard approach to life, nor was I sure he was mine, yet. However, I was doing my best to make both ventures successful. Despite having first met as teenagers twenty years ago, Charlie and I had only been dating for the last four months, while Making Waves, Cowes' newest sporting boutique, was a big jump up from Charlie's previous retail business in Ventnor. The shop focussed on high-end branded clothing and accessories aimed at the serious water sports enthusiast. I had worked in the shop regularly since it had opened just before Christmas.

After a successful career as a professional golfer, a persistent tendon injury had forced me to quit the competitive circuit the previous summer. Other than a vague *I'm taking time out to re-assess,* I hadn't told Dad how I was spending my newly acquired free time, but he must have received regular updates from Meg.

'You'll have heard of my old mate Stewie Beech, I take it?' he said as he fell into step. 'His death must be big news here.'

Everyone in Cowes knew Stewie Beech and I knew that today was the day of his funeral. What I didn't know was that he and my dad were friends.

The Isle of Wight was a sleepy little place out of season, but the death of the local restauranteur who had established a lucrative business by combining two of the island's top attractions, gourmet food and sailing, had been the talk of the town for the past couple of weeks. Stewie's restaurant was located on a restored 1920s wooden motor yacht and had a three-month waiting list for a table. *Absinthe's* regular clientele included premier league footballers and TV soap stars. Charlie's assistant manager Dexter dated one of the bright young things who worked as Stewie's waiting crew.

'Wasn't it a heart attack or something?' I slowed my pace, realising Dad was struggling to keep up.

'Apparently.' Dad gave a nod. 'I always thought Stewie was as fit as a fiddle, the last candidate for a cardiac arrest. He ran five kilometres every morning before breakfast and drank no more than two glasses of red wine a day.'

Dexter's girlfriend Amelie had said something similar.

'These things happen,' I pointed out. 'Being a chef can be very stressful.'

'Tell me about it,' Dad agreed. 'Horrible way to go though, all alone, stranded on the mudflats.'

I hadn't paid too much attention to the exact details, but I was aware Stewie Beech had been found dead on board a dinghy in Newtown Creek, approximately six miles from Cowes.

'Wasn't he fishing for the catch of the day or something?'

'Nobody seems to know exactly what he was doing there,' Dad replied. 'No need to be fishing, the restaurant didn't open on a Tuesday. Poor Pilar is mystified.'

Poor Pilar was Stewie's Spanish born wife, twenty years his junior and the real culinary talent behind the business, according to Amelie.

I pushed open the door of Making Waves and was pleased to see at least half a dozen customers browsing the merchandise. Charlie was occupied at the till. Dexter had taken the day off to accompany Amelie to Stewie's funeral. He hadn't mentioned the colour co-ordinated dress code.

I'd promised to cover the last couple of hours of business so Charlie could take his son to Heathrow Airport. Twelve-year-old Lucas was off to visit his mother Rowena in Athens over the half-term holiday. Charlie looked up and did a double take when he saw Dad. He'd never met my father but could probably deduce Ian Kane in his red smoking jacket and bold checked trousers was not a typical Making Waves customer.

I gave him a reassuring smile and beckoned Dad to follow me through to the staff kitchenette at the rear of the shop.

He wanted his coffee black which was fortunate as Charlie was down to his last dregs of milk in the fridge.

'It's been a bit of a day,' he remarked, plonking himself on a chair. He placed his carrier bag on the floor with a clunk and slid the flat package under his seat.

'How did you and Stewie know each other?' I asked, handing him a mug.

'We grew up in the same part of Leeds and went to catering college together.'

'Funny you should both end up working on the Isle of Wight – at different stages of your careers, of course.'

'Stewie's been here for years. He had previous restaurants in Yarmouth before moving onto that fancy yacht of his. I heard all about it at the service. The eulogy was a full career resume.'

He sounded bitter, although I wasn't sure why. After leaving Clifftops, my grandparents' hotel in Ventnor some thirty years ago, Dad had had a very successful career of his own, running a variety of restaurants and pubs across the north of England.

'What's in the packages?' I nodded at items he'd placed on the floor. 'Have you been shopping, or did you get left something in the will?'

'Sort of.' Dad bent forward and pulled down a corner of the plastic carrier to reveal a dark green bottle. 'Stewie left instructions for a bottle of absinthe to go to each of his friends.'

'Very generous. What about the other one?' I nodded at the brown paper parcel.

'It's nothing, just a painting Pilar wanted out of the house.' He manoeuvred the flat package further under his chair with his feet. 'Some old landscape. I offered to take it off her hands.'

'I didn't know you were an art lover.'

'I'm not. She said it had brought nothing but bad luck since the day Stewie bought it. You know what the Spanish are like, full of superstitions.' He shifted his weight on the chair. 'Anyway, that's enough about me. How is your wrist and what are your future plans?'

I was glad of the change of subject. 'My wrist is much better, thank you.' I rotated my hand to demonstrate its renewed flexibility. 'As for my future plans, it's early days but I'm involved with a new initiative aimed at making golf more accessible and attractive to young people, especially girls. In fact, I'm attending a junior coaching session in north Hampshire next weekend. Golf Sparks encourages youngsters to give the sport a go. We're hoping to take the programme out nationally into clubs as well as sports centres and schools later this year.'

'That's great, love. Do you miss the tournament circuit?'

'I thought I would, but I'm enjoying the quiet life for a bit. If Golf Sparks takes off as I hope it will, I'll be very busy. The only downside is the amount of travelling I might have to undertake. I want to put my roots down here on the island. I'm helping Charlie in the shop, I'm studying an online journalism course to improve my communication and social media skills, I go to the gym, and I've got my new house to keep me busy.'

'Oh yes, I was quite surprised when Meg said I'd find you working in a shop. I thought you'd be up to your neck in plaster and paint.'

Before I could explain the novelty of renovating my new house had soon worn off and I had passed the challenge over to a team of professionals, Charlie popped his head around the staffroom door. 'I've got to shoot off now, Eliza. Are you able to come and serve?'

'Yes of course. Charlie, this is Ian–'

'Pleased to meet you, mate.' Charlie grabbed his jacket off the coat hook. 'Sorry, but I've got to dash.'

As Charlie flew out of the door, Dad handed me his coffee cup. 'I'd better get going.' He picked up his carrier bag and reached for his parcel, tucking it under his arm. 'I thought I might stay on the island for an extra night or two. How about we get together tomorrow evening for dinner?'

I hesitated for a second. Dad rarely initiated meetings, it would seem ungrateful to refuse. 'Sure, why not? Meg too?' There was safety in numbers.

'Of course.' As he rose the painting slipped free from its wrapping and slid to the floor with a clatter. 'You couldn't pick that up for me, could you?' he asked after an awkward attempt to bend down. 'It's my knees. The NHS say I'm too young for replacements.'

It wasn't my father's knees which worried me, but his honesty. A framed canvas bearing a crude depiction of a male nude lay face up on the floor.

'It's not what you think it is,' he said, refusing to meet my questioning eye as I crouched down.

I wasn't sure what I thought about it at all. Why claim the painting to be an "old landscape" when it clearly wasn't? To spare my blushes? I was thirty-six, not sixteen. If Dad wished to collect portraits of naked young men that was his prerogative. On the other hand, I could quite see why Pilar might not want the painting in the house. It was the last thing I'd want hanging on any of my walls.

'I'll be in touch to let you know where and when for dinner,' he grunted, hastily re-wrapping the picture in the brown paper.

Baffled by his behaviour, I took up my post by the till and watched him saunter out of the shop without a backward glance, clutching the illicit piece of artwork to his chest like a hard-won prize.

CHAPTER TWO

'THIS STILL FEELS weird.'

'You're going to have to improve your pillow talk, Charlie.'

It was the following morning. Charlie and I were snuggled under the duvet.

'You know what I mean, Lizzie. You, me, together. Sometimes I can't get my head round it.'

I ran my fingers across his bronzed chest. 'You're not having second thoughts about us, are you?'

'No, of course not.' He gathered me in towards him. 'Quite the opposite. You're the best thing that's ever happened to me. I feel like I'm the luckiest bloke on the planet.'

Together like this, I had no reason to doubt Charlie's sentiments. When our paths had collided the previous summer, romance had been the last thing on either of our minds. After a couple of false starts, we'd finally got our act together after one of my sister Meg's charity fundraising events in the autumn, a night which would remain forever engrained and cherished in my memory. Thinking about Charlie always brought a smile to my face, thinking about that particular night with Charlie sent my whole body into a delicious ripple of sizzling tingles. We were treading cautiously. Waking up together was a novelty, as opposed to weird as he had not so eloquently put it. With Charlie's parental duties and the upheaval of moving homes and changing careers, opportunities to spend time together like this had been scant. Charlie was adamant he didn't want to risk Lucas catching us in bed together. Up until now overnight stays had been confined to a handful of occasions before Rowena had left for Greece, or whenever Lucas went on sleepovers with friends. I was looking forward to having him to myself for a whole week.

'Who was Father Christmas?' Charlie asked, when we broke apart several minutes later. 'That old bloke you were entertaining yesterday?'

It had been gone midnight before he had returned from dropping Lucas off at the airport. I'd been too sleepy for anything but the briefest of conversations. 'That was my dad.'

'Your dad? Why didn't you introduce us?'

'I was about to before you rushed off. Anyway, you'll have other opportunities to meet him. Tonight, for example.'

'Tonight?'

'Yes. He was back on the island for Stewie Beech's funeral. They were at catering college together. He's staying for another night and wants to take us out for dinner.'

'Meet the parents. That's getting serious, isn't it?'

Charlie had a natural aversion to the word "serious". I'd known his parents almost as long as I'd known him, becoming reacquainted with them over the summer when Lucas had attended my junior golfing academy and they'd been tasked with picking up and dropping off. When I'd accompanied Charlie to the family's traditional Boxing Day buffet I'd been introduced as Lucas' golfing instructor. He had so far not considered it necessary to give them an update on our status.

'Knowing Dad, more than likely he'll change his mind,' I told him. 'I'll get a phone call later saying he's on the train north.'

'What does Meg think?'

'Unimpressed when I spoke to her yesterday evening, but she agreed to come along. She's bringing Frank for moral support.'

My sister was a social worker employed by the local authority. She tended to keep her relationship with Frank, a volunteer at the island's aircraft museum and fifteen years her senior, very low key.

'How was the funeral?' Charlie asked. 'Must have been a big crowd.'

'I'm sure it was. Everyone had to wear red.'

'That explains the odd outfit. Or does he always dress like that?'

'To be honest, I wouldn't know. We've not seen an awful lot of each other over the years.'

My parents had separated when I was six and Meg seven; memories of our early family life were blurred. Meg and I had been dispatched at Easter and during the summer school holidays to stay with Dad at our paternal grandparents' house in Leeds, but when we were in our teens, the holidays had dropped off. Instead we were invited to visit at our own volition. Meg rarely did, but as I regularly travelled across the country to compete, I made a point of meeting Dad for lunch or dinner if I was passing through Yorkshire. An hour or two in his company was usually enough. I really didn't know him at all.

'Pretentious posh nonsense nosh,' Charlie said, interrupting my thoughts. He leaned back on his pillow, arms behind his head.

'Excuse me?'

'I remember it now. That's how one of those celebrity food critics described Stewie Beech's floating restaurant a few years back. I offered to take Rowena there when I was still trying to make things work. She told me not to waste my money.'

Charlie rarely divulged details of his relationship with Rowena. Now that he'd moved back to his old stomping ground in Cowes, I was very aware of her presence. It was easy to imagine

Rowena's cutting rebuffs to Charlie's attempts to save their relationship. Rowena and Charlie's split had been acrimonious. I so wanted to make him happy, to be everything Rowena was not – caring, loving, loyal.

'Oh Charlie,' I sighed, rolling into him again, filled with a rush of tenderness.

'Oh Lizzie,' he echoed, misinterpreting my sigh, or maybe not. 'As much as I'd love to linger, I've got a shop to open. We'll catch up properly later.'

Planting another kiss on my lips he swung out of bed and disappeared into the ensuite shower room to indulge in the invigorating delights of the South American rain forest. I was renting a modern three-bedroom apartment in Cowes while my house in Seaview was undergoing renovation. When Joel Campston, my builder, had offered me use of his sleek Airbnb at a discounted rate, I'd jumped at the chance. Joel's flat was just streets away from the family home Charlie shared with Lucas – the next best thing to moving in together, which would never have worked so soon into our relationship. The state-of-the-art shower was one of the many bonuses of the apartment and I'd already asked Joel to incorporate an identical system at Goldstone Villa.

I languished in bed until I heard Charlie leave. Entering the bathroom I picked up his used towel from the floor and returned it to the radiator, before stepping into the steaming shower cubical.

If Charlie and I did decide to live together at some point in the future, regardless of my selfless devotion, he was going to need some serious house-training.

'ISN'T THIS WONDERFUL,' Dad announced later that evening as we settled into our seats. He beamed around the table like a benevolent Old Father Time. He'd booked dinner in a tapas restaurant near the waterfront. I was pleased to see he'd discarded the smoking jacket and check trousers and was dressed demurely in chinos and a navy blazer. What he'd forgotten to tell us was that he would be bringing a companion along. Tess was a lean overly tanned platinum blonde in her early fifties.

Meg gave Dad a brittle smile. 'All we need is Mum and her latest boyfriend and we can play happy families.'

There had been no mention of Tess yesterday and I wondered if she'd accompanied Dad to the funeral. I'd managed to hiss 'you could have warned me' at him when we'd arrived at the restaurant, but he'd given me one of his infuriating *what are you worried about* shrugs. I wasn't worried about Tess, I'd long got used to the idea, however, inexplicable, that a certain type of woman found my dad attractive. I just had trouble remembering their names and didn't like putting my foot in it, as I had been known to the in the past. Offering one girlfriend condolences for the loss of another's parent had not been my finest hour.

'How long have you and Dad been seeing each other?' Meg asked Tess as the wine waitress appeared at the table brandishing the only bottle Dad had pronounced fit for purpose from the restaurant's extensive beverage menu.

'Ooh, let me think. Four months or so.' Tess gave Dad's arm an indulgent pat.

'Swiping right, were you?' Charlie asked.

'No, we met through work.' She deliberately raised her voice as the young waitress struggled with the cork. 'I'm an environmental health inspector.' The waitress jumped, splashing the wine all over Meg. Tess gave a peal of laughter. 'Only joking. I hired Ian as my head chef.'

'Your head chef?'

'Yes, I run my own pub on the outskirts of Harrogate.'

Last time I'd seen Dad he'd been the one running a pub.

Meg dabbed at her jumper with a serviette while Dad sniffed the wine. 'It's corked,' he announced to the waitress. 'Fetch another bottle, will you?'

I sensed it was going to be a long evening. Charlie squeezed my thigh under the table.

'Eliza tells me you and Stewie Beech were at catering college together, Ian,' he said. 'Did you ever get invited onto *Absinthe* for a meal?'

'I've heard all about it,' Tess cooed before Dad could answer. 'I wonder if the business will carry on? Have you seen that painting his wife gave us? Isn't it hideous? No wonder she wanted to get rid of it.'

'You didn't mention any paintings, Dad,' Meg said. 'What's this?'

'It's just a painting,' Dad replied, waving his hand dismissively.

Tess whipped out her phone. She had captured the nude in its full glory. 'You don't forget that once you've seen it, do you?' she said, cheerfully flashing the picture around the table. 'I'm wondering if it's by someone famous. The signature's just a squiggle. Looks like a B, possibly an A. It'll be one of these modern artists, won't it? Banksy or something.'

'I don't think Banksy is known for his life drawings,' Meg remarked under her breath. She refused the offer to study the snapshot in detail.

'Looks like one of those Birdie Adams' pictures to me,' Frank said, craning his neck for a closer look. 'Those red lips give it away. That's her trademark.'

'Who's Birdie Adams?' Tess asked, eyes wide.

'She was part of the 1980s figurative movement,' Frank replied.

'You sound like quite the art connoisseur, Frank,' Charlie remarked, his face twitching with amusement.

'I'm not, but it was all over the news a few years' back. A family in Ryde found one of her pictures in their loft. They were on one of those television shows where people bring their antiques to be valued. Turned out to be worth a small fortune. Birdie Adams stayed on the Isle of Wight back in the 70s and early 80s. After the show aired, everyone on the island was rummaging through their attics and garden sheds to see if they had one too. You should ask Lilian's friend Kurt Zeigler to have a look at it for you. He knows about art. He used to teach it.'

Another surprise. Kurt was a fellow resident of my grandmother's care home in Newport, a quiet but congenial elderly gent with a fondness for Fair Isle sweaters. I had no idea what he'd once done for a living. Frank had an uncanny knack for worming information out of people.

'How is Lilian these days?' Dad asked. 'I suppose I ought to pay her a visit while we're on the island.'

Meg raised an eyebrow. 'I'm sure she'd love to see you.'

'We'll pop in tomorrow.' Meg's sarcasm was lost on Dad. He threw Tess a look. 'Although not to talk about art.'

I couldn't help but wonder whether his reluctance to be drawn into a conversation about his painting was because he had his own suspicions about its worth. Pilar Beech was not going to give away a valuable work of art simply because she considered it unlucky – unless she shared my ignorance of the art world. I'd never heard of Birdie Adams and would Google her later. If her work was collectable, there were bound to be prints and imitations out there on the market. There was no reason to assume Stewie Beech had purchased an original.

Tess slipped her phone back into her handbag.

'Isn't Stewie Beech one of the sponsors for your BizziKids' nature camp?' Frank said after a few moments, giving Meg a nudge.

'He *was*.' Meg frowned. 'He pledged a large donation. I'll have to check with the treasurer to see if he actually made the payment. The camp won't be able to go ahead without it.'

'What's BizziKids?' I asked. Meg was involved in lots of good causes on the island but this was a new one on me.

'It's a club for families with children who've been diagnosed with ADHD,' Meg replied. 'The group receive no funding from the council and rely entirely on donations. We were hoping to take them to a nature camp in the New Forest at Easter.'

'Stewie was generous to a fault,' Dad sighed, shaking his head. 'Helped me out a few times early on in my career.'

'Yes, I understand he supported a lot of a charitable causes,' Charlie said. 'Not that I'm implying you were a charity, Ian. Sorry.'

'No offence taken, lad.'

The first round of tapas arrived. Dad took great delight in describing each culinary mouthful. Apart from his running commentary, with added remarks from Frank who was a tapas virgin, conversation remained stilted. As the meal neared its end, Tess took centre stage. We learned she had held down all manner of jobs, everything from dinner lady to traffic warden, before finding her forte in hospitality. She'd single-handedly brought up her two boys, Marlon and Harvey, who were both now involved in the tech industry.

'Probably gamers,' Charlie hissed into my ear.

'So what if they are, love,' Tess smirked. 'They're making a packet out of it.'

She had one grandson Sonny, who had just turned two. Sonny's mother had been consigned to history and was no longer part of either Marlon's or Harvey's life, whichever one was the father. Tess had the little boy overnight once a fortnight.

Meg stifled a yawn.

'You know what, love,' Tess remarked as Meg placed her hand over her wine glass to prevent a top up, 'you'd be a lot more pleasant if you let yourself go every now and then.'

'And you'd be a lot more pleasant if you kept your mouth shut.' Meg was stone-faced.

Beside me Charlie, in a valiant attempt to refrain from laughing, choked on the final Padrón pepper. Frank leapt from his chair to give him a hearty slap on the back.

Dad attempted to redeem the situation by ordering brandies and whiskies all-round. 'Still on the *Jim Beam*, Eliza love?' he asked with a wink. I was touched he'd remembered, but less touched when he requested the bill and asked the waitress to split it three ways. 'That all right with you boys?' he said, nodding at Charlie and Frank. I could feel the heat of Meg's smouldering outrage from across the table. I asked the waitress to split the bill into six. Dad handed over his card and assured Tess he had her portion covered.

'That was a jolly evening,' Charlie said after we'd said our goodbyes and headed out into the street. 'I think we both need something to take our minds off that disaster. What's it to be. Your place or mine?'

CHAPTER THREE

WE OPTED FOR Charlie's as it was closest. If I was honest, I disliked sleeping in Rowena's bed, in sheets she'd chosen, in a room decorated to her somewhat bohemian tastes. Charlie was oblivious to the reminders of his ex which filled the family home, having made little or no changes since moving back in. He left early the next morning and I didn't linger. With Lucas away, Charlie had accepted an invitation to spend Sunday on the water with friends from the local sailing club. I didn't resent the intrusion into our weekend; we had plenty of opportunities to be together during the week. After a brief debate on whether to give the kitchen a quick clean – a couple of days' worth of crockery was stacked in the sink as if Charlie had yet to remember he owned a dishwasher again – I headed back to my apartment for a soothing shower.

When I emerged from the rain forest fifteen minutes later, I had a new voicemail on my phone.

'Hiya hun, it's Tess. Your dad's had a bit of an accident. I've taken him to A&E at St Mary's hospital, but I've got to get back to Southampton to catch the train as I'm due to have Sonny tonight. Ian should be ready to collect later this morning.'

Seriously? It sounded horribly like Tess was inferring I should pick him up. Dad was her responsibility, not mine. Surely Sonny's overnight stay could be postponed? I dialled her number.

'Hi Tess–'

'Sorry to dump that on you, hun. You'll be able to look after him, won't you? I didn't want to miss the ferry.'

Look after him. It was getting worse. 'What's he done?'

'Tripped off the kerb on the way home from the restaurant last night. We thought it was just a sprain, but he didn't sleep a wink. His ankle's swollen up like a watermelon. The landlady at the B&B said we ought to get an x-ray to check it out. Turns out he's chipped a bone. They reckon he'll be in plaster for six weeks.'

I heard a Tannoy announcement in the background. She'd abandoned Dad some time ago if she was already at the ferry terminal in Cowes.

'How's he going to get back to Yorkshire?' I asked.

'That's just it, love, he can't. At least not until he can manage public transport on his crutches. Coming back to the pub isn't going to be practical anyway, not with all the stairs.'

'Right. I see.' I didn't like the way this conversation was going at all.

'I've packed up his stuff at the B&B and told the landlady you'll be over to collect it.'

'Can't he stay there?'

'She's already got the room booked out. You'll be able to put him up until he can put some weight on his foot, won't you? You've got lots of space in your apartment, or so that dishy boyfriend of yours was saying last night. Sounds delightful. Three bedrooms, two with ensuites, underground parking, lift, panoramic views. Ian'll love it.'

I was quite sure Ian would love it too, but I certainly wouldn't.

'Got to go, hun, they're boarding now. Keep in touch, 'ey?'

She'd gone.

This was my week with Charlie. I'd planned a cosy evening in at my place tonight, cuddled up on the sofa watching a film without being distracted by the photograph of him and Rowena which had pride of place next to his TV. I'd no idea why that particular keepsake had remained on display in the family house during Rowena's period of sole occupancy, or why Charlie had failed to remove it on his return. On the other hand, I had to remember it was Lucas' home too. Not that he seemed particularly attached to his mother, having chosen to remain in the UK with Charlie when she'd moved to Greece. Sadly, I knew from my own experience that family dynamics were never that simple. I didn't possess a single photograph of my parents together.

DAD WAS WAITING for me in the main entrance to the hospital in a wheelchair.

'Ah, there you are love. What took you so long?'

'Excuse me?'

His left leg was plastered up to the knee. 'It's just a temporary casing,' he explained. 'They want me back later this week to the fracture clinic. Hopefully they'll put me into an air boot.'

An air boot would be perfect – then he could manage the train journey back to Yorkshire. 'Have they given you an appointment?'

'They're going to ring me. Talking of which, my phone's just died. The charger's at the B&B. Have you been over there to collect my stuff yet?'

'No, I thought we'd do it on the way back to mine.'

'It's very good of you to offer to put me up, I do appreciate it.'

I hadn't offered. I'd been coerced.

Dad eased himself into the passenger seat of my BMW convertible and we set off back to Cowes. At the B&B the landlady handed me the plastic carrier bag which now contained half a bottle of absinthe and a holdall which I flung into the boot.

It was only when we were unloading in the car park beneath the apartment that Dad asked what I'd done with his painting.

'The landlady didn't have it. This was all there was, a holdall and your bottle.'

'That bloody bitch has taken it, hasn't she?'

'You mean Tess?'

'She was on the internet the minute we got back to the B&B last night. I should have guessed what she was up to.' He pulled his phone from his pocket, then swore loudly when he remembered it needed charging. 'She'll get a shock if she tries to sell it on.'

'A very pleasant one if it's by that artist Frank was talking about last night,' I remarked.

'I can tell you now, categorically, it's not a Birdie Adams. At least not a real one.'

'Oh?'

'It's a fake, a copy, and Pilar was right about one thing, it is bloody unlucky. Look at me.'

'Your broken ankle has nothing to do with bad luck and everything to do with booze. You tripped over because you were drunk.'

We reached the lift. Once up in the apartment Dad made himself comfortable on the leather sofa in the lounge, admiring the views of the Solent from the big picture window.

'You did all right with this place, didn't you love,' he called as I headed into the kitchen to make the requested cup of milky tea. 'Perfect spot.

You can show me your house in Seaview whilst I'm here, and I wouldn't mind a trip down to Ventnor, for old times' sake.'

I did not intend to spend the next few days being Dad's private chauffeur. As well as keeping Charlie entertained in the evenings and covering shifts at Making Waves, I had a full social calendar of my own. In any case, Dad needed to rest his leg.

'Goldstone Villa is a building site,' I called from the kitchen, 'full of tripping hazards. You'd be better off waiting to see it when it's finished.' Work was ahead of schedule, but the house wouldn't be ready until the summer. I loaded two cups of tea onto a tray and headed back into the lounge. 'Tell more about this picture. I'm intrigued. How do you know it's a fake?' Dad's claim had aroused my curiosity, especially after the story Frank had told us last night.

'Stewie had it valued a few weeks ago. He'd always assumed it was a Birdie Adams' original but turns out it's a worthless imitation. Pilar reckons the shock brought on his heart attack.' Dad lifted a mug off the tray and took a slurp of his tea. 'Are you sure you put three sugars in?'

'Definitely.' I settled into the armchair opposite him. 'Does she think Stewie was deliberately conned?'

Dad nodded. 'Stewie acquired the picture a couple of years back. Pilar doesn't know who sold it to him. Most likely somebody cashing in on the publicity after that TV programme Meg's bloke was talking about. Whoever conned him as good as killed him. The poor girl is distraught. That's why I took the picture. I offered to try and find out who did this. Now that bloody bitch has run off with the evidence.'

Tess had clearly done her homework. I hadn't got round to doing mine – Charlie had proved too much of a distraction.

'You've not exactly got an awful lot to go on,' I pointed out.

'I'll have talk to Pilar again, get some more details. The funeral wasn't the time and the place. We only had a short conversation while she was presenting me with the bottle of absinthe. Nice gesture that. Typical Stewie.'

Dad had been given a high dose prescription painkiller and he fell asleep as soon as he finished his tea. I texted Charlie warning him I had company, giving him an opt out clause for the evening meal which I still had to prepare, or rather purchase.

Charlie responded he was more than happy to keep to our evening plans with the addition of the gooseberry.

'*I thought your dad was great fun*', he added, ending his text with a winking emoji. He probably wouldn't be saying that after another evening in his company but leaving Dad snoring loudly, I slipped down into town while the shops were still open.

He woke up on my return and hobbled into the guest bedroom to phone Tess. It was impossible not to overhear every word of the heated message he left on Tess' answerphone. The walls in the apartment were not thick, which didn't bode well for Charlie staying over, or for a good night's sleep if Dad's earlier snoring was anything to go by.

'I've told her it's worthless,' Dad huffed when he returned to the lounge. 'But knowing Tess, she won't believe me. She'll think I'm trying it on.'

'What Tess said last night, about you working for her,' I ventured. 'I hadn't realised you'd changed jobs. What happened to the gastro pub in York, the one where I saw you last?'

Dad gave a shrug. 'You mean Turpin's? I fancied a change of scenery, that's all.'

I was under the impression Turpin's was one of his triumphs but held back making a comment. I didn't want to start dissecting Dad's life choices in case he started dissecting mine. Perhaps Tess had made him an offer he couldn't refuse.

I was very pleased to see Charlie when he arrived at six thirty bearing gifts of wine and a bunch of grapes for the patient. The day's sailing had left him with his trademark glow of windburn, salt infused dirty blonde hair and an intoxicating waft of sea spray – just the way I liked him.

'Dave and Fiona want you to tag along next time they venture out,' Charlie said, following me into the kitchen. 'They're off to Poole in a couple of weeks, but I told Fiona she wouldn't want the cleaning bill for the ruined upholstery. I think she understood.'

Dave and Fiona were a newly retired Scottish couple Charlie had befriended at a sailing club social. I had an unnatural aversion to waterborne activities and was grateful Charlie had declined their invitation on my behalf.

Both men seemed appreciative of the meal I served up, which was some consolation. It was the first time I'd ever cooked for Dad, although technically it was heating up, as opposed to cooking. He was full of praises. The upmarket frozen ready meal shop in Cowes was a lifesaver.

Over coffee he recounted the whole sorry saga of Tess' defection to Charlie. 'You're a man of the world, son. Any idea how a woman's mind works?'

'Not one bit, Ian,' Charlie replied.

Dad had returned to his prime spot on the sofa. I placed a row of cushions on the glass coffee table so he could keep his ankle elevated. 'I just hope whoever she tries to flog Stewie's picture to has the good sense to get an expert valuation before agreeing a price.'

'I'm surprised he didn't check its authenticity before acquiring it in the first place,' Charlie replied. He had pinched the armchair, leaving me the other end of the sofa. 'You'd have thought he'd need a proper valuation for insurances purposes. I assumed he was an astute businessman, but perhaps not. How well did you know him, Ian?'

'We were close as youngsters but lost touch in our early twenties,' Dad admitted. 'Five or six years ago we ran into each other in York. It was not long after he'd married Pilar. One of his boys was at university in the city. Stewie was visiting the lad and came to my pub. We'd been featured in one of those local lifestyle magazines they leave in hotel rooms. He read the article and looked me up. After that we met up whenever he was in the city. He even offered me a share in *Absinthe*, after all we had once talked about doing something similar together years ago.'

'You and Stewie Beech had contemplated going into business together?' I was surprised Dad had turned down the opportunity.

'We did work experience on a barge when we were at college. One of the guest lecturers had converted a narrow boat on the Leeds to Liverpool canal into an exclusive eatery. He took me on afterwards, full-time, but sadly he sold the place after a couple of years. Stewie and me talked about running our own floating restaurant. Just a pipe dream really.'

A pipe dream for Dad maybe, but Stewie Beech had succeeded in making his dream a reality.

'I didn't have the money to invest when Stewie made me the offer,' Dad continued. 'He'd already purchased the boat and the restaurant was up and running.'

'That yacht must have cost a fair bit,' Charlie mused. 'It certainly helped launch Stewie and Pilar into Cowes society. They seemed like a couple with a lavish lifestyle.'

'That sounds like Stewie,' Dad replied with a nod. 'I got the impression he offered me the share for old times' sake, not because he needed the additional finance. He didn't seem put out I didn't take him up.'

'If Pilar thinks Stewie was deliberately scammed, she really should go to the police,' I said.

'She said the police weren't interested. That's why I offered to help.'

'Now you've got Eliza on board I'm sure you'll be able to crack the case between you.' Charlie gave me wink before turning back to Dad. 'I take it she has told you about her sideline as a private investigator? Eliza is a secret super sleuth.'

'You kept that quiet, love,' Dad said. 'I'd appreciate all the help I can get.'

'Without the offending piece of artwork, it's going to be impossible to prove anything,' I remarked.

'You've never let lack of evidence hold you back before,' Charlie said with a grin. 'Eliza is a woman of many talents, Ian. I hope she's told you about her work promoting golf to young people?'

'I've heard a little bit about it,' Dad said with a nod. He shuffled along the sofa and put his arm around my shoulders. 'And the journalism, and the house renovations. I'm very proud of everything Eliza does, always have been. Not everyone can say they have a national champion for a daughter. She's my little star.'

It was many years since I'd been a champion of anything, but I appreciated the compliment. 'Aah, Dad, that's lovely. I'm proud of everything you've achieved too.'

'You shouldn't be. My life hasn't been a resounding success story like yours. Being a chef is tough and running a business in this industry, even tougher.' He shook his head.

'But you've done really well.' I gave him a friendly prod in the stomach. 'You've owned some fabulous restaurants and pubs. You cook great food.'

'And look at me now. Sixty, overweight and out of work–'

'You're not out of work. You've got the job in Tess' pub.'

'Umm. She's stolen my painting, love. I'm not going to go back and work for her now, am I?'

'You'll find something else,' I assured him. 'Why don't you buy another place like Turpin's, go back to being your own boss?'

'I don't have the money to buy my own place, I never have. Handouts, business loans, mortgages, partners, that's how I've always survived. Turpin's nearly broke me financially. I'm better off when I'm working for someone else. Everything I touch seems to have failure written all over it.'

The dad I saw on those fleeting visits north was congenial and jolly. Conversations were lightweight. I complimented him on his cooking, he praised my golfing achievements. I'd never heard him speak like this before. I was hit with a sense of shame. I had no idea he'd been struggling to make a living all these years when I'd had the money and means to invest.

'Why didn't you ever say anything? I could have helped you out.'

'I'd never ask you for money, Eliza. I'm your dad. I'm supposed to look after you, not the other way round.'

I felt tears prickling in the corner of my eyes, overcome with an emotion I couldn't quite define. The room fell silent.

'You know what, I'm going to shoot off.' Charlie jumped up from his chair. 'I've got some paperwork to do, and I think you need some dad and daughter time.'

'Charlie, you don't need to go–'

He bent to give me a kiss. 'I'll catch up with you tomorrow.'

Dad reached out and clasped his hand. 'Lovely to meet you again, son.'

'You too, Ian.'

Dad gave me a comforting squeeze as Charlie slipped out of the apartment. He cleared his throat. 'Do you know what, love, it's funny how things work out. I'm kind of glad I fell off that pavement now.'

The wobbly feeling returned as I felt myself welling up again. I rested my head on his chest. My voice was little more than a whisper.

'I'm kind of glad you fell off that pavement too, Dad.'

CHAPTER FOUR

Chrissy

CHRISTINE NOBLE HAD received the news of Stewart Beech's passing via a text. The sense of loss took her by surprise. She wasn't upset enough to burst into tears or throw herself distraught onto the bed, but the gut reaction had been unexpected. She thought she'd made herself immune.

She asked to be kept informed of the arrangements. It had taken some time; first the post-mortem, then the usual winter backlog at the crematorium.

Friday, 21 February, 11.00 am. Wear red.

Wear red. That was so Stew. The life and soul, joking to the end.

She made her excuses. Root canal treatment. The boys didn't press her. They knew how she felt about their father.

She wondered what would become of the business. Would sweet little Pilar soldier on? Stew had never been able to keep any of his multiple businesses afloat and Chrissy doubted *Absinthe* would prove the exception. Never one to let lack of funds hold him back, she was quite sure there would be debts for the widow to pay off. It was the boys she was sorry for. They'd get nothing. She knew how that felt.

On the day of the funeral she stuck to her normal routine, rising at dawn and tending to the animals in turn; Frida her young golden retriever, always first for attention, Tabs, her rescue cat, then the chickens and the geese, and finally her new arrivals, a pair of alpacas. After that she pottered in her polytunnels, sewing seeds and planting up.

She'd moved to Merryvale four years ago. The cottage was in dire need of fixing up, but it wasn't the property's interior that had interested her, it was the land that came with it. She had just over six acres complete with paddocks, stables, and various outbuildings.

Matt said he would visit at the weekend – if she wanted him to. Although she knew it was wrong to have favourites, she enjoyed her middle son's company best out of the three. He was a gentle giant, the calm sandwiched between two squabbling storms. He took after her in looks, which was a blessing, and was the only one of her boys not to follow Stew into the culinary arts. Callum worked as a sous chef at a Michelin starred restaurant in London, and Joshua, despite taking a degree in chemical engineering, now ran a trendy deli-cum-café-bar with his girlfriend in Winchester. Matt was a carpenter, a talented craftsman, sharing her love of nature and creativity.

He'd come out to her on his twenty-fifth birthday; she'd suspected he was gay long before that. There had been girlfriends over the years, but they'd never lasted. Matt was thirty now, still living by himself but comfortable in his own skin.

She told him only to come if he could afford to take the time off. Matt was self-employed, often working seven days a week.

'Don't be silly, Mum. Of course, I can take the time off.'

He took her to the local pub for a meal. They raised a glass and drowned their sorrows. She sensed Matt shared her conflicting emotions. She liked her local, where she was just mad Chrissy, a woman who spent more time with her plants and animals than people. She knew what the other regulars thought of her and how little they thought about her. It suited her to remain an eccentric enigma. One of the few benefits of ageing. You no longer cared what other people thought.

Matt didn't offer her a blow-by-blow account of the funeral service and she didn't ask. She didn't want a list of who had turned up to pay tribute; the new acquaintances Stew had cultivated in

Cowes, *the old friends*. It was best to not to know.

He talked about his latest orders and they discussed her aspirations for a bumper summer harvest.

'I want to concentrate on improving my strawberry crop this year,' she told him. 'I could put out a table and sell the surplus at the gate.'

'You'll need a proper stall,' he said. 'I'll make something for you.'

Chrissy smiled. Matt, just like his father, was full of good intentions but he didn't always deliver. The stall would go on the list with all the other home improvements identified at Merryvale, still awaiting attention. Chrissy wasn't bothered. Matt's paid commissions had to take priority and she was proud of his success.

He stayed over on the Saturday night and drove home on Sunday after a walk through the surrounding fields with Frida. Now it was Monday morning and time to restore her equilibrium.

With the animals fed and watered, she made herself a mug of steaming ginger tea before heading across the yard to one of the outbuildings. Another joy of Merryvale, the previous owner had converted a former stable block into a studio. Chrissy had her own private artist's retreat. She settled down at her easel, canvas in place. She hadn't felt the urge to continue this piece since receiving the news of Stew's death. It was a simple charcoal outline, but today she was going to add a splash of colour. She gave her ex-husband the briefest of thoughts before twisting open a new tube of Winsor & Newton. She took great delight in watching the paint ooze from the nozzle onto her pallet with a single squeeze. Quite fitting really. Carmine. She dipped in her brush and swiped a streak of red onto her canvas.

CHAPTER FIVE

Eliza

DAD HOBBLED INTO the kitchen wearing nothing but a pair of check boxers and carrying a bundle of laundry.

'I've run out of clean clothes,' he announced. 'I didn't bring an awful lot with me. Can you run this lot through the wash, and any chance you could pop out later and buy me a couple of new shirts? I'm going to be here for at least a week while we wait for the hospital appointment.'

'Maybe we can chase the hospital later on this morning,' I suggested. Lucas was only away for seven days. I wasn't sure how much more bonding Dad and I needed to do. I'd been overcome with sentimentality the previous evening, but it was surprising how quickly sentimentality evaporated when accompanied by a bag of dirty underpants. 'I'll pick you up a razor too while I'm out shopping, as you seem to have lost yours.'

'I expect your Charlie will be able to find me something suitable to wear in his shop, won't he?

Surplus stock or something. And I'll call Pilar and ask when she can see us. We need more information if we're going to get to the bottom of who killed Stewie.'

'I think you're being a little over dramatic. Until we, or rather you, find out who and where Stewie bought this picture from, we mustn't jump to any conclusions.' I wasn't entirely comfortable with being railroaded into help. Charlie may have over-played my role as amateur detective. I was naturally curious and solving puzzles provided a challenge once fulfilled by playing competitive golf, but both the previous cases I'd investigated had revolved around events in my grandmother Lilian's past, and neither had turned out quite the way I'd hoped.

I fetched my kimono from the bedroom and made him put it on. It just about covered his paunch. There was only one half-dressed man I wanted wandering around my apartment and his body was in a far better shape than Dad's.

Leaving him with a bowl of cereal, I headed over to Making Waves. Before snatching a quick hug in the stockroom, Charlie donated an XL fleece and two polo shirts from his customer returns collection.

'Your dad can have these. Hopefully they'll fit. I went online last night and ordered a waterproof cover for his cast. It'll make it easier for him to have a shower.'

'Thanks Charlie. That's very thoughtful of you.'

'You're welcome. It should arrive this morning. I've dealt with plenty of broken limbs in my time.' Charlie's medical knowledge far outweighed mine. He'd experienced all sorts of mishaps during his years as a scuba diving instructor and had first aid certificates galore.

I kept my arms firmly around his waist. 'I know Dad couldn't help having his accident, but this is supposed to be our week together.'

'Your Dad isn't Alistair Stonehouse, he's not going to stop me coming over, is he?' Charlie nuzzled my neck playfully.

I'd only recently learned my stepfather Alistair had warned Charlie off dating me as a teenager. I didn't resent the twenty-year wait because I'd had a brilliant career in the meantime, but even so, the thought of Dad snoring away in the room next door put a dampener on my plans for a fun filled week of unbridled sex with Charlie.

'No, I know but–'

'We'll just have to be inventive.' Charlie put a finger on my lips. He slid his other hand teasingly under my shirt before we were interrupted by his assistant, Dexter.

'Ah, there you are, mate. I've got a problem with the till.'

Dexter, a sandy-haired twenty-something with a degree in retail management, was a real asset to the Making Waves' team, and not just because of his professional skills. He shared Charlie's sporting physique and with matching navy polo shirts showing off their tanned biceps, the pair were a glowing advert for the healthy outdoors lifestyle the shop promoted. I left them sorting out the technical glitch and picked up some more groceries to keep Dad happy. The courier arrived at eleven and I helped Dad into the bathroom, insisting he remain in the kimono until he was alone. It was a good half an hour before he re-emerged, looking and smelling an awful lot more pleasant than he had earlier in the morning.

PILAR AGREED TO see us at two that afternoon and I wanted to be prepared. As a relative newcomer to the island, even more so to Cowes, I wasn't yet part of any social circle and was ignorant of local gossip. I tried to find out what I could about the Beeches online.

The Island Echo's news pages had reported Stewie's demise as the "Tragic Death of Local Entrepreneur". Details were sparse but it appeared he'd set off from the marina in Cowes in his motorboat around midday on a Tuesday morning in January, only to be discovered twenty-four hours later in Newtown Creek. The coroner had concluded Stewie had suffered a fatal heart attack whilst fishing.

According to its website, *Absinthe* was the top

gastronomic experience on the island, winning a string of accolades. Originally designed as an archetypical 1920s gin palace, the yacht had been part of the flotilla of boats used to rescue the British Army in Dunkirk in 1940. It had been fully restored to its former art deco glory by a previous owner who had rescued it from the River Medway in Kent in 2010. *Absinthe* now offered an intimate dining experience for up to twenty-five customers. The Beeches' ten course taster menu incorporated a fusion of traditional Basque recipes made with ingredients entirely sourced from the Isle of Wight.

Further reading revealed Stewart Beech had opened his first restaurant in Yarmouth in the early 1990s and had been married to his second wife, Pilar, for five years. Besides his love of cooking, Stewie was a keen athlete. There was no mention of the first Mrs Beech in the chef's online obituary, but the piece stated he was a father of three.

A picture of Stewie accompanied the write up. In a red shirt, suntanned and glowing, he posed on his pleasure cruiser with the chalk stacks of the Needles behind him. He looked at least ten years younger than Dad but was born in the same year. A hastily added banner on the restaurant's home page informed me that no further bookings were currently being taken.

The Beeches' house, Sandpipers, was located in Gunard, just a short drive from Cowes. I could have probably walked it quicker than the time it took to manoeuvre Dad from the sofa, down to the car park and in and out of my car.

The electronic gates opened to reveal Pilar waiting on the doorstep, the epitome of elegance in a belted grey silk dress and heeled knee-high boots. Still on the right side of forty with ombre hair tumbling past her shoulders and dark Mediterranean eyes, she greeted us in a throaty voice with a prominent Spanish lisp.

'Ian, so good of you to come, especially in the circumstances.' She threw her arms around his neck. Dad had explained about his injury on the phone.

He hugged her for far longer than necessary before releasing her and introducing me. 'My daughter, Eliza. Professional golfer and more recently, private investigator.'

'A private investigator?' Pilar stepped back with a frown. Her wrists jangled with bangles and three diamond studs adorned each ear. We were about the same height, but confronted with her slender beauty, despite my regular gym sessions, I felt gauche and ungainly. In addition, double denim was not the most professional outfit I could have chosen. I should have made more effort to look like a proper detective – a beige mac over a smart business suit would have probably done the trick, not that I possessed either item in my wardrobe.

'Eliza is going to help us find out who conned Stewie with that painting,' Dad explained. 'You said the police weren't interested. Between us we'll get to the bottom of this and bring the perpetrators to justice.'

His confidence was very convincing. Pilar clasped her hands in prayer against her chin. 'Oh Ian, I'm so grateful. Stewart always said you were a true friend. Come on through.'

We followed Pilar to a vast kitchen smelling of freshly brewed coffee. I thought the integrated barista machine in my rented apartment was high tech, the Beeches' appliance took up almost an entire wall.

She invited us to take seats on a rattan sofa in an adjoining conservatory. After a few minutes she joined us, bearing a tray of espressos and some delicious looking petit fours.

As soon as she sat down, she burst into tears. For a man with his leg in plaster, Dad could move very deftly when he wanted to. He slid along the sofa and encompassed her in his arms.

'Let it all out,' he soothed. 'You've had a terrible shock.'

'It's awful,' Pilar wailed. 'I wake up every morning alone. I don't know what I'm going to do.'

'Do you not have any family staying with you?' I asked. A box of tissues was strategically placed on a side table. I handed it to her.

She shook her head. 'My mother is in Bilbao. She looks after my elderly grandmother and cannot leave her. My father died when I was just ten.' She gave a hopeless shrug. 'My older brother is very protective, but he disapproved of Stewart. We are, how you say, estranged.'

Dad released his grip and shook his head. 'That's sad. Stewie was a good bloke.'

'I know,' Pilar agreed. She gave her eyes a delicate dab with her tissue. 'He was the best.'

'What about Stewie's sons?' I enquired. 'Are they not still here?'

'They left straight after the funeral.'

'You shouldn't be on your own at a time like this.' Dad took the crumpled tissue from Pilar and handed her another. 'Someone should be here with you.'

Was he about to volunteer? I wanted him out of my apartment, but I didn't want him making a complete fool of himself.

'What about friends?' I asked.

Pilar sniffed but didn't answer, keeping her attention on Dad. 'Do you like rabbit, Ian?'

'I've got a couple of good recipes, yes,' he replied with a slight frown.

'Wait one minute.' Pilar slipped off the sofa and disappeared into the kitchen where we heard doors being opened.

'Is she inviting us for dinner?' I whispered after a few minutes of bemused silence, wondering if she'd gone to retrieve said rabbit from a freezer somewhere.

Dad gave a shrug.

Pilar returned clutching a ball of white fluff. 'This is Alfonso,' she announced, sliding back into position on the sofa. She placed the trembling creature on her knee. 'I don't know what I'd have done without Alfonso since Stewart passed.' She ran her hands along the rabbit's back, his pink nose twitched appreciatively.

I cleared my throat before Dad could put his foot in it any further by suggesting Alfonso could provide even more comfort if stewed with carrots and onions. 'What can you tell us about this forged painting, Pilar? You don't know who Stewie bought the picture from, or where?'

As part of my research, I'd skimmed lengthy online biographies to find out what I could about the artist Birdie Adams. Information was confined to heavyweight cultural websites, but I'd learned she'd spent several summers painting on the Isle of Wight, which she described as a haven of tranquil creativity. She'd never married and had worked as a chemist before devoting her later years to art. I'd found a reference to the story Frank had mentioned. The painting discovered in a Ryde attic, similar in style to the one now in Tess' possession, had been featured on an episode of the popular daytime TV show, Treasure Trove on Tour. The programme's eagle-eyed fine art expert, Albie

Whittaker, had valued the painting at between twenty and thirty thousand pounds. Birdie had not been a prolific artist and much of her work remained in the hands of private collectors.

Pilar shook her head. 'He just he turned up with it one day.'

'Can you remember when this was?' I took out my phone and placed it on the table, pressing the record button. Just because I hadn't dressed like a private investigator, it didn't mean I couldn't act like one.

Pilar took a deep breath. 'It was two, maybe three years ago. I'm sorry I can't be more exact.' She turned to Dad. 'I hope you've put it in the trash, Ian?'

'It's gone off with the trash all right,' Dad confirmed.

That picture was the only evidence we had – and we didn't have it. Tess did. We could prove nothing unless we could get it back. I gave Pilar a sympathetic smile. 'I don't suppose you've any idea how much he paid for it?'

She shook her head, continuing to fondle Alfonso's ears. 'He never said and I didn't ask. We don't, didn't, scrutinise each other's spending. We have separate bank accounts for our personal finances.'

The Birdie Adams painting featured on Treasure Trove on Tour had been valued at a five-figure sum. If Stewie had paid a similar amount for his painting, there ought to be a record of the transaction somewhere. It was a lot of money to spend in one go without your partner knowing.

'I take it you have a business account for the restaurant?' Dad asked.

'Of course. He couldn't take any money out of that without me knowing. We also have a joint account for household bills.'

I wondered how receptive Pilar would be to a request to trawl through Stewie's personal bank statements – that's if she had access to them.

'When did Stewie discover the picture wasn't an original?' Dad continued.

'The middle of January. He took it to London. This was just days before...' She faltered and reached for another tissue. 'Just days before his heart attack.'

'I totally understand this is very difficult for you,' I said. 'Do you know why he decided to have it valued after all this time? Or where he went for the valuation?'

She shook her head. 'He told me he was seeing a specialist art dealer. I told you my grandmother is elderly. She needs full-time care. Mamá has found a nursing home for her, but it is expensive. I speak to Stewie and he tells me this painting could help with the costs. He does it for me, you see. He will sell this painting for me. And then, when he comes home from London, he tells me it is worthless. He was so angry. He goes into his study. I hear him making calls, shouting on the phone.' Pilar clenched her fist against her chest, sounding very angry herself. Alfonso took shelter, burrowing into a gap between the sofa cushions. 'Who would do this to us? To Stewart? He was a good man with a big heart, and this broke it. How do I tell Mamá the money we promised is not there?'

CHAPTER SIX

IT WAS IMPOSSIBLE not to sympathise with Pilar's plight. I suggested we take a break and offered to fetch her a glass of water. She directed me to the fridge.

'These phone calls you heard Stewie making when he returned from London, do you think he was trying to contact the people who sold him the painting?' I asked when she indicated she was ready to continue.

She gave a shrug. 'He wouldn't tell me who he was talking to. He brushed me away.'

'What about over the next couple of days? What did he do?'

'He was out a lot. He doesn't tell me where he goes or who he sees. Then on the Tuesday lunchtime, I hear him in his office, shouting again and then he storms out. He is putting on his coat, his jacket, his boots, and I ask *where are you going this time*, and he says out on the *Little Lady*. That is our motorboat. In Spain we have a saying, you never take a voyage on a Tuesday.' She threw her hands in the air. 'It's why we don't open the restaurant. He knows that. What was he thinking? It is only later when he doesn't come home…' Her words were lost in another flood of tears.

Dad leaned across to offer up another tissue, almost squashing Alfonso in the process. 'Now don't you worry, Pilar love, me and Eliza are going to find these fraudsters. They won't get away with it. We're going to need a list of all Stewie's contacts, personal and business, and if you have his financial records from around the time he acquired the painting, we should be able to see whether he made a cash withdrawal, or even better, a bank transfer for a substantial amount of money. Can you think just a little harder about the exact dates. Is there anyone else Stewie might have confided in about this painting? What about the boys?'

'I haven't spoken to the boys about this.' Pilar lifted Alfonso back onto the safety of her lap. 'I'm not sure they knew their father had the painting.'

'We'll have to talk to them,' Dad continued. 'Could you let us have their phone numbers?'

'Did they get on well with Stewie?' I asked.

Pilar gave a brief nod. 'Oh yes, he was close to his boys, and I always tried to make them welcome, but you know, I was their stepmother…there were difficulties.'

'Parenting is never easy.' Dad gave her a sympathetic smile.

'Talking to the boys would be helpful,' I agreed. 'And Dad is right about looking through financial records. You have access to Stewie's personal bank statements?'

'All our banking is online, but Stewart liked to print out the statements. He's old-fashioned. He likes, liked, paper records. I think I will be able to find them for you.'

'Thank you,' Dad said. 'What other close friends did Stewie have? Have you looked through his phone? Gone through his contacts lists, recent calls, anything that might lead us to these people?'

'I don't have his phone.' Pilar raised her voice again. 'That's another thing. I have to go to the police station to collect Stewart's things and it's not there. No phone. Where has it gone? He wouldn't go out on the boat without his phone.'

'Perhaps the police kept it?' I suggested.

'Why? They aren't interested. He die of a heart attack whilst fishing, they say. Case closed.'

'Who found Stewie?' Dad asked.

'It was Anton, our sommelier. I'm a heavy sleeper. When I'm not working I go to bed early. I didn't realise Stewart hadn't come home until the morning. Then I panic. I have this premonition something terrible has happened to him. I phone Anton and he calls Brian Riggs, *Absinthe's* skipper, to ask if he has seen Stewart–'

'Are Brian Riggs and Anton friends Stewie may

have confided in?' Dad interrupted. 'Make a note of those names, Eliza.'

I pointed to my phone. 'I'm recording, Dad.'

'Good girl, of course you are. So Anton and Riggs–'

'Riggs tells Anton he saw Stewart the previous day when he set off in the *Little Lady*. Riggs hadn't realised Stewart hadn't returned to the marina. They call the coastguard, take a boat and start a search. Then they find him, moored up in Newtown Creek–'

I interrupted again. 'Moored up? Not drifting?'

'Did Stewie take regular fishing trips?' Dad cut in before Pilar could answer.

She nodded. 'Yes, but like I said, not on a Tuesday because the restaurant doesn't open.'

'But no-one would have suspected anything was wrong when Stewie set off?'

Pilar shook her head, biting on her lip. 'I don't understand what he was doing. When they give me back his clothes, I see mud on his boots, grass on his trousers, as if he has gone ashore, hiking across fields.' She raised her voice again, throwing her hands into the air. 'Where does he go ashore? Why? What for?'

Dad put his arm around her shoulders. 'No more fretting,' he said. 'We can't bring Stewie back, but we're going to do our damnedest to ensure the people who did this to him, to you and your family, are brought to justice.'

I returned my phone to my bag and stood up. 'Thanks for taking the time to talk to us, Pilar. I think we've got enough information to go on for now.' It was a lie, but I had to stop Dad making more false promises.

Dad rose to his feet with a wince. 'How about I come back tomorrow to look through those bank statements? Meanwhile, could you compile a list of Stewie's closest friends, staff, business associates, anyone who you think might be able to help us. What else will we need, Eliza?'

'I think you've got it covered, Dad.'

Pilar placed Alfonso onto the floor and he hopped off happily towards the kitchen.

'You've just the one?' I asked.

Pilar nodded. 'Alfonso was a present from Stewart. I kept rabbits as a child.'

I'd read on the restaurant's website that Pilar had been raised on a farm. Rabbit was a popular ingredient in Basque cooking. I imagined the rabbits she'd kept as a child had regularly made their way onto the family's table.

'Are you planning on opening up the restaurant again?' Dad asked as Pilar accompanied us to the front door. 'I suppose you'll need to employ a new chef.'

If he was hoping to be offered a job, I suspected he'd already ruined his chances. I doubted *Estafado de Canejo* would appear on Pilar's menu anytime soon.

'I have cancelled all our bookings for the next month,' Pilar sniffed. 'I will have to have a serious think about the future.'

'You know where we are if you need us,' Dad said. 'I'm just glad I'm going to be useful while Eliza's stuck with me for a few weeks.'

A few weeks? Where did that come from? I'd hoped we'd be looking at days. I flashed Pilar a smile.

'We'll get cracking on this straight away,' I assured her.

'WHAT DO YOU make of that then?' Dad said as we returned to the car, the dainty vision in grey waving us off from the front door.

'She's grieving, struggling to come to terms with her husband's death and looking for someone to blame,' I replied. 'Stewie was conned three years ago. It's going to be hard proving anything. I feel sorry for her, but I don't think we, *you*, should get too involved.'

'Umm. I'm just glad I got that picture out of the way before she realised it was a portrait of Stewie. Then she'd be even more worried.'

I slammed my foot on the brake. 'What do you mean, before she realised it was a portrait of Stewie?'

'I mean, potentially, it could have been him. That must have been why he bought it. Vanity.'

In my mirror I saw Pilar step off the doorstep,

heading towards us, a puzzled look on her face. I held my hand up and gave her a reassuring wave before continuing out of the gates. As soon as we were out of sight and into a convenient spot, I pulled over.

'Why would Stewie Beech think Birdie Adams would paint a picture of him?'

'Because he modelled for her when we were over here on holiday back in the early 1980s.'

'You just happened to run into Birdie Adams while you were on holiday?'

'We met a group of girls when we were camping. One of them lived locally and Birdie was staying with her family. She used their barn as a studio. This girl posed for her all the time, or so she told us. She said the old lady was looking for new models. Stewie did it for a dare.'

'Why didn't you tell me this yesterday? No wonder you were so quick to take it off Pilar's hands.'

'I did the right thing though, didn't I?'

'I suppose so. When I saw you on Friday you said Pilar told you the picture was unlucky. Did you make that up?'

'No, I did not. Shortly after Stewie acquired the painting he got caught speeding again and lost his driving licence. Then he fell out with one of his boys. After that he got into a public slanging match with some restaurant critic or other who'd written a really bad review. On top of everything else, they had a hefty maintenance bill for *Absinthe*, engine failed or something, and they couldn't afford to miss a whole season of not taking her out. That's part of their USP, isn't it? Cruise, booze and food.'

Once again, I detected a trace of bitterness in Dad's voice. I wasn't sure *cruise, booze and food* was quite the tagline Stewie and Pilar had aimed for.

'Sounds like Stewie's run of bad luck was very much of his own making,' I remarked, checking my mirror to ensure the road was clear before pulling away. 'Tell me more about this holiday where you met Birdie Adams. Is that when you and Mum got together? I always thought you two met when you started working at Clifftops.'

'We did. This was before that. I came on holiday with some mates from Leeds. There were four of us.'

'Were you staying at Ryde? That's where they found that picture Frank told us about.'

'No, we were camping on the south of the island, just outside St Lawrence. After we got friendly with the girls, we moved our tents to this family's house. As soon as Pilar showed me the picture, I recognised it. I knew it was one of Auntie Birdie's, as they called her. They kept on about how famous she was the whole time.'

'Let's go and get a coffee somewhere. You need to tell me more about this holiday.'

CHAPTER SEVEN

Pauline's Pantry was my new favourite café in Cowes. I installed Dad in a window seat and made my way to the counter to order two cappuccinos and a cupcake.

'Did you all pose for Birdie Adams?' I asked when I re-joined him at the table. I wanted to eliminate the horrible scenario of a picture of Dad turning up at some point.

'No, of course not. I thought she was barmy, to be honest.'

'How do you know that picture is of Stewie?' Birdie's representations of the human form paid scant attention to detail, devoid of recognisable facial features apart from those lurid red lips.

'Stewie had no interest in art. He would never have bought that picture unless he believed it was based on his sittings. He modelled for the initial drawings but none of us saw the finished article.'

'I suppose it would explain why Stewie was convinced the painting was genuine.' I sipped my coffee while Dad took a chunk out of his cupcake. 'It could also mean whoever sold him that painting knew he'd once posed for Birdie.'

'Not necessarily,' Dad argued through a mouthful of chocolate chips. 'It could just be a coincidence. It was a long time ago and it's odd that that particular picture should surface so recently. We don't know it's based on Stewie's sittings, but I imagine he thought it was. We need to ascertain whether there have been any other art scams on the island in recent years. I'll have a search on the internet. See what I can find out.'

'That's a good idea, but as we've currently not got anything else to go on, let's start with thinking about everyone who was there with you that summer. Maybe someone who had a grudge against Stewie. Put your thinking cap on. Who else knew about this sitting?'

BY THE TIME we returned to the apartment, Dad had whittled our list of suspects – or rather the other house guests he recalled from his holiday – into four distinct factions: the lads from Leeds, a group of girls from Nottingham, the host family, and some "arty-farty" students from Brighton School of Art. Apart his own friends from Leeds and two of the girls from Nottingham, names eluded him. I wasn't sure if he genuinely had a case of memory loss, or whether he was being deliberately obtuse because he didn't want to believe anyone he'd encountered on that holiday could be responsible for what had happened to Stewie forty years later.

Of the girls from Nottingham, two had gone on to marry lads from Leeds. One, Pam, had married Dad's school friend Dennis Pacey, while the second, Chrissy, had become the first Mrs Stewart Beech.

'That's interesting,' I remarked. 'Did you all stay in touch?'

'Only for a bit. We went our separate ways shortly after.'

'Shame we haven't got any photos. That might jog your memory. I thought you were into photography?' It was one of the few facts I knew about my dad. I'd once admired a set of artistic black and white prints which had adorned the walls of one of his former restaurants and had been surprised to learn he'd taken them himself.

'We didn't go around snapping selfies back then like you youngsters do today,' he replied. 'Anyway, I have got photos. They'll be in an album somewhere in my sister Debs' spare room. Debs has got a stack of my old stuff.'

Debs was a distant memory from my childhood stays in Yorkshire.

'Why is Debs holding onto your old stuff?' I asked.

'Where else am I going to store it? I haven't got a place of my own anymore, have I?'

'What happened to that flat you used to own in Leeds? Don't tell me you've had to let that go too?'

'I'm not entirely feckless. It's rented out and right now is my only source of income.'

We fell into an uncomfortable silence. After a forty-year career in the catering trade Dad had very little to show for it. I was aware we had just witnessed all the trappings of success on display at the Beeches' residence. I decided not to press him any further. When he did hobble off back to Yorkshire, I would do what I could to help him out – whether he wanted it or not.

CHARLIE ARRIVED AT seven thirty with a takeaway and a welcome bottle of Merlot. After two glasses and a dose of painkillers, Dad retired to his room at nine.

He'd not mentioned hearing back from Tess, but I had her number on my phone following her call from the ferry terminal. She picked up after a few rings.

'Hello?'

'Hi Tess, it's Eliza here, Ian's daughter.'

Her tone changed in an instant. 'What do you want?'

'I wanted to let you know how he is and ask you about that painting.'

'I've got no idea what you're talking about. I've had enough of this abuse. First Ian, now you. I haven't got his flippin' painting and you can tell

Ian from me that I've packed his stuff into a couple of bins bags and taken it round to Marlon's garage for storage. I can't be without a chef for six weeks.'

'It won't be six weeks. He's having an air boot fitted in a couple of days and could be back at work next week–'

Tess ended the call. I tried ringing back but was cut straight off. I'd been blocked.

The following morning, Dad didn't emerge from his bedroom until Charlie had left for Making Waves. I had an appointment to check up on progress at Goldstone Villa and forestalled any attempt by Dad to join me by giving him the password to my laptop.

'You need to take it easy today and keep the weight off your foot. See what other cases of art fraud you can uncover. And maybe come up with some more names of those people you met on that holiday, then we can eliminate them one by one. Why not ask your sister to send down your photo albums? It might help.'

He gave a grunt. 'Good bloke, your Charlie. Known each other long?'

It was a deliberate distraction technique. 'We played golf together when we were teenagers at Clifftops,' I explained. 'We ran into each other last summer and hit it off.'

'He mentioned his son, he's been married before?'

'Not married, no.'

I gave Dad a brief run-down of Charlie's life to date, or what little I knew of it – *grew up on the island, parents still in Ventnor, went travelling in his early twenties and met fellow diving enthusiast Rowena Pallet in the Red Sea*. I'd asked Charlie early on in our relationship why he and Rowena had never married. He'd replied Rowena made it clear it wasn't important to her.

Wasn't it important to you? I'd wondered at the time. I was confused as to why that bothered me. I was well aware of Charlie's "commitment issue" as Meg regularly referred to it. I wasn't even sure marriage was important to me. At least, not until the right man asked.

'They returned to the UK when Lucas was about four,' I told Dad, quashing that particular train of thought. What was I thinking? I valued my independence. 'Rowena and Charlie ran a dive school together here in Cowes for several years. When their relationship broke down, Charlie moved back to Ventnor. Now Rowena has a new partner who is setting up a yacht charter business in Athens, Charlie has returned to Cowes to look after Lucas full-time.'

'He seems very fond of you. I like the idea of both my girls settling down. It's about time.'

Yet again I bit back the urge to comment. My father was a fine one to talk about settling down.

He pushed his unfinished bowl of muesli to one

side. 'I don't suppose you could run me to the barbers before I go over to Pilar's again this afternoon?'

'I'm glad you want to smarten yourself up, but you could be a bit less obvious.'

'What's that supposed to mean?'

'Pilar. You were all over her yesterday. It was embarrassing.' I couldn't shake off the horrible suspicion Dad's eagerness to find Stewie's swindlers was not entirely motivated by loyalty to his old friend, but a desire to impress Pilar with the aim of getting into her kitchen and/or even worse, her knickers.

'I can't help being tactile.'

'Is that what you call it? Anyway, when you do see her, ask her more about this fishing trip. It clearly concerns her and could be significant.'

'She's just being superstitious. Stewie gets all het up about his painting and goes off in his boat to chill out. Makes sense to me.'

I wasn't so sure. 'What about the mud on his boots, the grass on his trousers?' I reminded him. 'Ask her how many fish he caught.'

CHAPTER EIGHT

Joel Campston had estimated the renovation of Goldstone Villa would take six months. I'd fallen for the house because of its Edwardian charm and had initially wanted to retain and reinstate as many period features as possible. However, now that I was enjoying my sleek waterside apartment, Joel had the task of marrying the house's former elegance with easy living high tech modifications. I didn't doubt he would succeed, mainly because he was being assisted by Faye Cassidy, an old school friend who was now a major interiors influencer. Faye was hoping the refurbishment of Goldstone Villa would catapult her up the interior design ladder and onto mainstream TV. She and Joel were now an item and the project could make or break both their careers. We all had very high expectations.

I visited the house every couple of weeks to check in with Joel and ensure everything was going according to plan. After a quick walk around the site, I headed next door to catch up with my Seaview neighbour Jenny Murphy. Jenny worked from home as a website designer. She was a wheelchair user, and after her youngest son Kyle had left home in the autumn to work on the mainland, extended family and friends had rallied round to ensure she was kept entertained.

An unfamiliar black hatchback was parked on her drive. I hesitated on the doorstep. I'd told Jenny I would call in, but with my inspection next door completed quicker than anticipated, I was earlier than planned.

'Sorry,' I said as soon as she answered the door. 'Have you got company? Do you want me to come back later?'

'No, of course not.' Jenny beckoned me inside. 'I'm meeting with a client, but we've nearly finished.'

I offered to make coffees while she finished off her business meeting.

'That's a good idea,' she said. 'I'll only be another five or ten minutes. Go on through to the kitchen and say hello to Rodney.'

The large ginger Tom was curled up on the corner sofa. I'd originally adopted Rodney when his owner had abandoned him last year – before I knew Charlie had a serious allergy. With a cat's sixth sense, Rodney had hastily switched allegiance and taken up permanent residence in Jenny's kitchen.

A large bouquet of flowers had pride of place on the breakfast bar and a man's anorak hung over a stool. I made the coffees and settled onto the sofa. Rodney opened one eye and raised his head for a tickle. Pilar Beech was right, pets did bring comfort, but Pilar's childlike obsession with Alfonso seemed sad for a woman who was supposedly part of Cowes' vibrant social scene. The funeral had been well attended, so where were all those friends and acquaintances to offer support? Pilar had seized Dad's offer of help to trace Stewie's forgers, but surely she had closer friends to confide in?

'A penny for them,' Jenny said, entering the kitchen. Behind her I saw the tall, flush-faced figure of Phil Flowers, the Isle of Wight's most knowledgeable local history expert.

I'd introduced Phil to Jenny at Meg's charity fundraising event in October and had been willing the pair to get together ever since. When Phil announced he was looking to up-grade his Wight Wonders website, I'd given him Jenny's number, which he'd failed to acquire on the night.

'Phil, this is a pleasant surprise.'

'Hello Eliza.' His flush deepened.

'You took my advice. Is Jenny helping you out with a new website?'

'I'm bringing him into the 21st Century.' Jenny grinned. 'We're going to have some new features, a blog, maybe even a podcast.'

'A podcast?'

'Yes, once a week or month, we haven't decided yet. Phil will focus on a story from the island's past, maybe interview some relevant guests, that sort of thing.'

'Sounds amazing.'

'It will be,' Phil agreed. 'Thanks Jenny. I'll see myself out.'

'Do you have to rush off?' I asked. 'I'd quite like to pick your brains while you're here.'

Phil glanced at Jenny.

'Be my guest,' she said. 'I'll make another coffee.'

Rodney stretched and jumped off the sofa with a swish of his tail.

'Are either of you familiar with the artist Birdie Adams?' I asked. I'd downloaded a couple of typical Birdie prints from the internet, identical in style to the painting Dad had acquired from Pilar, although in both cases the models were seated, as opposed to standing in their full glory as per poor Stewie. 'She had a studio here on the island back in the early 1980s.'

'I have heard of her, but art's not really my thing.' Phil studied the pictures displayed on my screen. 'Wasn't she in the news a few years back? Someone found one of her paintings, sold it on for an absolute fortune.'

'Yes, that's her,' I confirmed. 'Unfortunately, it appears a friend of my dad has been the victim of scam, thought he owned a genuine Birdie Adams, only to discover it isn't. It could be related to or inspired by that particular incident. Do you know if there have been any other cases of art fraud on the island, particularly anything involving a picture by Birdie?'

'I'll have a look in the archives, see what I can find out,' Phil promised. The spare room in Phil's bungalow was a shrine to back copies of the island's newspapers. If there was anything to uncover, he was the man to do it.

'Thanks Phil. I'm grateful for your help, as always.'

'Why not ask some of the art groups on the island,' Jenny suggested. 'There's bound to be some enthusiastic art historians amongst their members who've heard of Birdie Adams. They might even know an amateur forger or two.' She gave me a wink. 'I expect you can get the contact details from local libraries.'

'Thanks Jenny, that's a good idea too.'

We chatted while Phil drank his coffee. He then made his excuses and left.

'You should have said he was here,' I hissed to Jenny, once he was out of the door. 'I didn't mean to interrupt.'

'You weren't interrupting. Anyway, it was good he was here. Hopefully, he can help you with your next case.'

I gave a nod to the flowers. 'Are they from him?'

Now it was Jenny's turn to flush. 'He's just a client.' She reached down to stroke Rodney who was winding around the wheels of her chair. 'You mentioned your dad? I didn't think you were close to your father.'

'I'm not, not really, but he's currently here on the island. He came over for his friend's funeral, the one we think was scammed. Dad has taken it upon himself to try and find out who sold him this fake painting. You've heard of Stewie Beech, the restauranteur?'

'Oh yes I have,' Jenny confirmed. 'I had a bit of a run in with him not that long ago, or rather I didn't, my sister Ruth did, on my behalf. She wanted to book a table on that yacht of his, but it's not wheelchair accessible. She wasn't impressed. The man had a serious attitude problem, he was totally unhelpful.'

'I thought venues had to be wheelchair accessible these days?' I said.

'They don't. There are exemptions. Anyway, as he so politely pointed out, even if I could get on board his yacht, I'd never be able to access "the heads" – that's nautical speak for the toilet, in case you weren't aware. Ruth retaliated with a comment that unlike men of a certain age, some of us were capable of holding in our bladders for more than a couple of hours. It all sort of degenerated from there.'

'Oh dear, I thought he'd be more sympathetic

than that. Didn't he do a lot of charity work?'

'Only when there was something in it for him. He regularly featured in the social pages of *Isle of Wight Life* with that stunning wife of his. They were always at some charitable event or other. He struck me as a man who liked to be seen to be doing the right thing, but not so happy to actually do it, if you know what I mean.'

'Oh right.'

Jenny's opinion of Stewie Beech left a different impression to the one I'd received from Pilar and Dad. Without a doubt, Stewie was a success story with a reputation for generosity, but had his need to court publicity exposed him to someone unscrupulous who'd taken advantage of him? It was another avenue worth exploring alongside those happy holiday makers from 1981. Hopefully by the time I returned to Cowes, Dad's memory might be in better working order.

CHAPTER NINE

Chrissy August 1981

THE HOLIDAY ON the Isle of Wight was Pam's idea. The perfect remedy for the horrendous turn of events in Nottingham.

Alan Wickstead had arrived in Chrissy's life three years earlier, just eight months after she'd lost her dear dad and far too soon for her mum to be dating, although her mum didn't see Alan's arrival into their lives as a "date". He was a new colleague at work, recently divorced, and feeling a bit low.

'I thought it would be nice for us to invite him over to share our takeaway,' she had said.

Chrissy hadn't thought it nice at all. With typical teenage petulance she'd refused to speak to Alan all evening, not even when he magnanimously left her the last prawn cracker. Three years later she remained mute in his presence as much as she could – hard now that Alan and her mum had just got married and he was making himself thoroughly at home in their house.

'You need to get away for a bit,' Pam said when Chrissy recounted the sorry tale of the wedding fiasco, blocking out the memories of the lilac bridesmaid's dress with puffy sleeves, the cringeworthy wedding reception at the Masonic Hall. 'Why don't you come with me and Rachel to this place on the Isle of Wight? There's plenty of room although we might have to share bunk beds up in the attic.'

Chrissy would have happily slept on the floor if it meant getting away from the middle-aged lovebirds for a couple of weeks.

Chrissy, Pam and Rachel had been friends since primary school. At sixteen they had gone their separate ways; Chrissy to secretarial college and then a job in the headquarters of major pharmaceutical company in Nottingham, Pam straight into a local insurance broker, and Rachel to technical college to study graphic design. Rachel was now in the first year of a degree at Brighton School of Art. Chrissy tried not to be envious. Her own ambitions in the art department had been sidelined by the need to earn a steady income so she could save up and leave her childhood home of 35 Lemon Road and all its bittersweet memories behind her.

Chrissy had become acquainted with a handful of Rachel's new art school friends during visits to Brighton, but she hadn't come across Sasha Mintrum, the friend whose house they would be staying at.

She booked two weeks' annual leave at the beginning of August, and happily waved her mum and Alan goodbye at the central station. Rachel had come back to Nottingham for the summer and the three girls travelled to the south coast together.

'Sasha can be a bit lairy,' Rachel warned. 'She'll say all this outrageous stuff to impress you. Take no notice. Once she sees you're not fazed by it all, she'll soon shut up. There's going to be a big group of us staying at the house. Sasha's family have got a barn where we can party, party, party.'

After a change of trains in London, the crossing to the Isle of Wight took just twenty minutes from Portsmouth Harbour station. As the passenger ferry docked against the pier in Ryde, Chrissy stood on deck, taking in the atmosphere. She was determined this was going to be her happy place. Sun, sea, sand and quite possibly sex, if Rachel was to be believed. For the best part of the journey south Rachel had given the low down on the art school lads who were very much part of the plans for the coming weeks. The boys were in a band called The Future and were using the Mintrums' barn to polish off their new set.

Chrissy heaved her rucksack onto her back. A vast swathe of golden sand stretched ahead of her. She spotted arcades, a pavilion, a boating lake. A sticky sweet aroma emanated from the fast-food kiosks, while squawking seagulls flapped overhead. A rusty London Underground train rattled along the rickety wooden pier to transport them to the esplanade station.

Sasha was waiting for them, a tall, slender girl with jet-black hair cut in a short 1920s geometric bob. Her leather trench coat, tartan shorts and Doc Martens seemed an odd choice of clothing for a hot summer's day. Chrissy wore a denim mini skirt and a sleeveless broderie anglaise blouse.

Sasha took the cigarillo out of her mouth and greeted them with a laconic 'chou'. She swung her arm through Rachel's and lead the procession to a waiting silver Rolls Royce parked on double yellows.

'Hi girls, call me Jonno,' the driver announced, springing out of his seat to open doors. He was in his late forties with the same jet-black hair as Sasha.

'Wow? Don't tell me we're going in that?' Pam exclaimed.

'Why wouldn't we?' Sasha drawled.

She directed Pam to the front passenger seat and indicated to Chrissy that she could have the privilege of travelling with her and Rachel in the back.

'Are the boys here yet?' Rachel asked as Jonno swerved out onto the main road, narrowly missing a cyclist. Chrissy wondered whether he'd seen the red light and deliberately chosen to ignore it, or whether he had a problem with his vision. Either way she decided this was the last journey she wished to take in his car – luxurious though it was.

'Not yet,' Sasha replied with a yawn. 'Do you like boys, Christina?'

'It's Chrissy, and yes, of course I do.'

'I thought you said she was a Christina?'

'Christine,' Rachel replied.

Sasha closed her heavily kohled eyes and leaned her head back on the seat. 'She looks like a Christina to me. I'll call her that anyway.' Rachel glanced sideways at Chrissy and mouthed *just ignore her*.

Chrissy fully intended to. There were only two people she had ever taken an instant dislike to her in her life, and it was an odd quirk of fate that the arrival of one had prompted her to become acquainted with the other.

Never mind. She was here to enjoy herself and she liked the sound of the boys who were due to join them. As for Sasha's drop-dead gorgeous brother Roland, according to Rachel he had to be seen to be believed, although if his manners were anything like his sister's, Chrissy had already decided she didn't care how good looking he was, she was going to steer well clear.

The drive took nearly an hour as Jonno accelerated, swerved and braked in turn, making frequent comments about the stupidity of every other driver on the road. They travelled along country lanes bordered by hedgerows and chocolate box thatched cottages. He finally slowed down as they came to a village with front gardens overflowing with exotic flowers and tropical palms.

'Nearly there, ladies,' he announced, much to Chrissy's relief.

'Wow, it's like being abroad,' Pam exclaimed.

Sasha rolled her eyes and mimicked Pam's exclamation parrot like.

'Don't forget to change your watches, girls,' Jonno joined in. 'We have our own time zone here on the island. We're forty years behind the rest of the UK.'

The Mintrums' residence was an imposing detached house, a mile or so out of the village. Half-hidden behind trees, the walls of the house were covered in ivy. Chrissy's first impression was that it belonged in the pages of a Gothic novel with its tall chimney stacks and obscured leaded windows.

Inside the Gothic novel gave way to domestic chaos. Chrissy had never seen such a mess. The front porch was littered with abandoned shoes, boxes of magazines and old newspapers. Not even pausing to remove her boots, Sasha dashed up a wide wooden staircase, while Rachel, Chrissy and Pam followed more cautiously. Children's toys were scattered on every step, together with items of clothing and even the odd piece of crockery.

'Come on, keep up,' Sasha called over her shoulder.

The attic room contained two sets of metal bunk beds complete with bare mattresses and a single pillow each. The bunks reminded Chrissy of those used in wartime prison camps. Rachel had forewarned them to bring sleeping bags.

'It's a good job you got here first,' Sasha said. 'The boys will sleep in the barn when they arrive.'

Chrissy wasn't so sure she'd got the better deal. She wouldn't mind looking in the barn to see if the sleeping quarters were more comfortable.

There was no clothes storage in the room, but some coat hangers had been thoughtfully left on the bare curtain rail for their use. Sasha said they should head straight outside to the pool.

'You have your own pool?' Pam's mouth gaped open again.

'Of course we do,' Sasha replied. 'Meet ya down there.'

Chrissy found a bathroom on the floor below. She'd often complained her mum spent too much time doing housework, but now she realised how lucky she was. It wasn't that Chrissy minded a bit of grime, a bit of a limescale, and whose bathroom didn't have the odd patch of mould, but...did Mrs Mintrum not know what bleach was for? Or a toilet brush?

She and Pam had bought matching bikinis. She'd chosen yellow polka-dots, while Pam had opted for red. They wrapped themselves up in their beach towels and headed outside.

The garden swept around the property. Chrissy was surprised to discover a well-kept lawned area at the back of the house, bursting with colourful flower beds. A white-haired lady sat at an easel under the dappled shade of a willow tree.

'Hello there,' Pam called out cheerfully.

'Don't interrupt her, she's working on a masterpiece,' Sasha hissed, having sneaked up on them unannounced. She had removed the trench coat and the Doc Martens and wore a plain black one-piece swimsuit coupled with her tartan shorts. Her body was as a slim as a boy's. At least I've got boobs, Chrissy thought with some satisfaction.

The swimming pool was set in an area of crazy paving. A pair of young teenagers occupied two wooden sun loungers, their heads bent in books, while a boy of about ten frolicked in the cloudy water.

Sasha made no attempt to introduce the others, so Chrissy could only assume they were younger siblings. She and Pam perched on the poolside, dipping their toes into the cooling water. Rachel and Sasha sat opposite, a transistor radio positioned between them.

'Scoot brat,' Sasha snarled at the boy as the duelling drums of Adam and the Ants blared out from the radio. Returning her scowl, the boy aimed his water pistol in a machine gun style volley around the pool.

Pam squealed but Chrissy took her cue from Rachel and Sasha and ignored the youngster's antics. She tilted her head towards the sun and remained optimistic. Things were bound to improve when the art school boys arrived.

CHAPTER TEN

Eliza

DAD WAS SNOOZING on the sofa. He woke up as I began to unpack groceries into the fridge. Used to catering for one, I was unprepared for impromptu visitors, especially ones with voracious appetites.

'Is it lunch time already?' he asked.

'How are you getting on with that list of names?' I replied.

'I've been racking my brains.' He waved a piece of paper at me. 'These are the lads I camped with, and I've remembered the name of the other girl, the one whose house we stayed at. It was Sasha.'

It was some progress at least. 'Have you rung your sister? Asked her to find those photo albums for you?'

'I don't see how that could help, and I can't imagine my mates Den Pacey or Mick Levine having anything to do with this either, before you ask.'

'Not even as a joke?' I suggested.

'An expensive joke,' Dad snorted.

'We won't know how expensive until you've checked through Stewie's accounts this afternoon, and you can only do that if Pilar has found the relevant statements. What was this girl Sasha's surname?'

'Umm. Not sure. Mitchell, Minter. Something like that.'

Dad might not think his memory needed jogging, but I did. His painkillers seemed to leave him half-comatose. Next time he fell asleep on the sofa I'd steal his thumbprint to open his phone and find Debs' number to ask her for the photo albums myself.

'I could show you where the house was. We could go later on, have a drive-by?'

'What? We just knock on the door and ask if they're harbouring any art forgers? It's not likely the same family will be living there after forty years.'

Dad looked disappointed. 'Surely it's worth a try?'

Perhaps a view of the house would be an aide-memoire. 'Maybe we'll go tomorrow,' I conceded, 'after we've been to Marsh House to see Nanna and her friend Mr Zeigler. My neighbour Jenny in Seaview made the very sensible suggestion that local amateur art groups might be able to help us out. If Kurt was an art teacher, he must have connections in the island's art world.'

Even as I said the words it struck me that my lack of knowledge of Kurt's former career also included a lack of knowledge of where he'd lived prior to moving into Marsh House. Many people retired to the island later in life. He could have taught anywhere in the country. However, Kurt was congenial and fond of Nanna. I was sure he'd help if he could.

'Have you had any luck on the internet?' I asked. 'Found any similar art scams?'

'There's been plenty of scams,' Dad admitted. 'Million dollars' worth of them. Art fraud is big business, but I've found nothing that appertains to the Isle of Wight or Birdie Adams.'

AFTER A STOP at the barbers, I dropped Dad off with Pilar at about two. I paid an expert to look after my finances and knew nothing about accountancy. I didn't feel I would have anything to offer by staying to help trawl through Stewie's bank statements, although following Dad's admission of a series of bad business ventures, I wasn't sure he knew much about accountancy either.

I spent a pleasant afternoon at Making Waves with Charlie before returning to Sandpipers. Pilar invited me in as far as the hallway.

'Ian *hath* been so busy,' she assured me. 'Papers everywhere.'

I could imagine.

'After you leave yesterday, I spoke to Josh, Stewart's youngest son. Of all the boys I think he was the closest to his father. I have given Ian the name of his café in Winchester. He is happy to talk to you.'

'That's great thanks. And you mentioned Anton your sommelier and the skipper, Riggs? I'd like to speak with them too.'

Pilar gave a little shrug. 'I don't think Anton will be able to tell you any more than I have. Riggs was closer to Stewart because they both liked fishing, but that was all.' She placed a hand on my arm. 'Stewart was a proud man. I don't think this…this thing with the painting is something he would have wanted people to know about. That is the trouble, I think, he tells no-one. The only person I have confided in is Ian.'

At the mention of his name, Dad hobbled into the hallway. A wad of papers tucked under his arm restricted his movement even further.

'Pilar dear, would you mind if I took this little lot away to discuss with Eliza?' he asked.

'Not at all, Ian.' She stood on tiptoe and planted a kiss on his cheek. 'Be my guest.'

'Find anything useful?' I asked, retrieving the papers so he could use the full support of his crutches for the walk back to the car.

'I'm not sure. Pilar gave me the last four years of Stewie's personal bank statements. I'll tell you more when we get home.'

On the short drive back to the apartment I asked when Pilar had first broached the subject of the painting. 'I just wonder why she choose you, of all Stewie's acquaintances, to trust and nobody else.'

'I was the one who mentioned it to her,' Dad explained. 'It was when she took me into his study after the funeral. I told you, Stewie had left instructions for his friends to have a bottle of absinthe.'

'He actually put that in his will?'

'Not in his will, but he'd left specific requirements for the service, including the red clothing, songs he wanted played, where his ashes were to be scattered, that type of thing.'

'I see. What songs did he want?'

'Celine Dion's *My Heart Will Go On*.'

'You're joking? That's not very appropriate for a man who died of a cardiac arrest. Surely, they didn't play it?'

'Of course they did. You can't not, it's what Stewie wanted. Anyway, it's a rousing tune. I think it was more the nautical connection, because of *The Titanic*.'

'That seems even more macabre in the circumstances.'

'Stewie didn't know he was going to die of a heart attack on a boat, did he? I left the wake early because I wanted to try and catch you and Meg while I was on the island. When I cornered Pilar to say goodbye, she took me into Stewie's study where she'd put the gift bottles. The painting was there, face up on his desk. I said, *oh my goodness, where did Stewie get that*, and it went from there. I don't think she knew what to do about it, poor girl, or who to approach. That's why I offered to help.'

'How many times had you met Pilar before this?'

'Half a dozen or so, whenever they came up to York. Me and Stewie might not have seen a lot of each other over the years, but we were able to pick up where we left off.'

Pilar had placed a lot of faith in someone she hardly knew. With a seeming lack of close acquaintances of her own, perhaps confiding in a long-standing friend of her late husband's wasn't such a random choice. Stewie had clearly trusted Dad. He'd offered him a share in his business. Pilar had admitted she was estranged from her older brother and her father was dead. Maybe Dad fulfilled the paternal role – although I wasn't going to burst his bubble and tell him that.

Back at the apartment he spread Stewie's bank statements onto the dining table. 'As far as I can see this account is pocket money spending, online shopping, direct debits for various subscription services, gym membership, payments to his boys, that type of thing. A set amount comes in each month and roughly the same amount goes out.

There are no big transactions either in or out relating to the period Pilar reckons Stewie acquired the painting.'

'I suppose it would have been too good to be true to find a bank transfer complete with a payee's name. Mr A Forger, or whatever.'

Dad gave a snort. 'I had been hoping.'

I was disappointed the bank statements had revealed nothing obvious. 'I don't suppose you found any diaries or notebooks while you were snooping about in Stewie's office?'

'I didn't get a look in the office. Pilar had already got these files out for me. I had to work at the kitchen table while she was cleaning out the rabbit. It lives in the utility room.'

'It would have been helpful if you could have had a good ferret around.'

'I would have liked to,' Dad agreed. 'Stewie probably kept his diary on his phone. Most people do these days. If only we had access to that we could check his last few outgoing calls. I'm sure he would have been trying to get hold of whoever sold him that painting. Stewie wouldn't let something like this go.'

'It is odd they didn't find his phone on his body. I wonder if it fell out somewhere, into the water or something. We should ask Pilar to go back to the police about it.'

'You don't have any friends in the force on the island? Private investigators need contacts, Eliza.

You'll need to cultivate a friendly copper if you want to take your investigative work seriously.'

The only members of the island's police force I'd come into contact with so far were unimpressed with my investigative work. I didn't want to get into a discussion about that.

'There is one thing that puzzles me though,' he said, pointing back to the bank statements. 'Every quarter a payment of £500 goes out to a P Pacey.'

'Lucky P Pacey. Wasn't that the surname of one of your friends?'

'Yes, my school friend Dennis.'

'The one who married the girl from Nottingham called Pam? Do you think this is her? Why would Stewie be sending money to Pam?'

'I don't know. It might not be *that* P Pacey.'

'Do the Paceys have kids? Perhaps Stewie is helping with college fees or something. We know how generous he is.'

Dad snorted. 'Not that generous. Over the last three years Stewie has given P Pacey more than he's given to his own kids.'

'What about payments to charities? Have you found many of those?'

Dad shook his head. 'Not on this account but they'd probably be from the business account, for tax purposes.'

'Oh I see.' Did my neighbour Jenny have a point? Perhaps Stewie wasn't quite the philanthropist he seemed.

'Do you know where your old friends the Paceys are now?' I asked as Dad gathered up the bank statements into a tidy pile.

'Den moved to Nottingham when they got married.'

'They weren't at the funeral?'

'No.'

'If Stewie was being that kind to them you'd think they'd turn up to say goodbye.'

'Absolutely, and Den would be first in line for a bottle of absinthe, I know that.' Dad pursed his lips together and frowned.

'If these payments go back three years, they'd have started around the time Pilar reckons Stewie acquired the Birdie Adams,' I remarked.

'Umm possibly.'

'You say Stewie kept this account with a minimum cash flow. He couldn't transfer money from his other accounts without Pilar's knowledge. Just suppose he borrowed the money to buy the painting. What if he borrowed it from the Paceys and now he's paying them back?'

Dad scratched his freshly shaved chin. 'There's no big sum coming into the account. If he did borrow money, he must have borrowed cash.'

'Cash would be ideal for the fraudsters. No paper trail.'

'How much was that Ryde Birdie Adams worth?'

'It was valued at between twenty and thirty thousand.'

'I can't imagine Den having that much spare cash to lend Stewie.'

'How do you know how much money the Paceys have? You haven't seen them for forty years. They could be millionaires. Look at it the other way, the Paceys were both with you that summer. They knew Stewie sat for Birdie Adams. Maybe they're the ones scamming him. Maybe they're the ones who sold him the picture and because he's a so-called friend, they agreed he could pay them in instalments.'

'Now you're just being ridiculous.'

'I'm just running through the possibilities. It's not as if we've got much else to go on. See if you can find the Paceys on Facebook. Maybe Pilar knows where they are. Meanwhile you need to chase up the fracture clinic about your appointment.'

'I will, love, but I'm not going anywhere until we've got to the bottom of this.'

At the rate we were progressing that could be several weeks. I found Dad the hospital's phone number and stood over him while he made the call. The clinic gave us the good news that Dad's appointment had been booked for Friday. Slightly disgruntled at this development, he retreated to the sofa and picked up my laptop. When Charlie arrived bearing gifts of takeaway pizzas, Dad announced he'd had no luck finding the Paceys on Facebook, but he had discovered his old school pal

Mick Levine was now running in bar in Majorca.

'Would he have stayed in touch with the Paceys?' I asked.

'Quite possibly,' Dad conceded. 'I wonder if Mick knows about Stewie?'

'Why don't you message him after dinner with the news,' I suggested. 'Drop in a casual *have you any idea where Dennis is* at the same time.'

Charlie and Dad would have happily scoffed their Pepperoni Delights straight out of the box. Although I would have once joined them, since becoming accustomed to the luxury of Joel's apartment, I'd upgraded my dining arrangements and placed plates, knives and forks on the glass table.

'Good old Mick, running a bar in Majorca,' Dad said. 'He was training to be a motorbike mechanic when I knew him.'

'Funny how none of you stayed in touch,' Charlie remarked, ignoring the cutlery and tearing off a slab of pizza.

'You grow apart, follow different paths,' Dad replied, following Charlie's lead. 'Are you still in touch with people you knew at eighteen?'

Charlie grinned at me. 'Yes, Ian, as a matter of fact I am.'

'You're a lot younger than me,' Dad said, missing the point entirely. 'Wait another twenty years and then see if you can say that. Mind you, it would be great to see Mick again. I've never been to Majorca.'

A few hours later, as Charlie and I lay in bed listening to Dad snoring on the other side of the wall, Charlie suggested we offer him the air fare and find him a flight to Palma straight after his hospital appointment on Friday afternoon.

'He says he's not going anywhere until he's got this mystery solved,' I whispered.

'You need to crack on with it then.'

'I would if I had something to go on. I'm worried he's trying to impress Pilar, and he'll end up making a right fool of himself. Why didn't Stewie go to the police the minute he found out he'd been sold a fake? Most people would.'

'Stewie was well known here on the island, I suppose he had his reputation to uphold. Would you want a crude nude depiction of yourself appearing all over the island's press? I expect he felt pretty stupid.'

'The story of the find in Ryde would have increased the value of Birdie's work. I reckon someone unscrupulous cottoned on to that and saw a chance to make some hard cash.' Dad's snoring subsided momentarily. I snuggled in closer to Charlie. 'What do you know about Pilar? The restaurant website doesn't give an awful lot away other than she's from the Basque region of Spain, is a self-taught chef and uses her grandmother's recipes.'

'They always say that, don't they?' Charlie mused. 'Did Lilian teach you any old family recipes?'

'No. Whenever we stayed at Clifftops we ate whatever we wanted from the bar menu. Grandpa Henry could cook the odd omelette, and by odd, I mean odd.'

The snoring resumed. Charlie rolled away from me and plumped up his pillows with a yawn. 'You should have a word with Amelie, Dexter's girlfriend. I'll check with him tomorrow, see if he can fix something up. She's worked for the Beeches for some time. Maybe she can give us an insight into something that can solve this puzzle.'

I liked the way he used the word "us", although I suspected Charlie's eagerness to see the case resolved had nothing to do with finding out who had defrauded Stewie Beech but because the novelty of Dad's presence had already worn off.

CHAPTER ELEVEN

D
AD LOOKED SMART for our trip to Marsh House Senior Living Centre the next morning, wearing one of his new shirts, courtesy of Charlie's surplus stock, matched with navy chinos.

'When was the last time you saw Nanna?' I asked, as we pulled into the residential care home's carpark.

'Thirty years ago,' he confirmed. 'She'll be in her eighties now, I suppose. I take it she's still got all her faculties?'

'Oh yes. You've nothing to worry about there.'

Nanna never had a good word to say about Dad, but then she'd rarely said anything complimentary about Mum either. She'd disapproved of Mum's marriage at the age of 21. She'd disapproved of Mum's divorce eight years later. I'd phoned ahead to let her know I was coming and was bringing a surprise visitor with me. I didn't mention Dad by name in case she told me not to bother.

As we walked through reception, we bumped into my friend Grace who was the centre's senior nursing officer. After a quick introduction to Dad, I confirmed I was still free to meet up the following day for our lunch date. Grace lived in Newport with her husband Richie and two daughters; we usually caught up at least once a month, depending on her days off.

Grace informed us Nanna was currently waiting to see the podiatrist in the clinical wing. 'But Kurt's in his usual spot.'

That was good, we could get the business over first. Having always seen Kurt in tandem with Nanna, I'd not given his physical appearance a great deal of attention. He carried himself well with no stooping. Slightly younger than Nanna, his white hair was neatly trimmed, and his sweaters were his trademark, beautiful Fair Isle patterns hand knitted, or so I'd been told, by his much-missed late wife.

Kurt looked up as we entered the conservatory. 'Ah, Eliza, lovely to see you. You've just missed Lilian. She's gone to get her feet done.'

'So I hear. We thought we'd wait here for her if you don't mind.'

'Of course I don't mind.' Kurt put down his book.

'This is my dad, Ian,' I said.

'I can see the family resemblance.' Kurt shook Dad's hand.

Not entirely flattered by his comment, I pulled over a couple of spare chairs and we sat down. 'Actually, it's quite good Nanna isn't here because I wanted a word with you about something rather delicate,' I began. 'I understand you used to be an art teacher.'

'That's correct,' Kurt said with a nod. 'I taught art for many years, the old O and A levels, GCSEs or whatever they call them now. Used to teach adult evening classes here on the island too, after I retired.'

'Have you always lived on the island?' I asked.

'I spent most of my life in Hereford. We moved here not long after the Millennium.'

'Have you heard of the artist Birdie Adams?' Dad asked. 'She lived on the island for a bit too, although it would have been before you arrived.'

'Birdie Adams?'

'You knew her?'

'Not personally, only by repute.'

I lowered my voice. 'The thing is Kurt, someone is copying Birdie's work. We were just wondering if you had any contacts here on the island who might be able to help us, practicing artists or historians, for example. We want to find the perpetrator. A friend of Dad's was duped into buying a fake Birdie.'

'And he subsequently died of a heart attack from the shock of it,' Dad added.

'Goodness!' Kurt's eyes widened and his face

paled. 'Are you sure?'

'That was just his wife's supposition,' I said, 'about the heart attack.' Kurt looked shaken and I didn't want him succumbing to the same fate. Any talk of forgery would be abhorrent to true art lovers. 'Do you know anyone who could help us shed some light on who might be behind something like this?'

Kurt took off his glasses and placed his hands together on his lap. 'You say this happened here on the island?'

'Yes, it did,' Dad confirmed.

'When exactly?'

'We believe Dad's friend bought the painting about three years ago. That it was fake only recently came to light.'

After a somewhat lengthy pause, Kurt cleared his throat. 'I'm a bit out of touch to be honest. I'm not sure I know anyone who could help you.'

'Oh that's a shame.' It was hard to hide my disappointment. I'd been banking on Kurt's help. Before I could say any more, Nanna shuffled into the conservatory with her wheeled walker. Her eyebrows shot up when she recognised Dad.

'Good grief, look what the cat dragged in.'

'Nice to see you too, Lilian.' Dad struggled to his feet.

'What have you been up to?' Nanna accepted his awkward embrace. 'No good by the looks of it.'

'I tripped off a pavement.'

'Were you drunk?'

Kurt seemed glad of the opportunity to escape and offered to fetch refreshments. I accompanied him to the ever-present tea trolley to see what was on offer.

'I didn't mean to be insensitive,' I said, when we were out of earshot. 'I was just hoping you might–'

'The fruitcake looks good today,' Kurt interrupted. 'I'll take Lilian an extra slice. Sometimes it can be a little dry. Depends which cook has been on duty.'

I'd upset him more than I thought. His abruptness was totally out of character. When we returned Nanna and Dad were sat in silence.

'He tells me he's staying with you for a little while,' Nanna said, as I handed out the tea and cake.

'Only until he gets his air boot fitted,' I replied.

'Maybe Lilian is familiar with the work of Birdie Adams,' Dad said, pretending he hadn't heard. 'You always used to know everything that went on here on the island, Lilian. Have you still got your finger on the pulse?'

'What do you want to know about Birdie Adams for?' Nanna turned to me. She took a large bite of cake before nodding at Kurt. 'This is good. Yvonne must have been in the kitchen yesterday.'

'That's what I thought,' Kurt mumbled, stirring his tea.

'You've heard of Birdie?' I should have guessed. Nanna had worked in the hotel industry on the island for sixty years. Dad was right. There wasn't much that happened here she didn't know about.

'She was related to that dreadful family in St Lawrence. There were girls at the same school as Jackie, one slightly older, I think, and twins a couple of years younger. The twins and Jackie were in the orchestra together. I didn't like her hanging around with them.'

'You didn't approve of anyone Jackie hung around with,' Dad reminded her, 'including me.'

Nanna continued to ignore him. 'Wasn't there a story about one of Birdie's paintings turning up out of the blue and fetching a fortune?'

'Yes,' I confirmed, wondering what instrument my mother had played in the school orchestra and why her musical talent hadn't ever been mentioned before. 'And a friend of Dad's got tricked into buying a copy. I suspect somebody jumped on the Birdie bandwagon, and Dad's friend fell for it. We want to find the culprits.'

'And bring them to justice,' Dad chipped in. 'We were hoping Kurt might have some insider knowledge.'

'Why would you think that?' Nanna asked, taking another bite of fruitcake.

'We thought he might have contacts in the art world,' I explained patiently. I gave Kurt an apologetic smile. He didn't catch my eye and seemed absorbed in his tea.

'Or even know someone who might have the talent to pull this off,' Dad added.

'He taught evening classes at Newport College, not the Royal Academy.' Nanna glared at Dad. 'I ask you. I doubt any of Kurt's part-timers would have had the ability to pass themselves off as Birdie Adams.'

'Oh I don't know,' Dad replied. 'You should see some of the stuff the old lady turned out. I don't think it required a great deal of skill.'

'Then it's more than likely one of those Mintrums is behind it.' Nanna licked her fingers.

'Mintrum, that's it,' Dad exclaimed. 'I'd forgotten the name. Just because you didn't approve of this family, Lilian, it doesn't make them criminals.'

'Huh. You clearly didn't know them as well as I did.'

'How well did you know them?' I asked. I sensed the longer we stayed the more the conversation would deteriorate into a sniping match.

Nanna made more huffing noises. 'Our paths crossed at school concerts and such. The children ran wild, they were unruly. As for the husband, took off with his secretary or something.'

'Can you remember exactly where this family lived in St Lawrence?' I asked.

Nanna shook her head. 'I believe it was a little out of the village, but I had no reason to ever go there. As far as I know Jackie didn't see the girls after she left school. Where did his friend get this picture from anyway? Have you thought about that?'

'We don't know where he got it from. That's what we're trying to find out.'

'You'd have to go through a professional dealer to acquire a painting by someone that famous. There's a couple of fancy galleries up in Cowes. Why don't you pretend you want to buy a Birdie Adams for yourself?' Nanna dusted some cake crumbs from her cardigan sleeve. 'Go visit the galleries and make them aware you've got good money to spend. Let them spread the word amongst their colleagues and if someone can miraculously conjure up a Birdie for you overnight, you might be on to something.'

I stared at her. Recent experience had taught me Nanna was not the bastion of propriety I'd always assumed her to be. 'Are you suggesting we set up some sort of sting?' I asked.

Kurt ran a finger under the collar of his shirt. 'I really don't think that would be appropriate.'

Dad choked on a mouthful of tea. When he recovered, he leaned forward and patted Nanna's knee. 'Oh Lilian, you wily old fox. You haven't changed a bit, have you?'

CHAPTER TWELVE

I WASN'T SURE Nanna's suggestion was even practical, let alone ethical. Dad, on the other hand, thought it was a brilliant idea.

'It's so simple,' he said as we drove away from Marsh House.

'It's not simple at all,' I argued. 'We'd have to pretend to be genuine buyers. I'm not known for my acting skills.'

'You don't have to act, just be yourself, Eliza Kane, former British Open Golf Champion, a woman with a substantial pot of prize-winning money. Makes sense you might want to invest in a piece of art.'

'I'm not against the idea of buying a piece of art, but why would I want a piece of Birdie's art? Anyway, I can't be me, can I? If this has anything to do with anyone who was staying at the Mintrums' house that summer, they'll recognise the name Kane. It might look suspicious.'

'Apart from the fact we don't know this has

anything to do with the Mintrums, if I'm having trouble recalling names of people I met once forty years ago, so will everyone else who was there. Other than the lads from Leeds, I suspect nobody at that house even knew my first name, let alone my surname.'

'The girls might,' I pointed out.

'Only the lasses from Nottingham. Nobody else took any notice of me.'

'One of those lasses from Nottingham married Stewie Beech and subsequently got dumped for a younger model. Has that thought not occurred to you?'

'What do you mean?'

'The ex-wife. What if she was out for revenge?'

'Chrissy wouldn't be behind something like this.'

'You said that about the Paceys. The girls were friends, remember. A woman scorned. Maybe they're in it together.'

'Stewie and Chrissy split up long before he met Pilar.'

'That doesn't mean she wouldn't have a grievance about the divorce, maintenance payments or something. Was she at the funeral?'

'No.'

'There you go then. A clear indication of some sort of animosity.'

After a lengthy pause Dad muttered, 'it's not unfeasible you'd want a painting by Birdie Adams because of the local connection. I think it's worth a try.'

'Seriously?'

Nanna's plan was a complete no-go as far as I was concerned. However, I had hoped for a more positive reaction from Kurt.

'Without Kurt's help we're going to have to contact these local amateur art groups ourselves,' I said. 'We can stop at the library in Cowes on the way home.'

'I thought we were going to look for the Mintrums' house first? No stone unturned and all that.'

I wasn't needed at Making Waves and even with a stop at the library, it could be a long afternoon at the apartment with no-one but Dad for company.

'Okay, let's head down to the coast. See if we can do some memory jogging.'

Contrary to my promise not to become Dad's private taxi service, he suggested a detour to Ventnor, followed by a drive-by of Meg's cottage. Ventnor was one of the island's more picturesque resorts, shabby but chic Victorian charm complemented by a small fishing harbour and a wide sandy beach. Out of season, it was very quiet. I followed the main road as it twisted and sloped towards the seafront, parking up in front of the concrete rotunda bandstand, a stark 20th century edition to the landscape. Dad insisted on getting out of the car to stand on the promenade.

'Not a lot has changed,' he remarked, a slight tremor in his voice.

The same couldn't be said for Clifftops, my grandparents' former hotel. The site had been sold off to a developer and planning permission was being sought to transform the hotel and adjacent golf course into a leisure village. The gravel track which led to hotel was already overgrown with weeds and brambles, and the building itself was hidden behind hoardings.

'Brings it all back, love,' Dad murmured, running a finger under his eye. 'Brings it all back.'

Meg's cottage on the nearby downs evoked a similar outburst of emotion. In thirty years, Dad had shown little or no interest in what was happening on the Isle of Wight. Whenever we met he rarely asked after Nanna, or Clifftops, or for news of our mother, making her home in Australia. He seemed keen to make up for lost time, overcome with nostalgia, or was it self-pity?

'You girls have done so well,' he croaked. 'I've been a terrible dad, haven't I? Leaving you both to fend for yourselves.'

'We haven't had to fend for ourselves.' I didn't like this maudlin version of my dad. I wanted the old lightweight one back. 'We had Mum, and we always had Nanna and Grandpa.' Now wasn't the moment to mention Alistair Stonehouse's influence on our lives, which in my case had been monumental. It was Alistair who had provided the paternal influence when I was growing up. He was the role model, the professional golfer who'd developed and encouraged my love of the sport. When I'd won the British Open the press had homed in on the family connection and Alistair had taken due credit. Dad hadn't had a look-in. That must have hurt. Coming to Ventnor had been a mistake. I was eager to move on. 'We were surrounded by people who loved us,' I said in a rush. 'You were always there, up in Yorkshire. You remembered our birthdays, Christmas. We used to love it when the postman arrived with all those packages.'

He didn't look convinced, but as we drove inland towards the village of Niton, his mood lifted. After a couple of U-turns, he let out a gleeful shout.

'That's the pub, The Water Mill. That's where we first met Chrissy and Pam. Shall we stop for lunch?'

I needed a break. After a hearty pie and chips for Dad and a chunky fish finger sandwich for me, I felt fortified enough to continue. We returned to the car and after driving no more than a hundred or so metres out of the village into farmland, he let out another whoop of excitement.

'That's it. This is where the campsite was.'

I pulled onto the verge. Many farmers allowed campers onto their spare fields in summer. Facilities would be limited, but campsite fees cheap.

Ideal for youngsters.

'It was a good half an hour's walk from here to the Mintrums' house,' Dad explained. 'After we met the girls, we pitched up in the garden.'

'I wonder if it's worth phoning Mum to have a chat about the Mintrums?' I suggested. 'I know Nanna didn't think Mum kept in touch with them, but you never know.'

'I don't think we should bring your mum into this,' Dad replied.

'I didn't even know she was musical.'

'Neither did I.'

'So you don't know what instrument she played in the orchestra?'

'Probably the triangle.' Dad kept his eyes averted, staring into the field.

'How long after that holiday before you started work at Clifftops? Did you enjoy it here so much, you decided to stay on the island permanently?'

'Not exactly. I went abroad for a year or so in between. I needed a bit of time to sort my head out.'

Had something happened that summer that had messed up his head? All their heads? A group of four friends, none of whom appeared to have stayed in touch. Was I over speculating? Dad was right, people did move on and go their separate ways. I'd only picked up my teenage friendships with Charlie and Grace because I'd returned to Ventnor when my golfing career came crashing to an end. The Leeds gang had been friends before texting and Facebook made it easy to keep up casual acquaintances.

I restarted the car and we drove on. Dad soon spotted a sign on the side of the road.

Waverley House next left.

'That's the place, Waverley House. That was where we stayed. It must be some sort of business now. Turn up that lane there, Eliza. Let's take a look.'

A short distance up a single-track road we came to a large pair of metal gates, beyond which stood a substantial grey stone property. A sign on the surrounding wall announced we had reached Waverley House Educational Centre for Recreational and Creative Arts. A mini-bus and several cars were parked on the gravel in front of the property, while on a grassy area to the side a group of people, including children, gathered in a circle.

'We'll have to look it up,' I said. 'I wonder when the Mintrums moved on.'

'They've spruced up the outside a fair bit, cut back the trees. I'd love to have a look around.' Dad's hand was already on the car door.

'We can't. It's half term this week. There are activities going on.'

'Even better. We can pretend we're potential customers, say we're teachers researching extracurricular opportunities.'

'Dad, no.' I leaned across to restrain him. 'We

can't be teachers one minute and wealthy art investors the next. Be sensible.'

'Oh, so you do think your grandmother's idea might work after all?'

Charlie's text arrived at a very fortuitous moment. *'Dex is meeting Amelie for a drink after work. Anchor Inn at 6.00 pm. Happy for us to join them.'*

'Let's head back,' I said. 'I want to stop at the library, and now Charlie has arranged for me to speak to Amelie who works on *Absinthe*. You can look this place up online when we get home.'

ON THE DRIVE back to Cowes, I mentally prepared excuses to deter Dad from accompanying me to the Anchor Inn. I needed some breathing space. Fortunately our stop at the local library proved fruitful. We left with a list of amateur art groups and a selection of Jo Nesbo novels. Complaining of discomfort, Dad was happy to remain in the apartment resting. He promised to make preliminary enquiries amongst the contacts on the library list, find out what he could about Waverley House and continue his Facebook search for the Paceys.

Dad had signed up for his library card with my address, much to my consternation. I wanted him to head to Harrogate after his boot fitting on Friday. I was away for the weekend and despite his insistence he wasn't going anywhere until we had tracked down Stewie's forgers, he could conduct online research just as easily from Yorkshire as anywhere. More importantly he needed to see Tess to demand his painting back. I set off for the Anchor Inn, bracing myself for an awkward discussion when I returned home.

I'd met Amelie a couple of times before. In her early twenties, she was typical of many young girls who came to Cowes to fulfil their love of sailing. The difference was Amelie's ambitions to emulate Ellen MacArthur who'd single-handedly sailed around the globe, or Shirley Robertson who'd won Olympic medals, had come to a grinding halt when she'd met Dexter. Rather than crossing oceans, Amelie crewed for Stewie Beech.

I arrived at the pub ahead of Dexter and Charlie, and spotted Amelie at the bar, chatting to an older girl with a yellow waterproof slung over her arm. The older girl's dark hair and pale complexion were a stark contrast to Amelie's sun-kissed blonde locks and glowing perma-tan, suggesting an indoors as opposed to outdoors lifestyle. The girls were saying their goodbyes. I wasn't sure Amelie would remember who I was, but after she and her companion threw each other a final air kiss, she beckoned me over.

'I was just telling Tufty about Stewie,' Amelie explained. 'She did a bit of waitressing on *Absinthe* a few years' back. She's been working in London, hadn't heard.'

I hoped for the girl's sake Tufty was not her real name. The brief snatch I'd caught of her accent and overall demeanour would suggest she was from the same breed as Amelie. Presumably after a stint of sailing-cum-waitressing Tufty had returned to her natural environment in the city.

'Everyone who worked for Stewie is very upset.' Amelie was half-way through a cocktail and accepted the offer of another. 'Apart from Anton, of course. He and Stewie didn't get on.'

'Oh?' Drinks purchased I steered Amelie to a table in a quiet nook. 'I thought it was Anton who contacted the coastguard? He was the one Pilar called when Stewie didn't come home.'

Amelie raised an eyebrow. 'She would, wouldn't she? Anton pretended to be upset, but now the coast is clear, don't be surprised to see him move in for Pilar.'

Interesting.

Charlie and Dexter walked into the pub. Tufty was putting on her coat in the doorway and she and Dexter exchanged a few words while Charlie headed to the bar.

'Are you suggesting...' I let the words hang in the air.

'Oh no, I'm not suggesting he and Pilar were at it, no,' Amelie insisted. 'Pilar was quite devoted to Stewie, but Stewie was old, wasn't he? At least twenty years older than Pilar, had to be, and Anton is the same age as her and much better looking. He was definitely jealous of Stewie.'

Even more interesting.

'What do you know about the business?' I asked. 'Was it good?'

'Oh yes,' Amelie enthused. 'Ask Pilar to show you the reservations book. We're always full. *Absinthe* is a unique concept. Stewie and Pilar worked hard to make the restaurant a success. Pilar's culinary skills are legendary. And don't forget the private catering business. That was flourishing too.'

It was the first I'd heard of a private catering business. 'How does that operate?' I asked.

'It's Pilar and Anton's little thing, food and wine pairings. They run it together and I help them out, waitressing. Fine dining in your own home.'

I wish I'd known; I would have hired the pair to cook for me. I wondered how Stewie felt about Anton and Pilar working so closely together. Did this now put Anton in the frame as a possible scammer, out to make a mockery of the older man? He'd found the body. If this was a murder enquiry, he'd be the main suspect. He was definitely next in line for questioning.

'Presumably Anton and Pilar do this on the days *Absinthe* isn't operating?'

Amelie nodded. 'The restaurant only opens Thursday to Sunday in winter, and the boat rarely goes out of the marina.'

'Do you know if Anton has an interest in art?' I glanced over to the bar where Charlie and Dexter were now chatting with the landlady. Hopefully

Charlie would have the sense to leave us alone together for as long as possible.

Amelie shook her head. 'Not that I know of.' She hesitated, fingering the stem of her cocktail glass. 'You know that was so odd about Stewie being found on the *Little Lady*.'

I was glad she had raised the subject. 'Yes, Pilar seemed puzzled by this too. Was it unusual for Stewie to go off fishing by himself?'

'Oh no, not at all, but I know Pilar suspects he was up to something. She told me there was mud on his boots, as if he'd gone ashore. There's not a lot of suitable places to land between Cowes and Newtown Creek. And you've got to be careful with the tides in the creek. It's very easy to get stranded.'

'What do you think he'd gone there for?'

Amelie shrugged and gave a small sniff. 'I've no idea, but it is awful to think of him dying like that, all alone. And he must have known too, I mean, that he was dying. The boat was tied to a buoy, so it wasn't as if he just died instantly and drifted. He must have felt his symptoms coming on and decided to rest, hoping he'd feel well enough to carry on for home a bit later...'

Her words trailed off and her eyes filled with water. No doubt if Dad was here, he'd have flung his arms around her. I squeezed her hand.

'It is terribly sad,' I agreed, signalling to Charlie and Dexter that now would be an appropriate time to join us. Talking to Amelie had been very useful. Anton the sommelier needed closer investigation, and we needed to ascertain exactly what Stewie had been doing in Newtown Creek. He'd stormed out of the house after a furious phone call. Could he have gone to confront his forgers?

CHAPTER THIRTEEN

Chrissy August 1981

SHE SOON BECAME accustomed to the chaotic set up at Waverley House. Sasha's younger sisters – auburn haired twins, unidentical in looks, shape or temperament, were called Immi, short for Imogen, and Dorcus. William, age ten, was the baby of the family. Mrs Mintrum, 'call me Prue', was a freckled and frazzled looking woman who told the girls to help themselves to whatever they wanted from the kitchen. After a quick check of the cupboards, Chrissy and Pam wandered down to the shop in the village to stock up with snacks.

With the twins and William banished to summer school holiday activities every morning, ferried across the island in opposite directions by poor Prue, Chrissy and Pam requisitioned the loungers by the pool. There was gossip to catch up on. Sue Noble and Alan Wickstead's wedding might have dominated Chrissy's summer, but the far more noteworthy nuptials of Prince Charles and Lady Diana Spencer had seen the entire nation glued to their TV screens. There were boys to discuss, not just the imminent arrivals from Brighton, but colleagues Chrissy and Pam fancied or didn't in their respective offices. They exchanged details of disastrous dates and contemplated future aspirations – anywhere but Lemon Road for Chrissy, a wedding dress to outdo Lady Di's for Pam.

Rachel and Sasha remained aloof, distancing themselves on the opposite side of the pool. Their conversations revolved around more serious topics; the state of country, political disquiet and inner-city riots, although there was a flurry of excitement with the news that big brother Roly was bringing a friend home with him. And not just any friend, but Jason Ross. *The Jason Ross.*

'You must have heard of Jason Ross?' Rachel said. Chrissy and Pam shook their heads. 'The music producer? Don't you girls keep up to date with anything? He's going to watch The Future perform. This could be their big chance.'

Chrissy spotted the elderly artist on the second morning in her towelling bathrobe going for a dip. "Batty old Birdie", she'd gleaned from Rachel, was some sort of relative.

Later in the day she approached the elderly lady beneath the willow tree. 'Are you painting a landscape?' she asked.

'No, I'm painting the twins by the pool,' Birdie replied. Chrissy stole a glance at the canvas but saw little to resemble the girls whose places she and Pam had stolen. The old lady's artwork was abstract in the extreme. 'Are you interested in art?' Birdie asked. 'Would you like to see my studio?' Chrissy accepted the offer and subsequently wished she hadn't. Birdie was obsessed with the human form. The untidy workroom was crammed with half-finished sketches and monochrome prints of naked figures and dismembered limbs. The twins were getting off lightly.

It was their third evening and the promised musical geniuses had yet to materialise. Chrissy and Pam decided to seek out the nearest pub.

'It's got to be better than hanging around here and listening to Sasha and Rachel banging on about people we've never met and are not likely to at this rate,' Chrissy said. 'We might be able to get some decent food there too.'

They took great care getting ready, indulging in preparations usually employed before a night in a Nottingham nightclub, not a country pub. When they reached the Water Mill, over-dressed and over-excited at their successful escape, the only food on offer was cod and chips or chicken in a basket. Both options were better than anything the girls could have cooked up in Prue Mintrum's kitchen. The pub was busy with holidaymakers, mostly families. Chrissy was on her third vodka and orange when four lads burst into the lounge bar and sat down at the newly vacated table next to them. Their boisterous northern voices provided a welcome taste of home.

'Which one do you fancy?' Pam whispered after several minutes of the two tables surreptitiously eyeing each other up.

'We could have two each,' Chrissy giggled. 'You have first choice.'

'The blonde one,' Pam said without hesitation. 'What about you?'

Chrissy had made up her mind the minute the lads had taken the table. After another round of eye contact, jostling and nudging, introductions flew across the tables and the offer of a drink was received. Ten minutes later they were squeezed up together, thighs already touching.

'Where are you staying?' the boy called Stew asked. 'We haven't seen you on the campsite.'

'At a friend's house,' Pam replied. 'It's got a pool. You should come over one afternoon.'

When Pam and Chrissy returned to Waverley House at midnight, Rachel and Sasha's classmates had finally turned up. The steady beat of a synthesizer broke up the misty night air. Framed against the backlight of the barn, Sasha and Rachel swayed to the music, arms above their heads.

'Shall we give it a miss?' Pam suggested. 'Not sure we need those art school boys now, do we?'

Chrissy nodded. Heading upstairs to her uncomfortable bunk, she thought of the blue-eyed lad from Leeds she'd met in the pub. Things were definitely looking up.

CHAPTER FOURTEEN

Eliza

BACK AT THE apartment Dad was browsing the internet.

'What have you been able to find out?' I asked, peering over his shoulder at the screen and to my horror seeing a property page for long term rentals in the Isle of Wight. Surely he wasn't thinking about staying here on a more permanent basis?

He hastily clicked open another tab. 'Not an awful lot. Still not heard back from Mick Levine. I tried calling Pilar to ask about the Paceys, but she hasn't replied. I've been googling Waverley House. The educational centre was established in the early 2000s. One of the directors is a William Mintrum, so the family must have retained an interest in the property. I've found some photographs. They've made a lot of changes.'

I glanced at the pictures Dad had pulled up on the activity centre's website. It all looked very busy with shots of children in muddy clothing swinging from trees.

'They've filled the pool in,' Dad said, 'and one of the barns has been converted into an accommodation block.'

'Do they list arts and crafts amongst the activities?' Charlie asked. He'd accompanied me back from the pub with a Chinese takeaway. I wasn't particularly hungry after our pub lunch, but Dad's eyes lit up at the smell of food.

'Yes they do, actually. Birdie Adams' studio is still there, in fact it's one of the highlights of a stay at Waverley House. They use nature to nurture creativity, according to the official blurb.'

'And paint a forgery in the style of Auntie Birdie?'

'They don't say that, but we can't eliminate this Mintrum bloke from our enquiries. He'd certainly be familiar with Birdie Adams' work.'

We ate the Chinese on our knees, Dad was apparently too exhausted to make the move up to table. I relayed my conversation with Amelie.

'She is as mystified as Pilar about this fishing trip,' I explained. 'If only we knew where he went ashore.'

'*If he went ashore*,' Dad said. 'How do we know his boots weren't muddy to start with?'

'Pilar wouldn't have mentioned it. It must have struck her as odd. Did you ask her if they found any fish in his boat?'

'No I did not.'

'There's not an awful lot of places to go ashore

between Cowes and Newtown,' Charlie remarked.

'That's what Amelie said. It's not only where he went ashore to consider, but why,' I stressed. 'Could he have been looking for his forger?'

'There's a holiday camp at Thorness Bay,' Charlie replied, 'but that's about it. Much of the land surrounding the creek itself is owned by the National Trust. It's a nature reserve, quite remote and a haven for wildlife, popular with birdwatchers. I dropped Lucas off there one day last summer for a day out with the Scouts.'

The northwest corner was one of the least populated parts of the island. It wasn't an area I was familiar with at all.

'If he did come ashore, there's a landing jetty at Hamstead to the west although there's nothing there but farmland,' Charlie continued. 'It would be quite a trek to get anywhere on foot.'

'Pilar did say he had grass on his trousers, as if he had gone for a walk through fields,' I pointed out.

'Alternatively, he could have landed at Shalfleet quay, further down.' Charlie frowned. 'Having said that, the quay is only accessible for a few hours around each high tide.'

'Amelie said something about the tides too,' I added. 'Is there anything at Shalfleet?'

'There's a pub, the New Inn, maybe a fifteen, twenty-minute walk from the quay. The village is further on.'

'Sounds more likely,' Dad said. 'We could always visit the pub to see if anyone saw Stewie in the vicinity and if he was with anyone. Add it to our list for tomorrow, Eliza.'

My list for tomorrow consisted of a shift at Making Waves and my catch up with Grace.

'There's going to be no more gallivanting until you've been to the clinic on Friday,' I said. 'We don't know for sure Stewie landed at Shalfleet.'

'Text me the date,' Charlie said, catching my eye. 'I'll check my tide table when I get home to see what times Shalfleet was accessible on the day in question. At least then you'd know whether a landing was possible.'

AN HOUR LATER there was a triumphant shout from the lounge as I loaded up the dishwasher.

'Found something exciting?' Charlie called. He was helping, or rather hindering me in the kitchen. Charlie's dishwasher stacking skills needed a lot more practice.

'Mick's just replied to my message.'

'That's a relief,' I whispered to Charlie. 'I thought for one minute he might have found himself a flat to rent here on the island. I caught him looking at the property pages earlier on.' I raised my voice. 'What does he say?'

Dad was concentrating on reading Mick's message. 'It's not good. Den Pacey passed away a year or so ago, prostate cancer. He's pretty sure Pam is still in Nottingham. Mick's bar is in Santa Ponsa, he's been out there for ten years or so. I'm welcome to visit any time.'

'Fantastic, you should go,' I said under my breath.

'Sorry to hear about your friend,' Charlie called, giving me a nudge.

'Yes, me too, sorry Dad.' I headed into the lounge. 'At least we now know why Den wasn't at the funeral, although not why Stewie is paying the Paceys those sums of money.'

'Unless he's helping them out. Treatment costs or something.' Dad rubbed his eyes.

'But then the payments would have stopped when Den died.' I sat next to him and gave his arm a comforting rub. 'It's sad, I'm sorry.'

Dad cleared his throat and placed his hand over mine. 'You get used to it as you get older, friends passing away. It's a fact of life, isn't it. First Stewie, now Den.' He brushed his hand across his face and sniffed. 'Today's been a bit of an emotional rollercoaster. Ignore me. I think I'll leave you kids to it and have an early night.'

I didn't have the heart to broach the subject of him heading home.

PILAR RETURNED DAD'S call first thing the following morning and announced she was flying to Bilbao for a few days. Dad was in the kitchen, cooking his breakfast. It was impossible not to overhear the conversation. He took all his calls on speaker phone – I was starting to wonder if he was a little deaf.

'Anton says it's not good for me to stay here on my own,' Pilar explained. Anton clearly had more influence over Pilar than Dad who had told her the same thing.

'I was hoping we could have another chat,' he replied. 'Does the name Pam Pacey mean anything to you?'

'Pam Pacey? No, not at all. Is she from one of Stewart's charities?'

'No, I don't think so. She's the wife of an old friend, Dennis Pacey. Have you heard of him?'

There was a dramatic humph. 'No, I've never met them, or heard talk of them. If they are old family friends you would be better asking the boys.'

'We will do. You said you spoke to the police about Stewie's phone?'

'Yes, it wasn't with his things. They say everything was bagged up from the boat but it would have been with him when he left the house. He never went out without it.'

Pilar sounded impatient, as if she was heading off to Spain that very minute and Dad's questions were delaying her departure. I shook my head to indicate there was no point pushing her. Pilar hadn't seemed that bothered by Dad's comment about recipes for rabbit at the time, but perhaps he had fallen out of favour.

'Have a safe trip,' Dad finished off. 'I look forward to seeing you when you're back.'

She ended the call without replying.

'Have you tried talking to Tess again?' I asked, watching him deftly crack two eggs into a bowl with one hand.

'No I haven't.'

'We really need that painting back. Whatever we do here means nothing without that picture as evidence.'

'Which is why we need a back-up.' He gave his eggs a quick whisk before tossing the mixture into a small saucepan. He had taken far less time to find his way around the apartment's fully equipped kitchen than I had. I'd hadn't seen the whisk or the pan before. 'I couldn't find any cream or butter in your fridge, by the way.'

'That's because I haven't got any.'

He gave an exasperated shake of his head and continued whisking. 'Lilian's idea of trying to trap these forgers into producing a second fake Birdie is not such a bad one. You ought to consider it.'

'Just like you ought to consider going back to Harrogate and sorting out this mess with Tess. And I don't just mean about this picture. Your life. Everything.'

He avoided my eye and tossed his eggs into the pan. Despite the lack of cream or butter, Dad's scrambled eggs looked far more appetising than anything I'd ever rustled up.

Pilar had given Dad Anton's number. I tried calling him but his phone went straight to voicemail. I wondered if he was driving Pilar to the airport.

CHAPTER FIFTEEN

MAKING WAVES WAS unusually busy. Charlie had decided on an impromptu sale to make way for some new spring stock. The shop had initially been sold as two small retail units, but after some deliberation I'd persuaded him to combine the two units together, giving him double the floor space. It was a gamble that so far appeared to be paying off. I had a sense of responsibility and gave up my time freely to help him out. Throughout January and February, traditionally quiet months in Cowes, business had been steady.

Our week together was nearly over. Lucas was landing at Heathrow tomorrow afternoon, and on Saturday I was heading over to the mainland for my Golf Sparks coaching weekend. It was quite likely we wouldn't see each other after tonight until early next week. A point I made to Charlie as we snatched a moment together in the staffroom.

'I know this week hasn't been quite what we'd wished for,' Charlie said. 'But that's how it is with families, Lizzie. You don't always get your own way.'

Was Charlie issuing me a warning? When you lived with other people you had to make allowances. Dad had been an absent parent since I was six years old. We were casual spectators in each other's lives, not active participants. I'd left home at the age of eighteen to travel the world competing and I wasn't used to sharing my space. Putting down roots, settling down with Charlie, if that's what I was planning, came with other considerations. Guys I'd dated in the past hadn't had baggage. It was just me, them and the next tournament to think about. I knew I should be grateful Lucas was nearly a teenager and relatively independent, but a steady relationship with a single parent required a certain amount of self-sacrifice. I didn't doubt my feelings for Charlie. I loved him, and Lucas was easy to get on with, but how would it work out if we were all together under one roof? I found Dad's constant presence in my apartment suffocating. When you lived with someone you had to make compromises. Maybe I wasn't cut out to be a family person. What did that mean for me and Charlie?

GRACE HAD ALWAYS been a good sounding board and I had lots to discuss. She was happy with the change of venue I suggested for our catch up. Charlie had checked his tide tables. Pilar had told us Stewie had left the house "around lunchtime". According to Charlie, the quayside at Shalfleet was accessible until about two o'clock that afternoon, perfectly do-able.

'But he'd either have to make a quick turna-round to catch the tide on its way out, or he'd be stuck there for at least six hours,' Charlie said.

I felt a moment of triumph when the landlord of the New Inn recognised the picture of Stewie Beech I showed him on my phone while I waited for Grace to arrive. All I needed to know was who Stewie was with, and I could pack Dad safely on a train to Yorkshire.

'Who he was with?' The landlord repeated my question with a frown. 'You think he's been here? No, I've never seen him here, I just know that's Stewie Beech, the restauranteur. Everyone in this trade on the island knows Stewie Beech.'

I tried to hide my disappointment. 'You've not seen him in the pub or in the village? I was hoping he might have been a customer. I'm trying to work out what he was up to on the day he died. You know they found his body on a boat in the creek? His widow is concerned.'

'I didn't think there was anything suspicious about his death,' the landlord replied. 'Heart attack, wasn't it?'

'Yes, it's not so much his death she's concerned about, it's the circumstances leading up to it. We think he may have moored up at the quay for a while.'

'Oh I see.' The landlord gave me a salacious grin. 'Like that was it. Leave me your number. I'll ask around. A few of my regulars keep their dinghies up on the quay. I'll see if I can find out if anyone spotted him for you.'

Over steaming bowls of the lunchtime special pumpkin soup, Grace helped put the world, or at least my relationship with Charlie, to rights.

'It's early days despite the fact you've known each other for years,' Grace said. 'You don't need to rush into anything. The crunch will be when you head back to Seaview and you're not living in such close proximity. Maybe that'll help you decide what you really want.'

If I was honest, I liked living in Cowes more than I thought. Although I was looking forward to the work at Goldstone Villa being finished, moving back was going to be quite a wrench. Perhaps that was telling me something.

'How's your dad?' Grace asked. 'After you left yesterday Kurt was in a right bad mood. He and your nanna had words.'

'No? Seriously?'

'Yes, I've never seen anything like it. He's normally such a placid man.'

I briefly explained about Stewie Beech's forgery and Dad's quest to track down the culprits. 'I'd hoped Kurt would be able to help as he used to teach art on the island. I thought he might know people, but he said not.'

'He taught at the FE college in Newport for a number of years,' Grace said. 'Surely he could put you in touch with some experts? How odd. Maybe he thought you were accusing him of being involved.'

'Why would he think that?'

'I don't know. Guilty conscience?' Grace raised her eyebrows.

Kurt had seemed irrationally defensive. 'Have you ever seen any of his paintings?' I asked.

'He's got some hanging in his room.'

'Portraits?'

'A couple yes, his wife, I assumed. And some abstracts. I suppose being a teacher you have to be able to turn your hand to anything.' She paused. 'The ideal skill set for a forger.'

Seriously? Kurt?

'What do you know about him?' I asked. 'He is quite young and with it compared to some of your residents. Why did he choose to live at Marsh House?' Rooms at the residential home didn't come cheap. Could Kurt have boosted his teacher's pension with a spot of forgery?

'I believe it was his niece's idea,' Grace replied. 'She seemed to think he couldn't manage on his own after his wife died. They didn't have any children, and the wife did everything for him. He wasn't domesticated, couldn't even boil an egg. The niece is in France, so not close enough to lend a hand. She thought he'd be better off somewhere like Marsh House. I don't think he had an awful lot of say in the matter. Sounds like he was used to being bossed around.'

'That's probably why he gets on so well with Nanna.' I sighed. Kurt was a henpecked old man, not a master criminal. Grace might be a good sounding board, but she also enjoyed putting a dramatic spin on everything. 'He must have his own reasons for not wanting to help,' I said. 'I've left Dad with the task of contacting local art groups to ask some discreet questions. The trouble is we've got no idea where Stewie Beech bought his painting, who from or how much he paid for it. The only other cases of art forgery we've come across have all been on the mainland, involving multi-million-pound scams. This case doesn't seem to fit the mould, which makes me suspect it could be personal.'

'You ought to pose as a buyer yourself,' Grace said. 'See if you can lure this forger out of the woodwork. The opportunity to strike again might be irresistible.'

'That's just what Nanna said.'

'Your nanna is very astute. Why don't you ask Faye Cassidy to help you? She's still working on your house, isn't she? She must have to source fancy ornaments for her interior makeovers. I expect plenty of her posh clients have asked for specific works of art. She's bound to have the right contacts. Ask her if she can track down a Birdie Adams.'

We were back to the theatricals, only this time Grace might have a valid point. Faye was very good at her job and if I could persuade her to make enquiries on my behalf, I'd be one step removed from any dubious dealings.

'Do you think she would agree to do it?'

'You won't know until you ask her. No time like the present. Give her a call.'

Faye rarely picked up at first ring. She liked her clients to think she was busy. I left her a message explaining why I wanted to talk to her, making it clear I wasn't chasing her up about Goldstone Villa. She returned my call within minutes.

'I didn't know you were interested in art,' was her first comment.

'I'm not.' I hadn't explained about the subterfuge in my message, just my desire to locate a painting by a particular artist. I lowered my voice, wary of discussing an illegal act of deception in a public place. 'We want you to pretend you've got a wealthy client who wants to buy some.'

'Now I'm more curious than ever.'

'Do you think you could help? Where would we start?'

'All my contacts are in London,' Faye replied. 'Do you want me to make some enquiries?'

'Without mentioning my name, yes. Would you be prepared to do that?'

'Just because it's you. We'll need to talk details. Give me a call this evening when I'm home and we can have a longer chat.'

'Sure, thanks Faye.'

'While I've got you though, I've literally just seen the most perfect Art Deco drinks cabinet on Etsy. It would be perfect for your front room.'

An Art Deco drinks cabinet was not on my current list of requirements, but Faye's exquisitely presented Instagram and TikTok accounts were all part of her career campaign. The purchase of the drinks cabinet was not so much for my benefit, as for hers. However, she was doing me a favour.

'Send me the link and I'll take a look.'

CHAPTER SIXTEEN

ON OUR WAY to the hospital the next morning, Dad announced he'd spoken to his sister Debs and she was going to visit Harrogate at the weekend and have a word with Tess.

'I've asked her to collect my stuff from Marlon's garage.'

'Do you think she'll be able to get the Birdie Adams back?' I asked.

'Umm.' Dad grimaced. 'I've asked her to do her best. I've been keeping my eye on eBay and the local Harrogate Marketplace. Nothing has come up as yet.'

Why hadn't I thought of that? 'If Tess thinks your painting is genuine, won't she be trying to sell it through more upmarket means?' I asked.

'There's nothing upmarket about Tess. More than likely she'll be off-loading it through one of Harley and Marlon's dodgy contacts.'

'Did you ask Debs about those photo albums?' Ever since I'd thought of contacting her myself,

Dad had been permanently attached to his phone.

'I've told you, there's no point. I think we should concentrate on Lilian's idea.'

'You'll be pleased to know my friend Grace agrees with you.'

Dad was delighted Faye had been roped in to help and praised Grace for her creative thinking.

'You think that's creative, you should hear her theory about Kurt,' I said.

Once Dad had stopped laughing, he agreed we could discount Kurt from our suspect list. 'Perhaps he just took offence at our suggestion someone on the island was involved,' he concluded. 'We'll be more tactful in future.'

Tact wasn't my strong point and I doubted it was his either.

The hospital appointment went without a hitch. I spent the afternoon covering for Charlie in the shop. The golfing weekend commenced at ten on Saturday morning, but I wasn't due to arrive until twelve, giving me ample time to pay a visit to Josh Beech in Winchester on my way.

The air boot cheered Dad up considerably. He assured me he felt positively light-footed and could manage perfectly well in my absence. I wasn't to worry about him over the weekend and he would continue his research in earnest.

Charlie had offered to entertain him for a couple of hours on Sunday. I called Meg at work and she promised to visit Dad on Saturday.

'Isn't he well enough to go home now?' she asked.

'Yes, but he won't. He says he's not going back to Tess. She's bagged up his stuff.'

'It's like dealing with a teenager,' Meg sighed. 'Tell him I'll pick him up at two. Maybe Frank can take him to the aircraft museum.'

I had to resign myself to the fact that Dad was not going to rush back to Yorkshire anytime soon, light-footed or not. But once we'd uncovered Stewie's fraudsters, he'd have no excuse to stay.

'By the way, at the restaurant last week you mentioned Stewie Beech was sponsoring a nature camp. Did you find out if he donated the money before he died?'

'I spoke to the Bizzikids treasurer,' Meg replied. 'Stewie told her he had a lump sum set aside for good causes but couldn't pay out until the end of January. The treasurer rang his wife to ask whether she was prepared to honour the pledge, but Mrs Beech burst into tears and refused to discuss the matter. We've no idea where we stand now.'

Dad had assumed Stewie would make charitable donations from his business account, but it sounded as if the restauranteur might have earmarked money from the sale of his painting to Bizzikids, as well as Pilar's grandmother. I told Meg briefly about the forgery.

'The families will be devastated if we have to

call the camp off,' Meg replied. 'Is there anything I can do?'

'I don't suppose you've got a telephone number for Auntie Debs, have you?'

'Auntie Debs? What's she got to do with it?'

Fortunately, before I could go into the gory details of Dad's involvement, another phone started to ring in Meg's office.

'I'll text you the number,' she promised. 'Got to go. Have a good weekend.'

I HEADED OVER to the mainland on the ferry at seven on Saturday morning. I'd forewarned Josh of my visit with a text explaining Pilar had asked me to investigate a suspected case of art fraud involving his father. His reply had been an instant '*not sure I can help, but happy to chat*'. We'd arranged to meet at his deli at nine. Josh was the youngest of Stewie's sons and Dad had met him a couple of times in York and again at the funeral.

'I thought he was studying engineering,' he said. 'Stewie seemed very proud of him. Not sure what he thought when he decided to run a deli instead.'

I wondered if Josh was the son Stewie had fallen out with during his run of bad luck after purchasing his picture. Was he disappointed Josh had decided not to pursue a career in engineering?

On my arrival in Winchester, I called Debs. She was surprised to hear from me but promised to look out the photograph albums Dad had "forgotten" to ask her for the previous day.

'How is he?' she asked. 'I hope he's not being too much of an inconvenience. I did tell him he could come and stay here for a bit, but it sounded like he was caught up in this thing with Stewie Beech.'

'Did you know Stewie too?' I asked.

'He and your Dad were once as thick as thieves,' Debs replied. 'They were always round each other's houses. They fell out big time not long after that holiday on the Isle of Wight.'

Dad hadn't mentioned any rows. 'Dad and Stewie met up again a few years ago and picked up their friendship,' I said to Debs. 'I'd assumed they'd simply drifted apart.'

'Ian was pretty laid back in his younger days so it must have been something big to have caused such a ruction,' Debs explained. 'He didn't talk about it. He bought himself a motorbike and took himself off to France for the next year or so. Mum and Dad were worried sick.'

'He went on his own?'

'His old school friend Mick went with him to start with, but then Mick's mum got ill so he came home. Ian stayed out there. He got enough work to get by financially. Stewie came here looking for him a couple of times early on. When Ian returned to the UK he got the job on the Isle of Wight, met your mum and it all ended happily ever after.'

'Well not quite,' I pointed out. My parents' marriage had barely lasted eight years.

'He settled down,' Debs said. 'I know he's my younger brother and all that, so I'm naturally protective, but I always think of your dad as a bit of a lost soul. He's just flitted through life, going with the flow, never taking control. He's not one of life's movers and shakers, if you know what I mean.'

I knew exactly what she meant. 'Do you remember a friend of Dad's called Dennis Pacey?' I asked.

'The Paceys lived in the next road to us when we were growing up. Funnily enough I'm seeing an old work colleague next week who knew the Pacey family well. She was a cousin or something.'

'I don't suppose you could ask if she knows where Den's wife Pam is now? Dad would quite like to get in touch with her. He heard Den had passed away.'

'I didn't know that. How sad. Yes, of course I'll ask.'

I thanked her and we promised to keep in touch. The conversation left me perturbed. Debs had described Dad as being laid back, but that wasn't how I remembered him. My parents had argued constantly. And then there was the row with Stewie. Dad had intimated he and Stewie had been the best of friends. Why had he lied?

DAD MAY NOT be a mover or a shaker, but Josh Beech, just like his father, had mover and shaker written all over him.

His deli-cum-café occupied a prime location just off Winchester's main high street. I recognised the young man serving behind the counter from the deli's trendy Facebook page. Josh Beech was shaven headed, heavily tattooed and dressed head to toe in black with an air of affability at odds with his intimidating appearance. I ordered coffee – the finest Colombian – and avocado on toast, which one of his many servers promised to bring over to my table. The café was bustling with youngsters grabbing coffees on their way to work and student types meeting up for a tasty hangover cure.

'What exactly is this?' he asked, joining me ten minutes later. 'It's the first I've heard of any art fraud.'

'Your dad hadn't mentioned a particular painting to you, by the artist Birdie Adams?'

'Never heard of her,' Josh said.

I retrieved my phone and showed him one of the pictures I'd downloaded from the internet from Birdie's collection.

'Your dad acquired a similar picture about three years ago. He might have paid a fair bit for it, believing it to be an original painting.'

Josh Beech shook his head. 'I've never seen anything like that before. Did he have it up in the house?'

'I believe so.'

'Didn't get invited over to Sandpipers many times to be honest,' Josh admitted. 'Probably explains why I don't recognise it. I didn't even know Dad collected art.'

'He had a personal connection to the artist, which is why he may have been persuaded to buy it. He didn't mention anything to you about being scammed?'

Again Josh shook his head. 'You said Pilar asked you to investigate this? Was she hoping to sell it on for a fortune?'

'Your dad wanted to raise some cash to help out with nursing home costs for her grandmother in Spain.'

Josh raised a pierced eyebrow. 'Really? I didn't know she had a grandmother in Spain. She's getting the whole family in on the act.'

'He had the picture valued just before he passed away,' I said after a slight hesitation. I didn't want to become side-tracked by Josh's personal grievances. 'Pilar reckons the shock of hearing it was worthless brought on his heart attack, that's why she's so keen to trace the forgers.'

Josh let out a snort. 'Dad was a walking time bomb. He had a heart defect. He could have dropped dead at any moment.'

'A heart defect? Pilar didn't say.'

'Knowing Dad, he hadn't told her, although he was on about ten pills a day, so she should have guessed. Not that she's the brightest button in the box. He probably told her they were vitamins.'

'Your dad was a keen sportsman, he ran—'

'Dad wanted to prove the doctors wrong, to cheat death,' Josh interrupted. 'He had his first heart attack about ten, twelve years ago, when he and mum were still married. That's when they discovered he had this condition. His own father died at fifty. After that Dad got paranoid, became this fitness freak determined to defy the medics. He had us all tested to see if we were at risk. We weren't. Then he and Mum split up. It was all very traumatic. I was fourteen, my dad had a near fatal heart attack, then within a few months my mum moved out. My teenage years weren't the best. Dad was very angry and not a lot of fun to live with.'

'I'm sorry. Your dad must have been bitter about your mum leaving him when he was ill.'

'Oh no, it wasn't like that at all. He kicked her out. Things hadn't been too good before his heart attack, but you'd have thought something like that would have brought them closer together. It had the opposite effect. Mum took herself off to a commune in Cornwall.'

Christine Beech was already on my list of suspects. Josh had confirmed a motive. I cleared my throat. 'Pilar seemed to think, out of the three of you, you were the son he was closest to. I was hoping he might have confided in you, maybe spoken to you after he received the news of the painting's value.'

'Dad didn't share confidences. He wasn't like that. He was a one-man band, self-contained. I was probably closer to him than the others. Matty's gay and Dad couldn't come to terms with that. Callum's worked in London since he was sixteen. The last time I spoke to Dad was just after Christmas. He's certainly never talked to me about any paintings. Did he lose a lot of money on it?'

'We don't know. There's no record of who he bought it from or how much he paid for it. That's why it's all such a mystery.'

Josh glanced over his shoulder at the clock on the bare brick wall behind the serving counter. 'I'm really sorry I can't help. I need to get back to work. Is there anything else?'

'Do you remember friends of your parents called Pam and Dennis Pacey? Pam's from Nottingham like your mother, I believe.'

'You'd be better off asking her then, not me.'

'I would, but I don't have your mum's contact details…' My words were lost as another gaggle of noisy youngsters came into the deli.

Josh stood up. 'Pilar's upset she's lost her meal-ticket.' He had to raise his voice to make himself heard. 'She's got the house and the business. You think she'd be satisfied with that. Why's she making such a fuss about a painting?

'My dad died of a heart attack, the autopsy, inquest or whatever, confirmed it. Nothing can change that. That it happened while he was out fishing and on his own, yeh, that's a shame, and it's a shame nobody found him sooner, but on the other hand, he died doing something he loved. That's how I'd like to remember him. Isn't that the best way to go, doing something you enjoy?'

It was a phrase heard regularly on golf courses. A sudden death was quite common amongst the elderly golfing fraternity. Had Pilar really been ignorant of Stewie's heart condition?

Josh's opinion of his stepmother had been scathing, but Pilar's culinary skills had contributed to *Absinthe's* success. She hadn't come across as a gold-digger. Josh was clearly peeved she'd inherited the house and the yacht. I had no idea how much either asset was worth, but I could hazard a guess, which did raise the awkward question of why an affluent man like Stewie Beech had been so reliant on the proceeds from the Birdie Adams' painting to fund the grandmother's care and potentially make the contribution to Meg's charity.

I left Winchester more confused than ever.

CHAPTER SEVENTEEN

IT WAS A relief to spend the rest of the weekend concentrating on golf. The Golf Sparks event was being held at a prestigious club nestled in the north Hampshire countryside. I had been invited to give a speech that evening at a private dinner to a selected audience of club members and local journalists, and although I wasn't nervous about public speaking, I hadn't done an awful lot of it.

Faye had recently introduced me to a PR Guru called Katy Pimm who she thought could help optimise opportunities like this to raise my media profile. Initially I wasn't convinced I needed the sort of help Katy offered. 'We'll soon have you back on Question of Sport,' Katy had said at our first meeting. 'And how good are you at ice skating?'

I wasn't good at all and hadn't realised the significance of the question until she later mentioned a certain TV reality show was looking for its next batch of contestants. I didn't want to be a

D list celebrity. I wanted to be Eliza Kane who got girls playing sport. Katy had since offered more sensible suggestions and was currently talking to people on my behalf. I didn't particularly enjoy being in the spotlight but knew it was essential to promote my cause. Katy had asked me to forward photographs from the weekend which she would distribute to her contacts.

As I prepared for the dinner, having contorted myself into my favourite confidence boosting black jumpsuit, I received a welcome message from Charlie wishing me good luck. Meg also texted to let me know Dad and Frank had got on like a house on fire and were currently discussing the afternoon's football results over a pint in the Navigator's Arms.

One final check in the mirror and just as I was about to head out of the door, an email notification pinged onto my phone from Phil Flowers. Dad hadn't been able to uncover anything pertinent in his online searches for art fraud, but Phil had access to a much wider range of resources. A brief glance at the message confirmed Phil had received some interesting information from a colleague on the mainland.

'It could just be a coincidence,' he wrote, 'but let me know what you think.' He'd forwarded his friend's email and included two attachments.

It would have to wait. I headed down to the hotel restaurant.

My speech, a little bit about me, my career, my involvement with Golf Sparks and how good it was to see the women's game becoming much more prominent, went down well. Earlier in the day I'd been interviewed by both local radio and TV stations, and there had been lots of photo opportunities for my social media accounts.

The Golf Sparks family was growing. I learned my old adversary Agnes MacDonald had agreed to participate in future events in Scotland.

'I'm not sure if that's a good thing or bad,' the chair of the organising committee confided over a nightcap in the bar. 'She is one of the UK's most successful female golfers ever, but she can be a bit fierce. I'm slightly worried she might put kids off the sport, rather than make them want to pick up a club.'

I agreed there was every chance Aggie might do more harm than good, but I had been concerned about the amount of travelling required to promote the scheme. Knowing Scotland was off the radar was a relief.

'Aggie is very passionate about golf,' I replied. 'Hopefully that passion will come across and inspire others.' I could tell from the chairperson's expression she found this prospect just as doubtful as I did.

IT WAS NINE in the evening before I arrived back in Cowes on Sunday, exhilarated and exhausted in equal measure. The whole weekend had been a huge success and I had ample material for Katy Pimm's PR company to work their magic with. Plus, with extra time waiting around for the ferry, I'd drafted my own feature to polish off and submit to various golfing magazines.

Dad was waiting for me, kettle at the ready.

'Put your feet up, love. I'll make you a cuppa. Or would you prefer a glass of the old *Jim Beam*?'

I would much prefer the bourbon, but it was always best to engage on social media when sober. I wanted to post more comments while I was still basking in my triumph, and that included messaging Agnes MacDonald to welcome her to the Golf Sparks clan.

Dad had enjoyed his afternoon with Charlie and Lucas, which had also involved a short walk to a local park.

'You'll be amazed at how quick I can go now that I've only got my boot on.' He beamed as he handed me a cup of tea. 'We bumped into one of Luc's friends, nice lad, Bailey. He's into photography. Had a fancy camera.'

I'd heard of Bailey and the fancy camera. Bailey also had an attractive newly divorced mother who was keen to recruit Charlie to take Rowena's place on the School Friends Committee. So far Charlie had put up admirable resistance.

'After that we had a game of frisbee.'

'You should not be playing frisbee, Dad.'

'Charlie, Lucas and Bailey played frisbee. I just watched.'

I decided not to risk an irrational bout of jealousy by asking if Bailey's mother had taken part in the game. Dad was very susceptible to the charms of attractive women. If she had been present, he would have mentioned it.

After frisbee he'd cooked dinner, a feat confirmed by Charlie in reply to my "honey I'm home" text.

'*BTW your dad cooks the best steaks ever*,' Charlie wrote.

I may have been wary of the downsides of family life, but I was now enjoying the benefits. Years of returning to a cold empty flat after tournaments, nobody enquiring after me, asking whether I'd won or lost, nobody to catch up with, *to look after me*, and here was Dad, tea towel over his arm fussing like an old mother hen, and Charlie, a text away.

Dad announced he had made exciting developments in his investigations over the weekend but insisted it could wait until the morning.

'Today is all about your achievements,' he said with a wink. 'I can tell you about mine tomorrow.'

HE LOOKED QUITE smug as he cracked his breakfast eggs into the bowl. A generous slab of butter was already melting in the frying pan. 'You know you left me with the task of approaching amateur art groups,' he began, 'well, you'll never guess what. One of the contacts the library provided is running a taster session at Waverley House this week. I've signed up. Can you run me down to St Lawrence tomorrow afternoon?'

'I thought we agreed we weren't going to Waverley House.'

'I want to find out more about Mr William Mintrum. He must be Sasha's younger brother. The class is run by a lady called Bethan Edwards, and even if I do bump into William Mintrum while I'm there, he won't remember me. He wouldn't have been more than nine or ten when we stayed there. As an extra precaution I've signed up to the course using my middle name, just in case.'

'Right. What is your middle name?'

'Malcolm.' Dad added some mushrooms to his pan.

I hadn't known. It must have been on documents somewhere, my birth certificate for example, ignored, dismissed from my memory. 'Anything else?'

'Yes, I've been back to look at those bank statements again.'

'Talking about that, Josh Beech knew the Paceys. He thinks his mum will still be in touch with them. We haven't got Chrissy's contact details, have we? Unless you've found her on Facebook?'

Dad shook his head. 'How was Josh? Did he

have any other useful information?'

'Sadly not, knew nothing about the picture, implied Pilar was some sort of gold-digger. Did you know Stewie had a heart condition?'

'Oh? No, I didn't.' Dad hesitated ever so slightly before retrieving a slice of sourdough from the toaster. His breakfast looked and smelt far more appealing than my muesli.

'According to Josh he could have dropped dead at any time.' I paused. 'Just out of curiosity, where did Stewie and Pilar meet? Do you know?'

'During Cowes Week, or so he told me. She was here with a catering company. This was before he bought *Absinthe*. He'd run restaurants for years but wanted to do something different. He knew the boat's owners were about to put her up for sale and he was mingling, as you do during the regatta. Pilar was working on one of the pop-up restaurants. One taste of her paella and he was smitten, or at least that's how he described it to me.'

Dad divided the contents of his pan onto two plates and pushed one towards me. 'Go on, I've made enough for two and I know you want to.' He rubbed his stomach. 'Got to watch my waistline.'

'Did they tell you that at the hospital?'

'I can't see my feet because of my belly, love. It's a sign I need to lose weight.'

I wondered if the mention of Stewie Beech's heart condition had touched a nerve. I helped myself to a forkful of scrambled egg. He must have used double cream. It was delicious, and the mushrooms were definitely not the supermarket norm. Organic without a doubt.

'Have you been out shopping?' I asked.

'I've stocked you up a bit,' he admitted.

I mopped up the last of the juices from the mushrooms with the sourdough toast. If I breakfasted like this every morning, Dad wouldn't be the only one losing sight of their feet. 'You said you found something else in the bank statements?'

'It looks like he was paying his boys an allowance, or rather only two of his boys, Callum and young Josh. There are no payments at all to Matthew. Pilar said he'd fallen out with one of his boys after he bought that picture. I wonder if it would be worth having a word with Matthew? See if there's a connection. Maybe they had an argument about it, maybe he accused his dad of wasting money, spending the inheritance and the like.'

'I think Stewie might have fallen out with Matthew because Matthew is gay. According to Josh, Stewie had trouble coming to terms with it.'

'Oh.'

'But that's good detective work, and no harm in chatting to Matthew. We've got his address, haven't we?'

'He runs a carpentry workshop in the village of Godshill.'

'Great. I'll pay him a visit tomorrow while you re-live your holiday memories at Waverley House.'

CHAPTER EIGHTEEN

Chrissy August 1981

SASHA AGREED THERE was no point the lads traipsing back and forth from their campsite every day. When they arrived in Dennis' Ford Capri to pick up Chrissy and Pam for a visit to the amusement park at Blackgang Chine, she ordered them out of the car.

'Tell me what you boys do,' she said, lining them up for an inspection.

'Me and Kaney are chefs,' Stew told her. 'We both work for the health authority in Leeds.'

'Tweedle Dum and Tweedle Dee.' Sasha ran her tongue around her lips. She had ditched her tartan shorts for a ruffled blouse and lederhosen. 'What about you other two?'

'I'm an electrician,' Dennis replied.

'And I'm a motor mechanic,' Mick finished.

'Trades people. Very useful.' She scrutinised the boys in turn, lingering in front of Stew as if she was assessing a specimen piece of prize livestock.

Pam had already ear-marked Dennis, who was

blond and stocky, not Chrissy's type. Stew and Ian were both over six foot tall, brown-haired with floppy fringes, and in Chrissy's opinion, much more attractive. They were both clear skinned and clean shaven, whereas poor Mick, the heavy metal freak, was in need of a serious haircut. 'And soap and a razor,' Pam had giggled after that first night in the pub. Sasha barely gave him a glance.

'When you come back from your little outing, bring your tents and pitch up where you like,' she said when she had finished her examination. 'We could do with some additional entertainment.'

Relieved the lads had passed the test, the two girls squeezed into the backseat of the car.

'Have you always worked together?' Chrissy asked, finding herself wedged between Stew and Ian. Stew was wearing a tight pair of nylon shorts, which left very little to Chrissy's imagination. Pam was squashed on the other side of Ian.

'Kaney got the sack from his last place, I managed to persuade my boss to take him on.'

'I didn't get the sack,' Ian said. His Leeds United football shorts were not quite as skimpy as Stew's but had an equally enchanting effect. 'The new owner wanted to bring in his own staff. It was a shame because it was a pretty posh eatery and I was really enjoying myself. The job at the hospital is just a temporary thing, until something better comes along.'

'Where would you like to end up?' Chrissy asked.

'I wouldn't mind a job here,' Ian replied. 'Sun, sand, seaside. You don't get a lot of that in Leeds.'

Stew and Ian jostled for her attention as they wandered around the amusement park. They showed off their prowess in the gaming arcades, egging each other on. Chrissy didn't have a head for heights or a stomach for high speeds, but with the lads' encouragement, she braved the roller-coaster. She felt exhilarated, and not just because of the adrenaline overload from the ride. The holiday was getting better and better.

On their return from Blackgang the lads set up their camp. Since the art students' arrival there had been continuous music and dancing in the Mintrums' garden as the band rehearsed for their big performance in front of the mythical Jason Ross, but like vampires, the students rarely surfaced until late in the day. The leader of the pack was a gangly youth with a permanent scowl and a thick wedge haircut who went by the name of Gideon. He complained Chrissy and Pam had no appreciation of culture, they'd never heard of the Velvet Underground, they were unfamiliar with the Brighton club scene. But that didn't matter now Stew and his gang were here.

It no longer mattered that the water in the Mintrums' pool was green and cold, or that Chrissy and Pam had no taste for art and intellectual conversation. It didn't matter that Rachel had hooked up and become inseparable from Angus,

The Future's synthesizer player, having given up on Roly, the original number one on her most-wanted list. It didn't matter because something far more exciting was happening. Chrissy was falling in love, or at least in lust. Something that made her heart and other places a flutter. Something that made her replay conversations and look for hidden meanings. Something that lifted her spirits and filled her with joy.

BIRDIE SAT AT her easel and complained about the noise. They were making it impossible for her to concentrate.

'Don't get your knickers in a twist, *Grandma*,' Stew yelled from his Lilo, can of beer in his hand.

'I wouldn't be surprised if she wears any, knowing how much she likes seeing people in the buff,' Mick sniggered from his spot on the grass. 'We've seen the pictures.'

Chrissy assumed the lads had sneaked into Birdie's studio. Highly unlikely the old dear would have invited them for a tour.

'Your accents are even worse than those girls,' Sasha called. She sat on the edge of the pool, her legs crossed. 'Where exactly were you dragged up?'

The lads were very proud of their northern heritage.

'Leeds is the best city in the world,' Stew exclaimed.

'Can't beat it,' Dennis agreed.

'Shows how little you've travelled,' Sasha remarked.

'Yeh? Where have you been then?'

'Paris, Amsterdam, Barcelona.'

'I say old chaps.' Stew mimicked her accent. He manoeuvred his Lilo closer to Sasha's side of the pool. 'I've been to Paris. Ooh la la.'

Sasha stretched out a leg and overturned his Lilo.

'I reckon that posh bird fancies me,' he said later, as they dried off beside the tents.

'I wouldn't be so sure about that,' Pam remarked. 'I think she's set her sights on Gideon.'

The next afternoon they left the art school boys lounging in the barn and took the bus to Ventnor. Rachel and Sasha joined them. They strolled along the promenade playing the slot machines, feeding chips to the marauding seagulls. Sasha bagged the seat next to Stew on the way home. Chrissy sat in the row behind, watching the back of Sasha's dark head deliberately coming to rest on his shoulder. What was she playing at? Sasha didn't *need* a lad like Stew. She was doing it deliberately, doing it because she liked winding people up, doing it simply because she could.

THAT EVENING, IAN lit a barbeque and Rachel and Sasha sang along with the band who had now adopted an Arabian Knights look to impress Jason Ross, wearing headbands, loose trousers and baring mid-drifts. Gideon offered everyone a puff on his not-so-secret stash of spliffs.

'He's hoping we'll be so stoned we won't notice how bad a singer he is,' Ian told her with a wink.

'It's absolute rubbish,' Stew agreed. 'Let's sneak off somewhere where we can't hear this shit. Who's with me?'

Chrissy woke at dawn in the unfamiliar surroundings of the tent, throbbing head, parched. She gathered up her clothes, anxious not to disturb the figure lying next to her, still lost in a heavy sleep. She tiptoed into the house across the dew-covered lawn, pausing in the kitchen to drink water straight from the tap.

Upstairs in the attic Pam and Dennis were squeezed together on the bottom bunk. Unable to keep the smile from her face, Chrissy clambered into the empty bed opposite. The holiday was getting better and better.

CHAPTER NINETEEN

Eliza

I WAS EAGER to tell Charlie about my successful weekend. After responding to the influx of social media messages, I headed over to Making Waves.

Following the frenetic activity of the sale, it was a relief to discover only one customer in the shop. A man in a navy puffer jacket stood at the counter with Dexter and Charlie.

'Ah, perfect timing.' Charlie beckoned me over. 'Here she is.'

The customer was in his early forties, with thick dark hair and eyebrows that met in the middle. He held out his hand. 'Anton Lorenz. I understand you want to speak with me.'

The sommelier. 'Oh yes, I would like a private word, thank you.' I noticed he had extraordinary long fingers. *Like an artist.* Or useful for pulling corks.

'I apologise for not returning your calls,' he said. 'I thought a face to face would be more civilised, but I wasn't sure quite where to find you. It was Amelie who mentioned the shop.' There was something disdainful about the way he said shop.

'You're welcome to use the staffroom,' Charlie said without hesitation. 'Dex and me need to sort out a new display. We can keep busy out here.'

The disapproving looks continued as I led Anton through to the kitchenette. I decided not to insult the sommelier's tastebuds by offering him supermarket coffee.

'I assume you wish to talk to me about Stewart Beech,' he said, dusting off the offered chair before sitting down.

'Yes, if you don't mind.'

'When I saw Pilar last week she explained you were looking into this business about the painting.'

'You knew about the painting?'

'No, at least not until last week.' Anton had the merest trace of a German accent. 'I called round to see how she was. That was when she mentioned it. And your enquiries.' He paused, putting his hands together as if in prayer. 'I am concerned. There are things Pilar does not know about Stewart, things that may arise during the course of your investigations which I would not want getting back to her. Do you understand?'

I nodded.

'Therefore, what I am about to tell you I am telling you for one reason only. I hope it will bring your enquiries to a speedy close without unnecessary upset.'

'Anything you tell me will remain confidential,' I assured him.

'I believe Pilar expressed her concerns to you as to why Stewart had gone off in the *Little Lady* that Tuesday afternoon.'

'She seemed quite mystified.'

'I can tell you exactly what he was doing.' Anton cleared his throat. 'He was seeing another woman.'

That was not what I was expecting.

'It had become a bit of a thing, this disappearing off to Newtown Creek,' Anton continued, 'on the pretence of fishing. Pilar would never normally have questioned it, after all, local fish plays an important part in our menu. I think on this occasion, the timing, knowing how furious Stewart felt about this forgery...well, she assumes it is connected, but it is not.'

I found my voice. 'You are saying Stewie regularly met up with a woman in Newtown Creek?'

Anton gave a brief nod. 'You are aware Stewart had lost his driving licence? He could hardly ask Pilar to take him to meet his lover.'

'I can see that might be awkward.' I cleared my throat. 'How did you know he was seeing someone else?'

'I suspected. It was easy to work out. Too many boat trips, but not a lot of fish. I picked up things, hints, clues.'

Anton was very composed. He sat straight backed, legs together. I wondered if he'd been in the military at some point.

'So, there you have it. That was why when Pilar phoned me on that Wednesday morning to say Stewart hadn't come home, I immediately called the skipper, Brian Riggs. I knew we had to find Stewart before Pilar called the emergency services. I didn't want anyone to discover him in a compromising situation.'

'Do you know who this woman is?'

Anton shook his head. 'No.'

'Presumably she lives in the vicinity of Newtown Creek?'

Anton shrugged his shoulders. 'It could be they chose that spot for their meetings because it is isolated. Perhaps she was married too and would not want to be seen or recognised.' He rose to his feet. 'You do not need to pursue this line of questioning any further. I have told you why Stewart Beech took his boat to Newtown Creek and it has nothing to do with this forged painting.'

'Thank you. You've been very helpful.'

He bowed his head slightly. 'My pleasure.'

'And with regard to this painting, you don't have any ideas–'

He cut me off before I could finish. 'None at all. I've told Pilar she should forget it.' Anton pursed his lips. 'I have suggested she remain abroad with her family for the foreseeable future.

It is for the best, don't you think?'

I accompanied him back into the shop floor and waited by the counter until he was out the door.

'What was all that about?' Charlie asked, leaving Dexter to finish off the window display.

'I'm not sure.'

Anton's confession had caught me totally by surprise. It seemed incredible to think Stewie was cheating on Pilar, but if he was, it made sense that Anton wanted Pilar out of the way to protect her. But as for asking no more questions, I was going to have to disobey orders. It was more important than ever to find out exactly where Stewie went ashore in Newtown Creek and who he met up with. If Stewie did have a secret mistress, there was every chance he may have confided in her about his painting.

When Dexter finished the window display, Charlie insisted we head to a sandwich shop for a bite of lunch, which actually meant back to his place, where there wasn't a sandwich in sight.

Fun though it was, we couldn't keep sneaking around like a pair of teenagers. Charlie was going to have to accept if we wanted our relationship to flourish, Lucas had to be prepared for the fact that I might occasionally "overnight" in Charlie's bed.

'You need to have a chat with him,' I urged, wondering if the stumbling block was not so much

Lucas, but Charlie.

'To be honest he's been a bit tetchy since he got back from Greece,' Charlie admitted. 'I don't really want to do or say anything that might upset him further.'

Although Lucas had set off for Greece with some trepidation, he'd been full of his adventures when Dad had seen him at the weekend.

'Dad seemed to think he'd had a good time,' I said.

'That's what he told me too. He's just been a bit...moody, I suppose. I think it's more to do with school.'

'He's not happy there?'

Lucas attended one of the top private schools on the island, the fees paid by Rowena's late father who had left the money in a trust specifically for the education of his grandchildren.

'I don't know. Something isn't right.'

Lucas was twelve going on thirteen and his hormones were probably running riot. Surely Charlie didn't need me with my absolute zero parenting skills to point that out?

'Let's do dinner one day this week,' Charlie suggested as we said our goodbyes. 'Out for a pizza with Lucas. He and your dad seemed to hit it off.'

'Everyone hits it off with Dad,' I replied. 'Just don't let Lucas get too fond of him, he doesn't tend to stick around.'

When I arrived back at the flat Dad was making himself far too comfortable and appeared to have every intention of sticking around. Only the two empty cups and a discarded chocolate bar wrapper on the coffee table gave any indication he'd left the sofa all morning. He expressed disbelief at Anton's accusation of infidelity.

'Stewie cheating on Pilar? No way! He was devoted to her.'

'I'm just passing on what he told me. If Stewie did have a mistress, we need to find her. He may have confided in her about these forgers during a bit of pillow talk.'

'Someone else would have known.'

'Why? People don't go bragging about their affairs to all and sundry. You've had plenty of girlfriends over the years. Don't tell me you've never had a fling with a married woman, or at least someone in a long-term relationship.'

A faint flush appeared on Dad's face. 'This isn't about me, it's about Stewie.'

'I know, I'm just saying why would anyone else know about it? Maybe this other woman offered him something Pilar couldn't.'

'Now what are you insinuating?' Dad snapped.

'Nothing. Why are you being so defensive?'

'I'm not. I just don't like the way you're talking about my friends.'

'Stewie might well have been your friend, but how well did you really know him? You didn't talk to each other for years. When I spoke to Josh Beech he was surprised to learn his dad was planning on paying Pilar's grandmother's nursing home fees. I get the impression Stewie kept a lot of stuff to himself. Maybe after working himself up into a frenzy about this forgery, he shoots off to seek solace in the arms of his mistress. And quite possibly over vigorously. Perhaps that was what brought on his heart attack, nothing to do with the shock of losing the money.'

'That's in very poor taste, Eliza.' Dad shook his head again. 'He must have been nuts. He had a beautiful young wife who adored him. That fantastic house. A unique business. Why put it all in jeopardy?'

'I don't know. Having it all clearly wasn't enough.'

'No.' Dad let out a long whistle of breath. 'Typical Stewie. It never was.'

WHEN HE CALMED down, he joined me at the dining table to browse Google Maps. We followed Stewie's journey along the coastline from Cowes to Newtown. After the village of Gurnard, there was nothing but farmland until the holiday park at Thorness. Was Stewie's mystery woman a tourist? I fleetingly thought of Pam Pacey, old family friend, recently widowed. Did she return to the island for her holidays? Could she be the mystery woman? Was that why Stewie was paying her money? Dad dismissed the idea instantly.

'Stewie and Pam? No way. I don't think this holiday park idea works at all. If Stewie had a quickie in a caravan, why then motor on round to Newtown Creek? Surely he'd have come straight home.'

The entrance to the creek itself was narrow, but the main channel subsequently split like fingers, winding through the nature reserve to the east and farmland to the west. The most eastern tributary, Clamerkin Brook, led to a firing range, with no suitable landing points. The causeway at Newtown, Shalfleet quay, or the jetty at Hamstead right on the estuary were the only possible places Stewie could have gone ashore.

'Is this woman a birdwatcher, a twitcher?' I wondered. 'Did they use a bird hide in the marshes as their lover's tryst?'

'Why couldn't he have just met her in a hotel room like every other adulterer?' Dad grumbled.

'He was banned from driving, remember. Boat must have been the most convenient form of transport. Perhaps his lady friend had a boat too.'

'Now you're being ludicrous.'

'Why am I being ludicrous? Women are allowed to own boats, you know. Emancipation and all that.'

'Very funny. Wouldn't he just ask this woman to pick him up from the end of his road or something?'

'Perhaps she didn't drive either.'

'Bus?'

'Not that frequent out to Newtown.'

'Taxi then.'

'This isn't London. He might be able to call a cab to take him out that way, but I wouldn't rate his chances of getting one back.'

'Umm.' Dad frowned. 'There's been a lot of publicity about Stewie's death. You think this woman might have come forward to put the family's mind at rest as to what he was up to in his final hours.'

'Maybe she's married, like Anton said.'

'You don't suppose Anton took Stewie's phone, do you? He's the one who discovered the body. If he suspected Stewie had been with this woman, he'd want to protect Pilar from discovering their texts.'

'It was Anton and the skipper Brian Riggs who called the coastguard. I'm not sure they actually boarded the *Little Lady* and examined the body.'

'But what if they did? Anton could easily have taken Stewie's phone. He wouldn't want Pilar going through Stewie's numbers. We need to question Riggs and find out exactly what happened when they found Stewie's boat.'

Once again Dad had made a sensible suggestion, but I wasn't sure Anton would hand over Stewie's phone, even if he had it.

'Okay, let's try and speak to Brian Riggs, but

don't get your hopes up about Anton. That reminds me, my friend Phil Flowers, the local history expert, sent me an email over the weekend. I've not had a chance to take a proper look at it yet.' With all the excitement of Golf Sparks, now trending in golfing social media circles, Phil's email had become hidden beneath a deluge of congratulatory messages. 'One of his colleagues on the mainland has apparently uncovered something interesting. I'll pull the message up for you to look at while I make us beans on toast.'

'Beans on toast? Is that the best you can manage?'

I left Dad hunched over my laptop. I hadn't even emptied the beans out of the can before he let out a shout.

'Blimey, your friend Grace is very good, isn't she? We misjudged her.'

'What do you mean?' I called from the kitchen.

'Come and read this. She's right about Kurt taking umbrage. He's got a conviction for forgery.'

CHAPTER TWENTY

Dad vacated his chair. 'I'll do the beans. You sit down.'

I read, then re-read, the email Phil had forwarded from one of his counterparts on the mainland. In 1965, two students from Winchester School of Art faced charges of attempting to pass off one of their own paintings as an original by the artist Francis Bacon. They claimed it was an experiment, never intended to be taken seriously. Phil's colleague had attached a scan of the local newspaper report on the incident. The article was grainy, but there in print were the names of the culprits: Kurtis Zeigler, an Austrian national residing in Winchester, and a fellow student, Ronald Albert Whittaker. Both men pleaded guilty, were fined and dismissed from their studies.

Phil had referred to a coincidence in his covering message.

'As far as I'm aware Phil doesn't know Kurt,' I said, reading the piece for the third time as Dad opened drawers and banged shut cupboards in the kitchen. 'He's never met Nanna.'

'Have you got any Tabasco, love? Or some Piri Piri?'

'How many times do I have to tell you, I don't cook. Why does Phil talk about a coincidence? There's nothing that links our Kurt to Stewie Beech or Birdie Adams.'

'Look at the other attachment. Perhaps that explains it.'

I opened up the second document and there it was. Another newspaper report, this time from the Island Echo of three years ago. I'd read it before. It covered the story of Roy and Donna Lemming of Queen Street, Ryde who had taken an old picture they'd had in their attic since "goodness knows when" to the filming of Treasure Trove on Tour, where it had been identified by the programme's art expert, Albie Whittaker, as a genuine Birdie Adams. "You could have picked me up off the floor," Mrs Lemming was quoted as saying on hearing Albie's estimated valuation of the painting's worth. Neither she nor Mr Lemming had any recollection of how they'd acquired the picture, although Mrs Lemming's mother, Elspeth Dawson, had once worked as a cleaner at a house St Lawrence where it was thought the artist might have stayed. The couple suspected the picture had been inherited from Mrs Dawson along with several other boxes of clutter.

Albie Whittaker was quoted as saying this personal connection to the artist gave the picture the provenance he needed to declare it genuine. He suggested the couple have a further rummage through Mrs Dawson's clutter at the earliest opportunity. "Some clutter indeed. Lucky Mr & Mrs Lemming," concluded the reporting journalist.

The coincidence wasn't Kurt. It was Albie Whittaker. The first rule of an investigation was to establish the facts – which I assumed Phil, being Phil, already had. It was safe to assume Kurt's co-defendant, Ronald Albert and esteemed TV art expert Albie were one and the same man. Did this now cast aspersions on Albie Whittaker's credibility and call into the question the authenticity of the painting discovered in Ryde?

While I contemplated this can of worms, a message pinged onto my phone from Faye. *'Success! One of my sources has got back to me already. Thinks he can put me in touch with a Birdie Adams expert. Currently waiting to hear back.'*

I'd half hoped Faye wouldn't be successful because I wasn't sure I could keep up the subterfuge. In less than an hour we had two new positive leads. I should have been jumping up and down with joy – but I wasn't.

WHILE WE DEBATED the Kurt dilemma, Dad took a call from his sister Debs. With the phone on speaker, I learned his possessions were now in her garage as opposed to Marlon's.

'What about the painting?' Dad asked. 'Did you quiz Tess about it?'

'Denies all knowledge of it,' Debs reported. 'She was lying though. I know a liar when I meet one.'

It was a shame Dad hadn't introduced Debs to Tess a bit earlier on in their relationship. Fortunately, Debs didn't get a chance to mention the photo albums because Dad was keen to commence an online enquiry into Albie Whittaker, delving into The Treasure Trove on Tour fan pages.

'Surely they'd never have him on TV if they knew about this conviction for fraud?' he remarked. 'And who is Francis Bacon anyway? Is he someone we should know about?'

We subsequently googled Francis Bacon and discovered that yes, we should have at least heard of him. He and Birdie were both part of the Figurative movement of artists, concentrating on depictions of the human form. Francis Bacon's work had disturbing and religious connotations, while Birdie's, although not easy on the eye, was marginally less disagreeable.

Had Albie Whittaker been committing fraud for over sixty years? Were he and Kurt still in cahoots? It was far too horrible to contemplate.

'We're going to have to tackle Kurt again,' Dad said. We'd lost our appetite for the beans despite his heroic efforts with black pepper and dried chilli flakes, and had resorted to glasses of *Jim Beam*.

'Let's talk to Phil first, see what else he can find out,' I suggested. 'Carry on looking at Albie. Before we accuse anybody of anything we need evidence connecting our forger, whoever he – or she – is, to Stewie. We cannot go jumping to any conclusions. You're at Waverley House tomorrow, and I'm going to visit Matthew Beech. I'll phone the skipper Brian Riggs and see when he's available for a chat. Let's continue to gather facts and not get carried away with suppositions.'

CHAPTER TWENTY-ONE

DAD'S ART LESSON started at two in the afternoon and he wanted to pick up some supplies in town beforehand. Judging by the amount of purchases he made, he was taking his undercover role far too seriously. When we returned from the shopping trip, I phoned Phil Flowers and arranged to meet him the following morning, and Brian Riggs, although unable or unwilling to commit to an appointment on the phone, begrudgingly admitted I could find him onboard *Absinthe*, tinkering with the engine, most afternoons. Dad was buoyed up after our evening of breakthroughs and had already become a fully paid-up member of the Treasure Trove appreciation society. Disappointingly none of the programme's avid viewers had so far made any mention of art fraud and I vetoed the idea of opening up a new online thread amongst Albie's fan base.

'You're right, the last thing we want to do is

alert Albie we're onto him,' Dad reluctantly conceded.

'I was thinking more of the legal consequences of defamation of character.' And the hoards of amateur detectives who might jump on Dad's bandwagon. The only case that needed solving was Stewie's. If Dad wanted to launch a vendetta against Albie Whittaker he could do it once he was back in Yorkshire.

After dropping him at Waverley House I set off for the picturesque village of Godshill. Having checked out his website I knew that Matthew Beech was no ordinary carpenter. You didn't visit his workshop because you were looking for someone to put your shelves up, you called on Matthew Beech when you wanted a unique piece of handcrafted furniture, a coffee table carved out of an entire tree trunk, or a bespoke hat stand made from a wizened piece of oak.

He worked out of a barn at the end of a rutted track. My car was not built for off-roading, so I parked in the village and headed to the workshop on foot.

The barn doors were wide open. Inside I could hear the whine of an electric sander. Matthew Beech wore a leather apron over a check shirt and jeans. He stopped sanding and took off his protective goggles as I approached his workbench. He was stockier than his brother with light brown hair, a neatly trimmed beard and blue-grey eyes he must have inherited from his mother.

'Hi, how can I help you?' he asked with a welcoming smile.

'My name is Eliza,' I said. 'I'm a friend of Pilar's. I just wondered whether I could have a quick word with you about your dad.'

Matthew gave a good humoured grunt. 'For one minute there I thought you might have been a new customer. Ask away.'

'Did he ever talk to you about a painting he owned by the artist Birdie Adams?'

'Did he ever talk to me about a painting? Did he ever talk to me at all would have been a better question. No, me and Dad didn't converse about art, I'm afraid.' Matthew shook his head, looking bemused.

I held out my phone to show him examples of Birdie's artwork. 'You don't remember seeing something like this in your dad's study?'

'I hadn't stepped foot in Sandpipers for three years until the day of Dad's funeral.' Matthew took my phone and studied the pictures for a few seconds. 'I don't remember seeing anything like this. Looks like something Mum might have done when she was doing her evening classes.'

'Your mum had art lessons?'

'Yes, at the Further Education College in Newport. This was when we were kids, before she and Dad split up. Dad always told her she was wasting her time, but she's gone on to become quite an accomplished artist.' He handed back my phone. 'If you don't mind me asking, what's this all about?'

I wanted to keep him talking, especially in light of what he'd just said about his mother. Kurt had taught at the FE College in Newport.

'I'm afraid it seems Stewie might have been a victim of art fraud. Have you heard of Birdie Adams before?'

He shook his head. 'No, can't say I have. Art fraud? Are you sure? I always thought Dad was a complete philistine. He was very critical of anything Mum ever brought home.'

'He bought a picture in good faith, but a recent valuation revealed the painting to be a fake, someone imitating Birdie's style. Pilar feels the shock and stress contributed to his heart attack. She is keen to trace the people responsible.'

'Dad did have a heart condition.'

'So I understand.'

'I wish I could help, but as I said, me and Dad weren't exactly on speaking terms. I suppose it's too obvious to say did he not keep the receipt?'

'If only.' I smiled at him. 'It would have been a lot easier, wouldn't it?'

'I'm surprised he had the money to waste on artwork.' Matthew paused, returning my smile. 'Josh was under the impression *Absinthe* wasn't quite the goldmine Dad had hoped it would be.'

Another hint things were not as rosy for the

Beeches as it seemed. I'd picked up on Josh's grievance against Pilar but he hadn't mentioned specific money troubles. Did this explain why Stewie had been so reliant on raising cash from his picture?

My encounter with Josh had taken place against the frenetic backdrop of breakfast service in the deli. Here the smell of sawdust and varnish permeated the air, we were surrounded by hand-crafted furniture and off-cuts of timber, cows grazed in the field outside. An aura of calmness surrounded Matthew, his demeanour was open and honest, inviting confessions and confidences. 'I understand Pilar was hoping the money raised by selling the picture would go towards her grandmother's nursing home fees,' I explained.

'People do buy art as an investment. Pretty rubbish to then discover your investment is worthless. I suppose the shock could have brought on the heart attack, especially if Dad had banked on using the money for something specific.' Matthew's shoulders sagged. 'Why would somebody cheat him like that?'

'That's what we'd like to find out. Pilar heard him shouting on the phone in his study just before he left the house and set off in the *Little Lady* that Tuesday. He'd been very angry since he returned from having the painting valued.' I hesitated for a second. 'Pilar seemed to think it odd that he went to Newtown Creek. Have you got any idea why he might have gone there?'

Matthew gave a shrug. 'Dad liked fishing. It was his way of relaxing. I just don't know why she didn't raise the alarm earlier. They didn't start looking for him until the next day, and when they did, he'd been dead for nearly twenty-four hours. I know we didn't get on, but it's not nice to think of Dad dying all alone out there on his boat.'

I'd heard such contrasting views about Stewie Beech, I wasn't sure whether I liked the man or not. But regardless of my opinion, he'd been a victim of crime, a crime which had quite possibly triggered his death. I sensed Matthew was struggling with his own mixed emotions. We didn't choose our fathers, after all.

'I am sorry,' I said. Dad's touchy-feely approach was becoming infectious. I had to physically fold my arms to control the urge to reach out and comfort him. 'It must be awful to lose a parent, even when you are estranged. I'm lucky I've still got both my mum and dad, although my mum's in Australia, and we don't actually see each other that much. Up until a couple of weeks' ago I hadn't seen much of my dad, either. My parents divorced when I was a child.' I stopped myself. What on earth had come over me? Matthew Beech was grieving. He wasn't the least bit interested in my family history. I waved my hand dismissively. 'Sorry. I'm rambling. Ignore me.'

Matthew smiled. 'No worries. You said you were a friend of Pilar's?'

I nodded.

'That probably explains it. You look familiar. We must have met before.'

Perhaps that was it, That was what drew me to him. I knew him from somewhere, although if we had met before, it was not through any connection with Pilar.

'Do you play golf?' I asked, wondering if our paths had crossed on a course somewhere. He was probably five or six years younger than me so I wouldn't have known him from my days playing on my grandparents' course at Clifftops. I was rarely recognised out of golfing circles. The women's game received little coverage in the media and press. My interviews from the weekend had yet to be broadcast on the local TV and radio stations, although I had been assured they were scheduled for this week.

'No, never,' he chuckled, 'but you are local?'

'I grew up in Ventnor, but my dad knew Stewie from way back, they were at catering college together in Leeds. Which reminds me, I don't suppose you remember old friends of your parents called Dennis and Pam Pacey?'

Matthew grinned. 'Den and Pam, that's a blast from the past. Yes, I do remember them. We used to meet up when Mum took us back to Nottingham.'

'Would you know if Pam's still in Nottingham?'

Matthew shook his head. 'No, but Mum's probably still in touch. I can ask her next time I see her.'

'Do you go down to Cornwall regularly?'

'Cornwall?' Matthew looked momentarily puzzled then he laughed. 'You mean the commune? No, she's been back on the island for about four years now. She's bought her own place at Cranmore, a smallholding, grows her own fruit and veg, keeps chickens. Merryvale, it's called, on the main road. Maybe she'll be able to help you with Dad's painting. She's quite knowledgeable about art, she even has her own studio. Pop in and see her, I'm sure she won't mind.'

I didn't know Cranmore, but I knew where it was – the northwest corner of the island, not a million miles from Newtown Creek. First the connection to Kurt. Now the location. *She has her own studio.* Forget TV celeb Albie Whittaker. Wronged wife Christine Beech jumped to the top of my list of suspects.

'Thanks. I'll do that. Nice to meet you, Matthew. You've been really helpful.'

'Great. Call me Matt. Nice to meet you too. Eliza, did you say?'

'Yes,' I held out my hand for him to shake. 'Eliza Kane.'

His hand fell away from mine. He opened his

mouth but then shut it again. I gave him an encouraging smile, wondering if there something else he wanted to say, but he picked up his safety goggles from the work bench as if he was keen to get back to work. I was disappointed at the awkward end to what I thought had been a friendly conversation. When I reached the door, the whirr from his sander had not restarted. I turned and gave him a wave. He stood watching me, goggles in hand, but didn't return the gesture.

CHAPTER TWENTY-TWO

DAD WALKED ACROSS the Waverley House car park clutching his sketchpad and the tin of pastels he'd picked up at the art supplies shop that morning.

'Well?' I asked, as he clambered into the car. 'Aren't you going to show me your masterpiece?'

'It was a class for beginners.' He kept his pad firmly shut.

'Did you meet Mr Mintrum?' I decided to keep quiet about my visit to Matthew Beech and let Dad tell me about his afternoon first. My suspicions about Christine needed time to digest.

'No, the class was taught by the delightful Bethan Edwards.'

'Tell me more about Bethan.'

Dad's use of the term delightful usually set alarm bells ringing. Perhaps with Pilar hot footing it off to Spain at Anton's command, he was now going to try his luck elsewhere.

'It was a hugely entertaining afternoon. Bethan

Edwards can talk the hind legs off a donkey.'

'Sounds just your type,' I teased.

He shot me a look. 'Anyway, you'll be pleased to hear that I was able to strike up several conversations in which I divulged my admiration for the work of a certain Birdie Adams.'

'Well done.'

'I knew you'd be pleased.' Dad smirked. 'Bethan then asked if I knew that Birdie Adams had stayed at Waverley House in the past, and that Bethan's partner, William Mintrum, was a relation? I feigned all knowledge, of course.'

'Ah ha, partners. That's interesting.'

'Isn't it just. I had the whole story. Do you want to hear it now, or shall we wait until we get home?'

'Don't keep me in suspense.'

By the time we reached Newport the traffic would be at a rush hour crawl. Dad was relishing the opportunity to tell his tale and it would probably be far more entertaining than Isle of Wight radio traffic bulletins.

'Birdie Adams was William Mintrum's great aunt,' he began. 'She was the single sibling of William's maternal grandmother, and Jonathan, William's father, was an only child. Birdie never married and Jonathan's family were the only family she had. Did you know Birdie originally started out as a chemist working for ICI paints?'

'I did actually.' I'd ploughed my way through

several of Birdie's bios online. 'She went back to art college as a mature student in the 1960s, but her work didn't start achieving acclaim until the early 70s, by which time she herself was in her 70s.'

'According to Bethan she spent several summers here on the island staying with the Mintrums. She must have been well into her 80s when I met her, but that was when her work was at its height.'

'Presumably as her only relatives, the Mintrums, subsequently inherited her fortune when she died?'

'Naturally William's father expected to be left her fortune. But here's where it gets juicy. He didn't. Birdie created the Adams Foundation for Struggling Artists. All assets including a flat in London, her entire collection of work, sketch books, half-finished pieces of art, anything left at Waverley House, was subsequently auctioned off by the executors with the proceeds going to the Foundation. The Mintrums themselves didn't get a penny.'

'That must have caused a rumpus.'

'It did. Jonathan had been relying on Birdie's fortune after some dubious speculative investments.'

'And when it didn't happen he ran off with his secretary instead.'

'Basically. He was a hedge fund manager or something in London, came home weekends.

When he could no longer support the lifestyle to which he had become accustomed, rather than stay and face the music, he ran off to the south of France with one of the girls in the London office.'

'What year are we talking about? Birdie died in 1990.'

'It was when her dear Will, as Bethan referred to him, had just started uni.'

'Would Will remember Stewie had stayed with them that summer?'

Dad shook his head. 'I wouldn't have thought so. I told you, he was just a kid, but that doesn't mean he couldn't be our forger. Some of his artwork was on display and it was very good. He'd be very familiar with Birdie's style. We have to consider him a suspect.'

I'd let Dad have his moment. I'd tell him about Christine Beech later.

'Did you find out what the rest of the family are up to?'

'They seem to have scattered far and wide. Only one of Will's sisters lives on the island still, although Bethan didn't say which. The older brother died a few years ago. I'm assuming both the elder Mintrums are also now deceased. I didn't think I could ask for a rundown of all their life histories, but I did drop in a casual *and are any of them involved in the art world*. Sasha studied art at Brighton, remember, creativity runs in the family. Anyway, according to Bethan, one of the sisters is married to someone who dabbles, but Bethan didn't elaborate, another is an actress. By that time I felt I'd asked enough questions. I could tell some of my fellow students were getting a tad irritated about the amount of attention Bethan seemed to be giving me. To be fair, I was the only real novice. I needed the most help.'

'You do seem to have struck quite an accord. Good job.'

'I thought you'd be pleased. Bethan's Welsh, hails from Carmarthen.'

'Fascinating. Do we know how Will came to acquire the house, if he's the youngest?'

'He doesn't own it, he's a director in the consortium who run the activity centre. The family had to sell up when Jonathan Mintrum absconded. Bethan said the property has changed hands a few times, one owner ran it as a B&B, another a private nursing home, before the consortium took it over.'

We'd negotiated the centre of Newport and were on the road to Cowes. 'When are you going back for another lesson?' I asked.

'Funny you should say that, but I thoroughly enjoyed the afternoon. I hadn't realised how relaxing art could be. I might well sign myself up for a series of classes when I retire.'

It was the first I'd heard of Dad's plans to retire. I decided not to press the matter. If I ignored it, the notion that Dad might be considering a more permanent move to the Isle of Wight would hopefully go away.

He remained quiet over dinner as I recounted my visit to Matthew Beech. It was a lot to take in.

'So Chrissy is on the island?' was his only comment when I finally finished.

'She has her own art studio. We have to put her down as our chief suspect.'

'Along with Will Mintrum, Kurt and Albie Whittaker.'

How many suspects did we need? Dad appeared to be overlooking a major fact – motive. As far as I could see Chrissy was the only suspect on our list who had one. They all possessed the means with their artistic talents, but what about the opportunity? How did our forgers make contact with Stewie?

'I'm not convinced Stewie would knowingly have bought a picture from Chrissy,' I said, thinking out loud. 'According to Josh their divorce was acrimonious. I wonder how she approached him.'

'Chrissy wouldn't be behind this.'

'Why not? She was thrown out of her home without a penny. Maybe she saw it as revenge.'

'You know that for a fact do you?'

'No, I don't. But Stewie kicked her out, Josh was adamant about that.'

Dad pushed his plate into the middle of the table, his meal unfinished. 'We need to find something that connects Stewie to one of the others, evidence of a meeting or something. If only I could have a rummage through Stewie's office. It's a shame Sandpipers is protected by a six-foot high wooden fence. With Pilar away–'

'Don't even think about it,' I snapped. 'If you're going to break in anywhere, go back to Harrogate and have a rummage through your friend Tess' place. Without that picture it's going to be pretty hard to prove anybody forged anything. Evidence of meetings means nothing without evidence of the fake artwork.'

'Umm. Not if your friend Faye can come up trumps.'

'Can you stop making that noise?'

'What noise?'

I glared at him. '*Ummmm.*' I pushed my plate into the centre of the table to join his. 'If you're so convinced Will Mintrum is our forger, why don't you ask your friend Bethan if she's got access to any of Birdie's work, pretend you'd like to acquire one of her pictures for yourself.'

'Don't you think that'll look a bit odd. I've only just met her. I can't come on too strong.'

'I'm sure that's never stopped you before.'

'What's that supposed to mean?'

Arguing was getting us nowhere. I heaved a sigh. 'I did learn something else today. Matthew hinted *Absinthe* wasn't making money. That must explain why Stewie needed to raise cash by selling the Birdie Adams. Remember how Pilar reacted when you asked if she knew Pam Pacey. She was worried Pam was from a charity. I wonder if Stewie over committed on his good deeds and poor Pilar is having to fend everyone off.'

'Um…' He stopped himself in time. 'I suppose. But I thought the restaurant was doing well. You can't book a table, there's a waiting list and all that.'

'Hype?' I suggested. 'You said yourself how hard it is to be successful in the hospitality trade. Maybe that's why Stewie offered you that share in *Absinthe*. He needed an injection of cash, even back then.'

'He wasn't upset I didn't invest. Plus, if the restaurant was failing three years ago, I doubt he'd have been able to sustain it for this long.'

'Three years ago? Why didn't you say? I thought it was when you first met. Three years ago he bought that painting, remember. What if Stewie was offering shares in the restaurant to his friends, but he really wanted the money to buy the Birdie Adams? Did he ask you for cash?'

'We never got that far into the conversation.'

'I know you dismissed the idea of the Paceys lending him the money, but he might have convinced them to buy so-called shares. They might not be the only ones. Perhaps we ought to check those bank statements again to see what other individuals he pays out to on a regular basis, quarterly, twice yearly, like dividend shares.'

'You think he'd fleece his friends like that?'

I gave a shrug. 'I don't know. I'm just tossing around ideas, and to be honest, it doesn't matter how he financed this purchase, it's *who* he paid for it we need to find out.'

CHAPTER TWENTY-THREE

Chrissy August 1981

THE SECOND WEEK at Waverley House passed in a delicious, dreamy whirl. Chrissy rose before anyone else so she had first pick of the bathroom and the hot water which always ran out by nine. In the kitchen she grabbed the milk from the fridge before it turned sour, and whatever piece of fresh fruit was left in the fruit bowl. Then she re-joined the lads at their camp for breakfast.

The art students mooched in their barn while Chrissy, Pam and the lads radiated between the pool and sight-seeing trips, cramming themselves into Dennis' car and singing along to Radio One as they negotiated the island's scenic roads. The knowledge that Leeds was not far from Nottingham took away some of the dread of returning home.

Stew was thinking of staying on for an extra week. He urged the others to do the same.

'Some of us have got jobs to go back to,' Chrissy pointed out. She and Pam were on the wooden sun loungers. The boys lay on towels spread on the grass, apart from Stew who perched on the end of the diving board.

'Phone in sick. That's what I'm going to do.'

'For a whole week? You'd need a doctor's note,' Dennis pointed out. He and Pam had made a date to meet up again in Nottingham in a couple of weeks.

'My boss would get too suspicious if I phoned in sick after two weeks' annual leave,' Pam replied.

'My place too.' Chrissy would definitely get the sack if she announced she wanted another week off, doctor's note or not. Her job was her ticket away from her mum and Alan. She couldn't afford to lose it, no matter how tempted she was at the thought of another week on the island.

'What about you, Kaney?' Stew asked. 'You going to stay on with me?'

'I'm not sure, mate.' Ian rolled onto his stomach. 'It's going to look a bit odd if I go back to work without you. They weren't that happy about us having the time off together in the first place.'

'Certain people in Leeds will be missing him too much if he stays here any longer,' Mick laughed, giving Ian a friendly punch. 'And I don't just mean the lads at the cricket club.'

Ian returned Mick's punch with a kick.

'You're more than welcome to stay,' Sasha said joining the group. Rachel as always was in her wake, together with Angus, the synthesizer whizz, and Gideon who was carrying a portable stereo cassette player. Sasha was in her plain black one-piece today. Chrissy wondered how she avoided getting tanned. Her milky white legs hadn't changed colour in two weeks. Chrissy had moved through various shades of red before she'd reached an acceptable shade of brown.

'The boys have made a tape for us to listen to,' Sasha announced. 'This is the set they're going to play for Jason Ross.' She jumped up onto the diving board to join Stew. Chrissy noticed the scowl on Gideon's face. Gideon was in leather and looked hot and bothered beside Stew in his Speedos. 'Auntie Birdie's looking for a new model, by the way. What about you Christina? She likes a fuller figure.'

Chrissy pretended she hadn't heard. Auntie Birdie's studio was the last place she'd want to spend the afternoon.

'It's very easy,' Sasha continued. 'You don't have to do anything but sit there or stand. She'll pay you. Any of you boys fancy giving it a go?'

'I'm fine thanks,' Mick replied from his towel.

'Yeh me too,' Dennis laughed.

'Surely you're not afraid of a bit of nudity?' Sasha looked at each boy in turn.

'Have you done it?' Stew asked.

'Frequently. So's Gideon. It's fun, you'll enjoy it. Go on, I dare you.'

Chrissy knew that would be it. Anything Gideon could do Stew could do better. Sasha was playing them off against each other.

'Here we go,' murmured Pam, hiding behind the magazine she was pretending to read.

'If it gets me away from having to listen to this dirge I'll happily give it go,' Stew announced, puffing out his chest.

'Wait here.' Sasha tapped him on the shoulder. 'I'll go and see if she's free. Then you can start straight away.'

Twenty minutes later to the encouraging cat-calls of the Nottingham lads and the muted jeers from the art school boys, Stew re-appeared beside the pool in a white bathrobe. It appeared Auntie Birdie was ready and waiting.

'SO HOW WAS it?' Chrissy asked later that evening. Ian was cooking sausages.

'Piece of piss,' Stew replied. 'I stood there in the nuddy and she drew pictures.'

'You wouldn't get me doing it,' Dennis said. 'It would be like showing your privates off to your nan.'

'It's art,' Stew said, taking a swig from his can of beer.

'When do we get to see the finished result?' Pam enquired. She and Chrissy were sharing a bottle of Pomagne.

Stew gave a shrug. 'She didn't say.'

'Going to do it again?' Ian asked.

'I might. She gave me fifteen quid.' He put his hands behind his head and thrust forward his pelvis. 'I think I've got what it takes to be a male model.'

'When she sells it for a fortune, you'll be famous,' Dennis laughed.

'I'm going to be famous anyway,' Stew replied. 'I'm going to open the best restaurant in Leeds one day. Kaney here'll be my sous chef, won't you mate?'

Chrissy didn't catch Ian's reply. She thought Stew and Ian were the best of friends but over the last few days she'd noticed some sort of tension creeping in between them. She hoped it wasn't because of her. She didn't want to come between friends, but neither did she want to stop spending time with the lads. It was their last few days and she wanted the dream to continue.

CHAPTER TWENTY-FOUR

Eliza

O N OUR WAY to see Phil Flowers in Ryde, Dad asked me to take a detour, the reason for which became apparent when he directed me to a block of flats a couple of roads back from the seafront, one of which had a prominent "To Let" sign stuck in its front window.

'Dad, you're not seriously thinking–'

'I'm just looking at what's available. No harm in keeping my options open.'

As far as I could see Dad didn't have options. His life was in Yorkshire, it had always been in Yorkshire and that was where he needed to be heading.

'Auntie Debs says she'll put you up.'

'When did you speak to Debs?'

We continued on in an uncomfortable silence.

Phil met us at the front door of his bungalow and invited us straight through to his new and improved office in his late mother's former bedroom.

'Is the new website up and running?' I asked.

'Jenny's done a marvellous job,' Phil enthused, calling up the site on his desktop PC. 'I don't know how to thank her.'

'Why don't you take her out to dinner?'

Jenny had worked some magic. The local history website had a far more professional appearance. Phil's fingers hovered over his keyboard.

'Oh…I'm not sure that would be appropriate.'

'Why not?'

He reddened. 'Well, er, I'll have to have a think–'

'Nonsense,' argued Dad. I'd given him a brief rundown of how I'd first met Phil in the car on the way here, mentioning Jenny in passing. 'Got to take the plunge one day, man.'

The website and the bungalow weren't the only things to have had a make-over. It was quite noticeable that Phil had smartened himself up too. His hair was combed, his tie straight. He put his head down to concentrate. 'Right, so where were we? Mr and Mrs Lemming and their painting.'

Dad looked over Phil's shoulder while I pulled up a chair beside him.

'I know you asked me to look into cases of art fraud, and there's nothing to suggest for one minute that this couple were involved in anything untoward,' Phil said, 'but as soon as I saw the name Whittaker I had to ask myself whether it was the same man my colleague had uncovered in that case in Winchester. I think it's safe to assume it is. He's a member of the Institute of Chartered Surveyors, so his credentials are valid. Seems to have worked as an auctioneer for many years before he started on TV, so well respected.'

Dad nodded in agreement. 'I've looked him up online. Doesn't say anything about studying at Winchester School of Art. I suppose he's conveniently deleted that episode from his CV.'

'Wouldn't this conviction have hampered his career?' I asked.

'He pleaded guilty and received a fine,' Phil said. 'A conviction like that would soon be spent. It seems he and his fellow student conducted an experiment to see how easy or difficult it would be to reproduce a painting by a well-known artist. They must have faked a provenance–'

'What's a provenance?' Dad interrupted.

'It's the history of an antiquity, something that proves its authenticity, or ownership. In the case of the Lemmings of Ryde, the fact that the mother-in-law had worked as a cleaner for the family Birdie Adams lodged with was enough evidence to assume it was a genuine piece of the artist's work.'

'That's a joke for a start,' Dad spluttered. 'I saw that house, I knew that family. There was no cleaner. There should have been mind, the place was a tip.'

I shot Dad a glare before turning back to Phil. 'The fact that Mrs Lemming's mother worked as a cleaner, or was acquainted, shall we say, with Birdie, validated the painting's authenticity?'

Phil nodded. 'It was assumed Birdie Adams either gifted the picture to Mrs Lemming's mother, or Mrs Lemming's mother may have simply helped herself. Either way, the fact that she was a regular visitor to the artist's place of work–'

'I've told you that's highly unlikely,' Dad interrupted again. 'What providence did this Albie Whittaker use when he was a student?'

'*Provenance*,' Phil corrected. 'It's not clear from the newspaper report. Similar cases have involved forged letters, receipts, that type of thing. A historic family connection makes everything credible. One example I found on the internet involved a Dutch couple who used the cover story of a relative hiding Old Masters from the Nazis during the War to validate their fraudulent work. It was all very believable. No one doubted a genuine Holbein could turn up in a bunker by the North Sea, given the country's history.'

'Can we assume this Albie Whittaker bloke is untrustworthy?' Dad asked. 'Has his name cropped up in connection with any other dodgy valuations?'

Phil shook his head. 'Not that I can discover. However, I've tried to find out what I can about the Lemmings and it seems they've conveniently disappeared.'

'Should we read anything into that?' I asked.

'If I received a five-figure sum for an old painting which my mother-in-law may have stolen from a famous artist, or alternatively may be a forgery, I might be inclined to disappear too,' Dad said.

'Funnily enough I couldn't find anything about the painting being sold on,' Phil added. 'I assume it changed hands somewhere, but I can't find anything online to confirm that.'

'So we can assume the Lemmings and Mr Whittaker were in on this together?' Dad persisted.

'We don't know they were in on anything.' I so wished I'd left him at home with his sketchpad. In between perusing the property pages, he'd been doodling away since his return from the art class.

Phil was being remarkably patient. 'I'm not sure what any of this actually proves, other than a renowned art expert dabbled in a bit of forgery himself sixty years ago. I thought it was interesting but probably not remotely related to the incident with your friend. We may be casting totally false aspersions on Mr Whittaker. Don't forget he had an accomplice.' Phil clicked open another page on his computer. 'Kurtis Zeigler. Could just be a coincidence, but after a bit of digging around, I discovered there's a gentleman of a similar name used to teach adult education art classes at the college in Newport. A convicted forger here on the island sounds a far more likely candidate to be behind your scam than a prominent TV expert. It might be worth contacting the college to see if they have any idea of his current whereabouts.'

Dad opened his mouth to speak but I gave him a kick. I thanked Phil for his help and promised to keep him updated.

'What if Will Mintrum or Kurt, or both, do the artwork and Albie authenticates it,' Dad said as we walked back to the car. 'Clearly the Lemmings were in on it too. I told you, the Mintrums did not have a cleaner.'

'Just because they didn't have a cleaner when you were there, it doesn't mean they didn't have one ever. Anyway, I thought you were camping in a tent in the garden. How often did you go into the house?'

'For food, for the loo. Several times a day in fact. It was filthy. Chrissy said she'd rather sleep in the tent with–' He stopped.

I glanced at him. 'She'd rather sleep in Stewie's tent than in the house? It was that bad?'

'Yes, something like that.'

'Someone in the family would have contacted the TV company to say this cleaning woman didn't exist if the Lemmings were lying.'

'Not if they're all in this scam together.' Dad's face was stony.

'The whole family? Seriously? All the Mintrums, Kurt, Albie, Mr and Mrs Lemming? Be realistic. Christine Beech took art lessons at the college of FE. Kurt taught there. He could have put the idea into her head.'

'This is nothing to do with Chrissy.'

'So you keep saying but she has the means and the motive. And she currently lives in the vicinity of Newtown Creek. We just need to work out how she persuaded Stewie to buy one of her forgeries.'

Dad flung open the car door and threw himself into the passenger seat. 'Let's go and see Kurt.'

CHAPTER TWENTY-FIVE

We agreed in the car that I would do the talking. Dad didn't know Kurt as well as I did. It was important not to rush in with wild accusations. We'd already upset him once.

Nanna and Kurt were playing crib in their favourite spot in the conservatory. Kurt looked up as we approached and took off his glasses. 'I wondered when you'd be back,' he said with none of his usual perkiness. 'Lilian was right. Some people are too sharp for their own good. I'm assuming you're here to talk about me and Albie Whittaker.'

'It's all right.' Nanna had a hand on his arm. She scowled at me. 'He's told me everything.'

At least we could get straight to the point, unpleasant though it was. Dad went to fetch another chair.

'He seems to be managing very well with that thing on his foot,' Nanna remarked. 'Isn't it about time he went home?'

'Yes,' I agreed. I wasn't going to pile on the

misery by telling Nanna he didn't have a home to go to.

Kurt cleared his throat. 'Before you start, can I just say it was a long time ago, and I'm not proud of what I did. I'm sure you can understand why I've tried to keep it hidden.' It sounded as if he had been preparing his speech. 'I haven't seen Ron, or Albie as he now likes to call himself, since 1965, and it's a good ten years since I taught evening classes here on the island. I was being perfectly honestly when I said I don't know anyone who could help you.'

'Kurt,' I said, leaning forward. 'I totally understand. Please don't think we've come here to hound you.'

'Why are you here then?' Nanna demanded. Eliciting the relevant information from Kurt could be harder than anticipated with Nanna in one of her obstinate moods.

'There's a chance the cases are connected,' Dad said.

'I highly doubt that,' Kurt retorted.

'Maybe you could give us an insight into how art scammers operate,' I suggested.

'I wasn't a scammer. Ron, or rather Albie, asked me to help him prove a point.'

'It was all Whittaker's idea,' Nanna added. Loyalty had always been one of her strengths – and weaknesses. Kurt had made his confession to her and she would champion his cause to the bitter end.

'What exactly happened?' I asked.

Kurt took a gulp. 'There was a lecturer at the art school, nasty little man, Augustus Tindall was his name. I'm not sure why he went into teaching because he didn't like students, that was for sure. He told Ron he was wasting his time at Winchester, that he'd never be able to make his living in the world of art. Ron wanted to prove him wrong, but Ron's idea to prove Mr Tindall wrong, was by doing something wrong himself. He came up with the idea of creating a fake Francis Bacon, which he would then convince Gussy Tindall was an original. Francis Bacon was a prolific artist and around this time he was in a destructive relationship with a younger man. Ron knew the young man in question, not well, I hasten to add, but well enough to a establish a false provenance. Bacon was temperamental, notorious for destroying his own work and it could well be that a piece thought to have been destroyed had been passed on by his lover. Once Gussy Tindall declared our painting genuine, Ron would come clean, proving his point that yes he could make his own way in the art world. The last laugh on the tutor, so to speak.'

'Why did you help your friend do something knowingly illegal?' I asked.

Kurt shook his head. 'I was desperate for money. Ron paid me to paint the picture. My family were Austrian immigrants, they'd left Vienna with nothing. My father died when I was just a year old and my mother made a lot of sacrifices to ensure I received a good education. She'd been so proud when I got that place at art school. Then I blew it by getting my girlfriend pregnant. In those days when you got a girl pregnant, you got married. I didn't have two pennies to my name, I barely had enough to look after myself, let alone Madeleine and a baby. I was in a desperate situation. I already had two part-time jobs to make ends meet, I was living in a bedsit and Madeleine worked as an au pair for a wealthy family. They would dismiss her the minute they found out she was expecting. Madeleine was French, and Catholic, she couldn't turn to her own family for help. We needed to get married, we needed a decent place to live. Ron offered me a way out.

'I knew it was wrong. I didn't tell Madeleine what I was doing because I knew she would be appalled. It was the worst decision I've ever made in life. Ron told me his aim was simply to prove a point to Mr Tindall, but as our project got underway, I realised he wanted to do more than that. I should have stopped him.'

Nanna leaned across and gave Kurt a reassuring pat on the arm. 'Everyone makes mistakes.' She glanced up. 'None of us are perfect. We all have our flaws. Isn't that true, Eliza? Ian?'

'Oh absolutely,' we said in unison.

Kurt was eager to continue. 'I admired Bacon's boldness and I had, I admit, done a few pieces mimicking his style. Like a lot of young men I was under the false impression I was a budding genius. In a way I was flattered Ron had asked for my help. I should have known better.'

'Whittaker coerced you into it,' Nanna said with a nod. 'Took advantage. You were never to blame.'

That wasn't entirely true, although I could see Kurt had been vulnerable.

'If only Ron had limited himself to showing our masterpiece to Gussy Tindall,' Kurt said with a sniff. 'But once he'd proved his point, dazzled by his own brilliance, rather than come clean, he decided to try and sell the piece on the open market. He took the painting to an auction house and was arrested within days.'

'He didn't have to dump you in it, though, did he?' Nanna interrupted. 'He could have kept quiet.'

'He tried to bluff his way back out of it. Said it was a prank.' Kurt sighed. 'We were each fined and kicked out of art school. I was so ashamed. I couldn't tell my mother, and as for poor Madeleine...well, she lost the baby shortly afterwards. I'm sure it was because of the stress. It was the most horrible time of my life.'

It was the longest speech I'd ever heard Kurt make. He was such a quiet, unassuming man. He had to be telling the truth.

'I'm so sorry mate,' Dad said.

'That's such a tragic story.' I struggled to find my voice. 'What happened afterwards? Were you able to continue your studies elsewhere? And what about Madeleine?'

'I learned my lesson the hard way,' Kurt said. 'Madeleine stuck by me. I was truly humbled, and very lucky. I didn't want to stay in Winchester where everyone knew me and what had happened. Madeleine was able to get a job in a private school in Herefordshire as a French teacher. We married, but she couldn't have any more children. After a few years of mundane manual jobs, she encouraged me to take a teaching qualification. I spent the next thirty odd years doing something I loved and instilling a love of art in others. When I retired from teaching full-time, we moved to the island and I taught adult classes at the college here in Newport. I'm proud of my career and of the talent I've been able to nurture. I saw it as making amends for my own foolishness.'

'Did you ever teach a student called Christine Beech?' I ventured, avoiding Dad's eye. 'She would have taken classes here in Newport.'

Kurt's face lit up. 'Oh yes, I remember Christine. She was a wonderful student, very keen to learn. It was a joy to watch her evolve as an artist.'

'I don't suppose you ever mentioned this incident with the Francis Bacon painting to her?'

Kurt frowned. 'I'm so ashamed I've never told anybody. Why on earth would I?'

'Because somewhat incredulously Eliza is convinced Christine Beech is our art forger,' Dad replied.

'That's preposterous,' Kurt spluttered.

I could feel two pair of admonishing eyes bearing down on me. Nanna's face remained impassive.

'She has the means,' I pointed out with a pout, 'and the motive.'

'Motive?' Kurt spluttered again. 'What possible motive would Christine have to commit an act of fraud?'

'The victim was her ex-husband.'

'You're telling me she divorced that clown who spent years telling her how useless she was? Well done, Christine.' Kurt put his hands together. 'On second thoughts, perhaps she is your forger, although it's hard to imagine that gentle girl being the vindictive sort. Better things to do with her time I would imagine.'

Dad put his head on one side and gave me a stupid *I told you so* grin.

'I'm glad we've got that cleared up,' Nanna said decisively. She patted Kurt's arm again. 'You've been very brave to talk about it. I hope Eliza and Ian appreciate how distressing this has been for you.'

'I'm truly sorry, Kurt,' I said. 'I don't suppose you…er…stayed in touch with Albie?'

Kurt cleared his throat. 'As I said, I haven't seen him since, apart from on TV of course. I have to admit it was a bit of a shock to recognise him, and quite galling to see him being feted. Mr Tindall will be turning in his grave.'

'I never took to him,' Nanna said. 'I know he's popular but he comes across as a smarmy know-it-all.'

'Would you trust his valuations?' Dad asked Kurt.

'You're thinking about that painting they found in Ryde, aren't you?' Kurt said. 'I haven't seen that particular episode, but I've heard about it. I highly doubt Ron, Albie, would want to get caught up in anything controversial in case this earlier escapade came to light. On the other hand, would he even care? He had a very cavalier attitude to life. He never once got in touch to ask after Madeleine.'

Dad shifted on his seat. 'Albie Whittaker is quoted as saying he believed the Birdie Adams found in Ryde was genuine because the owner's mother-in-law had previously cleaned for the Mintrums. Would word of mouth be enough to convince an expert the picture was genuine? Surely they'd want more proof?'

'A personal connection would be enough,' Kurt said. 'In any case, I'm assuming the television company would have checked that out. What was the name of the family who owned the painting? I can't remember.'

'Lemming,' Dad said.

'And the mother-in-law, the cleaning woman

was called Elspeth Dawson,' I added, as the name came back to me.

'Elspeth Dawson?' Kurt scratched his head. 'Goodness me. That's strange.'

'Do you know her?' Dad frowned. His theory of there being no cleaner was about to fly out of the window and I felt a moment of sanctimonious victory.

'I used to know someone of that name,' Kurt replied, 'but it can't possibly be the same one. Elspeth Dawson was a student with us at Winchester. The poor girl died midway through our first year. Fancy Mrs Lemming's mother having the same name.'

CHAPTER TWENTY-SIX

Silence fell. We exchanged glances. Without a doubt we were all thinking the same thing.

Nanna was the first to speak. 'That's a big coincidence.'

'Albie Whittaker gave the Lemmings a false provenance.' Dad was unable to contain his excitement. 'There was no cleaner.'

'But why use Elspeth's name?' Kurt's brow was furrowed.

'Because men aren't known for their imaginations?' Nanna suggested.

'There could be two Elspeths.' Doubt was written all over Kurt's face.

'It would be risky making up a story like that,' I said. 'There could be people watching who knew Mrs Lemming's real mother.'

'The Lemmings have since disappeared,' Dad pointed out. 'That might not be their real name either.'

'I can't believe the TV company would not

have run a background check.' Kurt shook his head.

'If they're professional fraudsters, they'll have fake ID.' Dad sounded more joyful than ever.

'But what about the Mintrums?' Nanna asked. 'They'd remember the name of their own cleaner. If any of them were watching–'

'The Mintrums will be in on this,' Dad cut in. 'You said so yourself when we first mentioned Birdie Adams. In fact, it was the first thing you said.'

Nanna's eyes narrowed.

'Have you got a picture of these Lemmings?' Kurt asked.

'I've seen a photo of them in one of the online newspaper reports.' I reached for my phone, then remembered both Nanna and Kurt wore glasses. 'It would be easier if we had a laptop with a bigger screen.'

'Let's go to the library,' Kurt said, 'have a look on the computer there.'

He was out of his chair before I could stop him. I followed in hot pursuit, while Dad and Nanna brought up the rear. I could hear them bickering as I tried to keep up with Kurt.

'Christine Beech,' Nanna hissed. 'Why do I know that name?'

'You don't,' Dad hissed back as our procession snaked out of the conservatory. In reception, Grace was putting on her coat.

'Ah just the person,' Kurt said. 'I don't suppose you've got time to help us in the library before you leave?'

'What's going on?' she asked.

'Kurt is on a mission,' I explained. 'We need a computer.'

'Sounds intriguing. Is it anything to do with you know what?' She tapped the side of her nose.

'Quite possibly.'

'I'm just clocking off my shift, I don't want to miss this.'

The library was empty apart from one elderly lady dozing in a corner with a large print copy of a Jilly Cooper novel face down on her lap.

Grace, who was more familiar with the residential home's antiquated computer system than either Kurt or Nanna, quickly found the article I'd already viewed online.

The photo was black and white, but Roy and Donna Lemming, a couple in their fifties or sixties, were non-descript. Neither had any distinguishing features. The picture was taken from the TV show, Birdie's painting was poised on an easel between the couple and a beaming Albie Whittaker, complete in tweeds and a trilby.

'That's it?' Nanna asked, taking off her glasses and squinting at the screen before putting them back on again.

'Surely these participants are vetted by the production company,' Grace said, having been brought up to speed as to what we were looking for. 'They'll have a whole team of researchers investigating their family heirlooms before they get to see the experts.'

'Must have fooled all of them,' Nanna remarked.

'False credentials,' Dad insisted. 'This will be a professional set up.'

Kurt let out a long sigh. 'This is so disappointing. What can we do about it?'

'Nothing,' I said. 'The Lemmings have disappeared, together with all traces of their painting.'

'Is it worth contacting the TV company to find out if they know what happened afterwards?' Grace suggested. 'If the painting was subsequently sold on at auction, the auction house would have a record of it.'

'An auction house would have carried out their own evaluation,' Kurt put in.

'Maybe they took Albie Whittaker's word for it too,' Dad replied. 'We should tackle Albie Whittaker. Tell him we know he provided a false provenance live on TV.'

'No doubt he'd say it was a genuine mistake and blame it all on the Lemmings.' Nanna gave a shudder. 'I've met people like Albie Whittaker before. Nasty piece of work.'

Kurt turned to Dad. 'Do you seriously think this could be related to the incident involving your friend?'

'It's impossible to say,' Dad replied. 'Both cases involve paintings by Birdie Adams. It could be we're not just looking for Stewie's forgers, we're looking at an entire forgery ring with your friend Albie Whittaker at its core.'

We left Nanna and Kurt in the library. Dad was revelling in the whole dramatic turn our investigation had taken. 'Let's go straight to the marina and speak to this skipper Riggs,' he said. 'We really do need to get hold of Stewie's phone and go back over his movements those last few days.'

Despite Nanna's observation that he appeared to be managing well, he dawdled beside me, his limp quite pronounced.

'Let's not Dad. You look tired. You've been over-doing it. I'm going to take you back to the apartment to rest.'

To my relief, he didn't protest. After dropping him off, I headed to Making Waves in search of some light relief under the pretence of checking what plans Charlie had made, if any, for us to meet up for dinner later in the week. Dad's conviction that Albie Whittaker, the Lemmings and the entire Mintrum family were involved in some huge conspiracy was getting out of hand. I remained convinced Christine Beech was a far more likely candidate for our forger, however virtuous she might seem. I'd seen that moment of doubt flit across Kurt's face when I'd mentioned the victim had been her ex-husband. However, I had no evidence apart from my theory of a discarded wife with a talent for art. We needed solid proof to connect either of our nominated forgers, be they organised gang or woman scorned, to a transaction with Stewie before making any accusations. So far we had nothing.

I was surprised to find Amelie helping Charlie and Dexter unpack a box of wetsuits.

'Are you the new assistant?' I asked.

'I just popped in to see Dex,' she replied. 'We're supposed to be going over to the mainland for a gig when he finishes tonight but I completely forgot I can't go because I'm looking after Pilar's rabbit.'

'Alfonso?'

'Yeh. You know she headed off to Spain, right? She asked me if I'd go round twice a day and feed him. Dex has got tomorrow morning off and wants to stay over.'

'We'll be back by lunchtime,' Dexter argued.

'Pilar was very precise. Alfonso needs his tea at six and his breakfast at eight. She's got CCTV on the front door. She'll know if I don't go.'

'She's left you a door key?' I asked.

'I've got the key to the front door and the code to the gate.'

'I'll do it.' The words were out before I could stop them. The opportunity to get inside Sandpipers could not be missed. 'I'll cover for you, tonight and tomorrow morning.'

Amelie sighed. 'That's very kind of you, Eliza, but she'll know you're not me. She'll see you on the webcam. She can be a bit odd about things like that.'

Dexter grabbed a baseball cap from a nearby display stand and thrust it on my head. 'Give Eliza that hoodie you always wear with the *Absinthe* logo. Pilar won't know the difference. You're the same build and those CCTV pictures are always fuzzy.'

'I'm not sure.' Amelie hopped from foot to foot. 'What do you think, Charlie?'

Charlie gave a shrug. 'I'm sure it won't matter if Eliza takes your place.'

Amelie looked relieved. 'You will go at six on the dot, won't you? She's left his food in the utility, and you have to empty his litter tray and let him have a run around the kitchen. I usually stay for ten, fifteen minutes. Don't forget to lock up when you leave.'

'I won't.'

'Hang on here while I go and fetch you my sweatshirt and the key.'

While I waited Charlie asked if I fancied a drink at the sailing club for lunch. Judging from his expression this had the same connotations as his previous invitation to the sandwich shop. At some point we were going to have to sit down and have a serious conversation about the not-so-adult manner in which we were conducting our relationship, but right now, after the morning I'd had, there wasn't anything I wanted more that the shot of endorphins provided by a romp in Charlie's bed.

CHAPTER TWENTY-SEVEN

Dad was on the phone when I eventually returned to the apartment. He hobbled out of earshot and into his bedroom when he heard me come through the door. That didn't bode well. I refreshed the laptop he'd abandoned on the sofa and just as I suspected, a property page popped up.

He emerged a few minutes later. 'You took your time. I don't suppose you could run me down to Newport?'

'You're supposed to be resting. I need to be back here by six. I've got a date with Alfonso.'

'Who?'

'Pilar's rabbit. Dexter's girlfriend Amelie is looking after him while she's away and I'm covering for her tonight and tomorrow morning. I've got two fifteen-minute slots while Alfonso has his daily exercise to look for clues.'

Dad flopped onto the sofa. 'That's fantastic. Can I come with you?'

'No, definitely not. The front door is covered

by CCTV and I've got to pretend to be Amelie.' I showed him the baseball cap. 'Pilar will recognise you.'

'At least you're in. You need to look for a diary, calendar, notebooks, and the joint accounts if possible, just in case Stewie did take the money out of those.'

That was an awful lot to look for in fifteen minutes. 'Why the rush down to Newport?' I asked.

'Oh…nothing. It can wait for another day. This is far more important.'

It was a twenty-minute walk to Sandpipers from the apartment. As I turned into the road, I slipped the baseball cap over my head and strolled up to the gate. My fingers trembled as I keyed in the code Amelie had given me. I wasn't breaking in; I was here on legitimate business. Pilar would not want Alfonso to starve.

I expected to find a traditional hutch in the utility room, but Alfonso lived in a little wooden house, complete with a seed tray of grass and a picket fence. I found his carrots and cabbage leaves in the fridge and emptied a portion of dried food from the bag on a shelf, as instructed by Amelie, into his food bowl, before topping up his water bottle.

With Alfonso tucking into his supper, I had ten minutes left. There was nothing wrong with having an innocent wander. After all, Pilar wanted this case solved. She'd allowed herself to be bustled out of the country by Anton, which wasn't exactly helpful.

Amelie had explained the alarms were not set and there was no CCTV in the house itself. The study was located across the main hallway and to my relief, the door wasn't locked.

The surface of the walnut desk in the centre of the room was completely clear. Not a laptop, iPad, piece of paper, or a pen in sight. Behind the desk was a large filing cabinet, to the side a bookcase. Pictures covered one wall including several photographs of a smiling Stewie with various celebrity patrons. There was a painting of a pub, which could possibly be his former home in Yarmouth, a large canvas photoprint of *Absinthe*, and a faint mark where something else had once hung, presumably the Birdie Adams.

The desk had one drawer which slid open easily enough to reveal a routine selection of stationery items, pens, pencils, staples, a couple of memory sticks, but no notepads, no diaries. I turned my attention to the filing cabinet. Locked. I returned to the drawer, hoping to find a key but there was nothing. I tugged at the filing cabinet again. It didn't budge.

The bookcase was full of the usual crime and thriller suspects, together with non-fiction titles on sailing and the geography of the Isle of Wight. No cookery books though. Stewie was a chef. Where did he keep his recipes? Not that I needed a recipe, but…

I thought of Charlie's study, scraps of paper strewn across his desk, sticky notes, invoices, receipts. Stewie had been dead for over a month. I'd been too optimistic. Pilar had had plenty of time to clear everything away. And why would she leave valuable business accounts unsecured for anyone to see, especially if her finances were not good?

Dad was on standby back at the apartment. I couldn't go back empty-handed. I returned to the desk drawer and slipped the memory sticks into my pocket. I glanced at my phone again, only five minutes left. *Quit while you're ahead, Eliza.* My enthusiasm to snoop was wearing off.

'Come on Alfonso,' I called, walking back into the kitchen. 'Alfonsooooooo'.

There was no sign of the rabbit. I checked his house, empty. The double doors to the conservatory where Pilar had entertained us were locked. Alfonso had to be in the kitchen somewhere unless he had followed me into the hallway. In which case he could be anywhere in the house.

I should have shut the kitchen door. Did I leave him roaming the house in the hope that when I returned at eight tomorrow morning he'd have hopped back into his comfortable residence in the utility room? All the other doors off the hallway were shut, which meant the only place Alfonso could have escaped to was up the stairs.

Any other rabbit I'd ever met, although to be honest I hadn't met that many, would probably have left a little trail of droppings for me to follow. Alfonso was fully toilet trained. If every door upstairs was shut, I'd meet him on the landing. If doors were open, I could have a large task on my hands.

Only one door was open and it led to the main bedroom. I felt like the worst kind of intruder. My heart hammered against my chest.

Come on Alfonso. It wasn't funny anymore. The master bedroom was sumptuous, a magnificent four poster bed draped with a voile canopy. An abstract seascape dominated one wall, on another a large photograph of Stewie and Pilar on their wedding day took pride of place.

Alfonso was here somewhere. Having learned my lesson downstairs, I pulled the door shut to prevent his escape. Kneeling down, I peered under the bed, grateful for the fading embers of daylight. I didn't want to have to start turning on lights in case that alerted the neighbours. The space under the bed was empty.

From the items on top of the ornate night stands it was easy to work out which side of the bed was Pilar's, and which had once been Stewie's. Not for one minute did I think Alfonso had the dexterity to open a bedside drawer and hop inside, but …

Stewie's desk had been functional, devoid of personal items, but here in his bedroom, distasteful as the idea of a sneaky rummage seemed, there could be clues. It would only require a quick peep. Concealed amongst several pairs of identical socks, I found a Rolex watch, a leather wallet and a dated Nokia phone. The phone was long dead and there was no sign of a charger. I didn't have one at home, nor would I be able to find one for this particular antiquity in Cowes between now and eight tomorrow morning. I doubted Stewie had used the device for several years, although that did beg the question of why keep it.

I grabbed the wallet and shoved it in my pocket, mindful of the minutes ticking by. I then continued my search through the adjoining dressing room and into the ensuite.

Alfonso was sat on the cream bathmat, waiting for me. I'd outstayed my welcome by a full ten minutes and would have to brief Amelie with a plausible explanation to give Pilar if she questioned the timings on the doorstep camera. I didn't want to get her into trouble.

With Alfonso firmly ensconced in the utility room, I jogged back to the apartment where Dad was waiting in a state of animated anticipation.

'Well?'

I handed him the memory sticks. 'That was all I could find in the study. Everything else was locked.'

'What? Not even a file, a piece of paper?'

'Not a scrap. Those were loose in a drawer. I doubt they're going to contain financial records. More likely Stewie's holiday photos.'

'We won't know until we take a look.' Dad inserted the first stick straight into my laptop. 'Let's just hope they're not password protected, although I could have a couple of guesses.'

There was no need. A list of jpegs flashed up on the screen.

'You're right about photos,' Dad grunted, clicking away with the mouse. 'It's food though, not holiday snaps.'

'I've risked my life for food porn?'

'I think that's a bit of an exaggeration, love. You didn't risk your life, although I was bit a worried about you. You were a lot longer than I thought you'd be.'

'Alfonso went walkabout.'

I stepped away and poured myself a large glass of wine from the fridge. 'Do you want one?'

'It's too early for me,' Dad replied to my surprise. 'Let's have a look at the second flash drive, see what's on there.'

I stood at his shoulder and watched yet more images of delicious looking plates of food explode onto the screen. Stewie and Pilar had an extensive menu repertoire.

'He must have snapped every dish he'd ever cooked,' I said between gulps of wine. 'Who does that?'

'Lots of people, I believe. Ever looked on Instagram?'

My own Instagram account contained pictures of virtually every golf course I'd ever played. Dad had a point.

'Hold on a minute, there's something else here.' He clicked on the mouse. 'Some sort of spreadsheet.'

'Accounts?' I asked hopefully. I wouldn't feel quite so guilty if my snooping produced results.

'I doubt it. They'd be on a specialist programme. This is a list of suppliers by the look of it, colour coded.'

'Colour coded suppliers?'

'Maybe he ranked them good or bad. I don't know.' Dad sounded disappointed.

'Download a copy,' I suggested. 'Meanwhile, let's see what's in this wallet.'

'Where did you find that?'

'In Stewie's bedside drawer.'

He opened his mouth as if to say something then shut it again.

At least a dozen business cards were wedged into the wallet's many compartments, along with discount and store loyalty cards. 'Looks like Stewie was a bit of a hoarder.' I spread the wallet's contents onto the countertop. Two train tickets dated in January from Southampton Central to London Waterloo, dental and hair appointment cards, memberships to two different gyms, the sailing club, and last but by no means least, a folded page from a notepad, the sort waiting staff used for orders. The word *Tufty* had been scribbled across the middle, followed by a telephone number. That rang a bell.

'I suppose he used these train tickets when he went to get the picture valued,' Dad said.

'Shame he didn't keep a note of who he was meeting on that day. It would have been more helpful.'

'Perhaps that's Tufty,' Dad suggested. None of the business cards appertained to any art dealers, most were food wholesalers or catering suppliers.

The order pad was the clue. 'Tufty's the name of one of his former waitresses,' I said. 'She was chatting to Amelie when I went to meet her last week in the Anchor Inn.' I stared at the piece of paper, willing it to explain itself. Why would Stewie have kept Tufty's number?

'Could she be our mystery woman?' Dad asked.

'She's younger than me and according to Amelie wasn't aware of Stewie's death. I wouldn't have thought so. She works in London.'

'Ah, London.' Dad pointed at the train tickets. 'Stewie could have gone to see her up there.'

'In that case he wouldn't have needed to go to Newtown Creek for a liaison, would he? This has got us nowhere.'

Dad spread the business cards out in a row and took pictures of them on his phone. 'Email me a copy of those spreadsheets. You never know, something might jump out at us later.'

He offered to cook a risotto for dinner, only to discover although we had the rice, we didn't have anything else to go in it apart from some frozen peas.

'You should have said earlier, I could have brought you back some of Alfonso's greens,' I remarked.

'Not to worry,' he insisted. 'I'll start it off, you keep stirring and adding the stock while I'll nip to the corner shop and pick us up something to go with it.'

He headed out of the door. A second glass of wine later, I heard his annoying guitar rift ringtone emanating from the sofa. Determined to fend off more estate agents, I retrieved his phone from behind a cushion and answered the call with a cheery 'hello'.

'Ah, I was hoping to speak to Malcolm.'

'Malcolm?'

'Malcolm Kane. This is his number, right?' The caller had a strong Welsh accent. 'He came along to my art workshop on Tuesday. My name is Bethan Edwards.'

I walked back into the kitchen and gave the rice a prod with my wooden spoon. 'Oh Bethan, hello, yes. I'm Mal's daughter.' Dad was so much more a Mal than a Malcolm. If he could role play so could I. 'He's not here at the mo, can I help?'

'I was calling to see if he wanted to sign up for a series of lessons. Tuesday was a taster afternoon and he seemed keen.'

'Oh, he's very keen.'

'That's wonderful. Can you also let him know the life drawing class we talked about is on a Thursday evening at the Arts Centre in Newport.'

Never answer the phone when drunk, Eliza. Don't let the rice dry out, give it another glug of stock. 'That'll be perfect. He's wanted to undertake life drawing lessons for so long.' The risotto bubbled with gratitude. 'Dad is a great admirer of the works of the artist Birdie Adams. He was saying you were related.'

'It's wonderful to meet someone as enthusiastic as Mal,' Bethan replied. 'Few people have heard of Birdie, and she's such a talent. It's not me who's related to her, but my partner Will. She was his great aunt. Sadly, I never got to meet her myself.'

'It must be fascinating to have that family connection.' I moved away from the hob into the furthest corner of the kitchen, lowering my voice. 'Actually Bethan, whilst I've got you, Mal has a big birthday coming up soon, and I just wondered how easy it might be to find a Birdie original for him, you know, as a special gift. Do they ever come onto the market?'

'Rarely.' Bethan sounded a little taken back.

'I thought, you know, with your partner being related and all that, you might have some insider knowledge on how I could get hold of one for him.'

There was a slight hesitation. 'An original Birdie won't be cheap. I'm not sure if you're aware of their value. Potentially you could be looking at tens of thousands.'

'Money isn't a problem, Bethan, and Mal's worth it.' I returned to the hob and gave the risotto another generous slosh of stock. 'I'd want it as a surprise though. Could I leave you my number?'

CHAPTER TWENTY-EIGHT

DAD WASN'T AWAKE when I slipped out of the house at eight the following morning for my return visit to Sandpipers. I hadn't mentioned Bethan's call and left him a note to remind him we were dining with Charlie and Lucas that evening. I felt even more like a thief as I replaced the items I'd "borrowed" the night before. Alfonso appeared unscathed after his adventure. I kept the kitchen door firmly shut while he took his exercise.

From Sandpipers I headed to Making Waves via Pauline's Pantry. I had promised Charlie I would cover Dexter's morning shift. When I arrived with coffees and croissants, Charlie was examining a new delivery from Spaniel Sportswear. Spaniel had sponsored me when I'd competed on the professional golfing circuit. They were picky about which outlets sold their brand, but I'd managed to secure Making Waves an exclusive deal to stock their aquatic range. Charlie wanted to give the swimwear a prominent spot in the store.

While he concentrated on arranging the new merchandise, I received a text from the TV reporter I'd met at the weekend to say our interview would be shown on the local news channel that evening.

'Even more good news,' I told Charlie, helping him attach the minutest and least practical bikini I'd ever seen over a naked manikin.

'Brilliant, come over early and we can sit down and watch it together before we go out to eat,' he enthused.

He didn't think it was quite so brilliant when I spent the next hour on my phone updating all my social media accounts to let my followers know. Mid-posting I was interrupted by a call from an unknown number. Wary of answering unsolicited calls I let it go to voicemail, only to subsequently discover my mystery caller was the landlord at the New Inn in Shalfleet. I'd almost forgotten I'd left him my number.

'I don't usually permit staff to make personal calls on the shop floor,' Charlie remarked as I called the landlord back.

'There is only you and me in the store,' I hissed. It was a blustery day and most of Cowes had battened down the hatches. Dark clouds outside threatened rain. 'I'll go and hide in the staffroom if it bothers you. This could be vital information.'

'No, go on, I'm all ears.'

I put my phone on speaker and placed it on the counter.

'I'm not sure if this is going to help to you,' the landlord explained. 'You remember I told you a couple of my regulars keep boats up on the quay. I had a chat with one of them yesterday. Rob Hedges often sees Stewie Beech coming into the creek fishing, and he saw him on that Tuesday. In fact, he saw him moor up at the quay.'

A confirmed sighting was great news.

'He says Stewie Beech landed around two o'clock,' the landlord continued, 'just caught the tide in time. It stuck in Rob's head because he remembered thinking it would be several hours before the boat could launch off again. People who don't know often get stranded. Had it been a stranger, he'd have warned them, but he knew Stewie Beech would be aware of the tide times, being a fisherman.'

'I see.'

'Stewie must have come back after dark, because they found him out in the main channel, didn't they? Rob reckons he wouldn't have been able to move off much before eight o'clock.'

That gave Stewie several hours to wander around Shalfleet. 'I don't suppose your friend saw where Stewie went after he moored up? Did he see him meet anyone, or see what direction he walked off in?' I asked.

'Rob didn't say. He was getting his dinghy ready to put up for sale on Gumtree, so he took several photographs. He says you can see Stewie Beech's boat in the background alongside the quay in one of them, if that's any help. He's sent me a copy. Would you like me to forward it on to you?'

'Oh yes please, thank you.'

I slipped my phone back into my pocket.

Charlie let out a sigh. 'That's good news. So where did he go and why?'

'If Anton the sommelier is to be believed, Stewie Beech was having an affair.'

'He was meeting this other woman?'

'It would make sense. But I've also found out the ex-wife has a smallholding at Cranmore. If Stewie was stuck on dry land for all those hours, he'd have plenty of time to get there.'

'It's three or four miles by road but there could be a short cut cross country. Why would he go and see his ex? Had they got back together? It does happen.'

It did, but both Matthew and Josh had intimated the couple's separation had been bitter. Christine wasn't at the funeral. Traipsing across fields would explain the grass on Stewie's trousers. Was this enough evidence to confront Christine Beech?

I gave Charlie a brief rundown of my suspicions. Christine had a grievance against Stewie, she knew about art, she even had her own studio. She was at Waverley House that summer and knew Stewie had sat for Birdie Adams. Dad's conspiracy theory about the Mintrums, the Lemmings and Albie Whittaker had several flaws. Why would so many people come together to risk their livelihoods, their credibility, just to swindle Stewie Beech? It had to be something personal.

'Knowing of the animosity between them, I don't think he would have bought the painting directly from her,' I told Charlie. 'She could have used a third party to bring the picture to Stewie's attention.'

Charlie glanced at his watch. 'You want to go and quiz her, don't you?'

I gave him a half-grimace half-smile. That was why I loved him. He knew me so well. 'Would you mind? We're not exactly rushed off our feet, are we?'

'Dexter is due in at two. Go on, I'm sure I can manage.'

'You're the best, Charlie.'

'No,' he said, and he cupped my face in his hands and gave me a kiss on the lips. 'You're the best, Lizzie. Now off you go and get this solved.'

CHAPTER TWENTY-NINE

Chrissy August 1981

ROLY MINTRUM HAD finally turned up together with Jason Ross. When Chrissy bumped into Roly breakfasting in the kitchen, she decided it was just as well Rachel had found solace with Angus. She'd have been wasting her time holding out for this particular hero. Prue Mintrum, for once not on taxi duty but busy preparing copious rounds of toast, didn't seem the least perturbed at her eldest's penchant for *Rive Gauche*, painted fingernails and eyeliner. Chrissy decided the poor woman probably hadn't even noticed. She'd been left to run the household single-handed.

There was more discord than ever amongst the lads from Leeds and the art school boys. There'd been a huge hoo-ha the previous day when Stew had accidentally knocked The Future's precious music tape into the pool. Gideon had accused Stew of a deliberate act of sabotage.

'You shouldn't have left it lying around,' Stew argued. 'It's not my fault. I didn't see the thing.'

'That's got all our best bloody tracks on it,' Gideon fumed. 'You great northern twat.'

Stew and Gideon had faced each other, fists at the ready. The situation had only been diffused by the arrival of William, newly released from his school holiday activities, charging out the house with his fully loaded water pistol. Gideon's wrath had turned elsewhere.

The doldrums set in. Only two days left and then back to the mundanity of Nottingham. Stew wanted to spend the evening in Ventnor. He didn't want to stay at Waverley House watching The Future's grand performance. He was in a bad mood. He'd been posing for Auntie Birdie again, earned another fifteen quid, but the novelty of being a model was wearing off.

Dennis didn't want to drive to Ventnor, he wanted to stay cosying up with Pam.

'Why don't you drive us there in Den's car,' Stew suggested to Ian.

'Because I want to have a drink,' Ian replied. 'And I don't want to lose my licence.'

'We've hardly seen a police car since we've been here. I don't know what you're worried about.'

'Then drive Den's car yourself.'

'You can't go to Ventnor and miss the show,' Sasha announced. She had a habit of creeping up on them when they least expected it. 'It's the band's big night. They need an appreciative audience. You girls need to be up dancing with me and Rach. And you boys, you need to look like you're having fun. Let me find you some decent clothes to wear.'

'I'm not dressing up like a flippin' poofter,' Mick retorted.

Sasha put her head on one side. 'Now Michael, that's not polite, is it? Why don't we think about doing something with that hair? After all, from the back, you're the one who looks like a girl.'

Chrissy hadn't been bothered about going to Ventnor.

'It really doesn't matter,' she said to Stew. 'If you don't want to listen to the band, I'm sure we can come up with another form of entertainment.'

'Don't you worry, I've got a plan.' Stew put his arms around Den and Mick, drawing them in. 'If we've got to stay here, let's make it a night to remember.'

THE BAND WERE on their third number when there was a woosh as the lights in the barn went off and the music died. Gideon's vocals faded into the night.

'Fantastic,' Sasha giggled. 'A bloody power cut.'

'Flick the switch back on someone, will you,' Roly called.

Chrissy's eyes became accustomed to the darkness. Where was Stew? She could make out Ian and Mick smoking in the doorway to the barn. The lads had complied with Sasha's desired costume change after a hilarious rummage through the Mintrum family dressing-up box. Perhaps not quite the Brighton Blitz nightclub scene The Future might have hoped for, but Ian looked the part in three-cornered hat and Matador style bolero, while Mick had donned a boiler suit and a child sized fireman's helmet. Chrissy, defying orders, had opted for her favourite pedal pushers while Pam had borrowed Rachel's velvet knickerbockers and stuck a feather in her hair.

The boys in the band were checking their leads, swearing amongst themselves.

'It could be all over the island,' Pam whispered. 'Look, the lights in the house have gone out too.'

'What I heard was okay,' Jason Ross remarked. He was less *Rive Gauche*, more Patchouli oil. He leant on Roly's shoulder. The two men had had their arms draped around each other all evening. 'But I wouldn't have minded hearing a bit more.'

'Just give us a few minutes and we'll get it sorted,' Angus called.

It was lighter outside the barn than in, a clear night with an almost full moon. Pam and Chrissy headed into the garden. Prue came out of the house in her dressing gown and slippers, carrying a torch.

'Where's Roly?' she called. 'All the electrics in the house have gone.'

'Something must have tripped,' Mick suggested.

He nodded back towards the barn. 'This lot probably overloaded the system.'

'Can you fix it?' She shone the bright beam of light into his face. Mick flinched.

'It's the other one who's the electrician, Ma,' Sasha said. 'Where's he?'

'You talking about me?' Dennis, who'd done his best to emulate The Future's Arabian Knights theme with a pair of harem pants and a tea-towel, sounded a little out of breath.

'Oh you?' The beam of light from Prue's torch changed focus. 'Can you fix it? Have you got your toolbox with you?'

'I don't tend to bring my tools on holiday with me, Missus.'

'It'll be a fuse or something I expect,' Chrissy said. She'd had a crash course in household maintenance from her dad when he was in the early stages of his terminal illness. 'Where's your fuse box?'

They followed Prue into the house, stepping cautiously to avoid the hazards on route to the front hallway where the fuse box was located high above the front door.

'I'll need a ladder to look at that,' Dennis said.

'There's a step ladder in the coal shed,' Prue confirmed. 'One of you boys go and fetch it.'

'I don't know where the coal shed is.' Stew had now joined the group in the dark hallway. Sasha had found him one of Jonno's suits to wear and he looked like a 1940s spiv. Upstairs, a child was crying.

'It's just outside the back door and to the left.'

'You've got a bloody big house, Missus, and in case you hadn't noticed, it's very dark out there. Have you got another torch I can borrow?' Dennis tried to contain a snigger.

'Prue, Prue, what's going on?' Prue's torch picked out a ghostly apparition in a long white robe on the landing above.

'Go and see to William will you, Auntie,' Prue called. 'We're trying to fix the electrics.'

They waited in the hallway while the lads went in search of the coal shed. Upstairs William could not be placated by Auntie Birdie, and the twins joined the commotion, one of them taking a tumble, as it was an inevitable someone would on the detritus left on the stairs. Fortunately, there was no major damage.

Precariously perched on top of an old wooden ladder with the torch between his teeth, Dennis confirmed Chrissy's initial diagnosis.

'Have you got any fuse wire?' he asked the assembled crowd.

'Kitchen drawer possibly,' Prue replied. Against all advice William made his way downstairs, heaving great big sobs. Chrissy wasn't sure whether it was the darkness that scared him, the motley crew gathered in the hallway, or Auntie Birdie's attempts at pacification. Auntie Birdie was led back to bed by the second twin, in Chrissy's revised opinion, the only sensible member of the entire family.

After a futile torchlit search of the kitchen, it was another hour before Dennis, by some miraculous piece of good fortune, discovered a reel of fuse wire in the glove compartment of his Ford Capri amongst the cigarette packets, chewing gum and used condoms, as he so delightedly informed Prue Mintrum.

'Five minutes and your electrics will be as good as new,' he assured her.

With the power back on in the barn, the band returned to their instruments. Roly Mintrum and Jason Ross were nowhere to be seen.

CHAPTER THIRTY

Eliza

A WHITE BERLINGO van sat on the gravel in front of Merryvale Cottage, which despite the dismal weather still retained an air of country charm. Battered rose hips framed the front door and browned seed heads bobbed furiously in the front garden. The cottage was situated in a hamlet, but it was further from Stewie's landing point than I'd anticipated. He would have had quite a trek. *But he had time to take a trek.*

As I stepped out of my car I was greeted by a chorus of cackles and quacks. I didn't even need to ring the bell on the front door before a woman appeared at the five-bar gate that separated the front from the rear and side of the house.

'Hello there, can I help you?'

For some stupid reason I was expecting an older version of Pilar. I wasn't prepared for the short, elfin-faced woman in paint splattered denim dungarees and baggy purple fleece. Her mousey greying hair was scooped into an untidy ponytail.

'Christine Beech?' I enquired tentatively.

'Yep, that's me.' When she smiled, dimples appeared in her cheeks.

'My name is Eliza. I spoke to Matthew on Tuesday. I was hoping you might be able to put me in touch with an old friend of yours in Nottingham, Pam Pacey.'

I could hardly come out with a direct accusation of forgery and had decided to use Pam to open the conversation, with the aim of luring Chrissy into a confession.

'Pam Pacey? Why are you looking for Pam if you don't mind me asking?' As Chrissy drew closer, grappling with a boisterous golden retriever, I could see the skin on her face was soft and unblemished. Her clear blue eyes were devoid of any make-up.

'I'm carrying out an investigation on behalf of Pilar Beech, Stewie's wife.'

'Pilar's more likely to know where Pam is than I am. When couples split, friends take sides. Den and Pam decided to stick with team Stew, I'm afraid. I haven't seen or heard from Pam for several years.'

'Oh. That's a shame. Pilar didn't have an address for her.'

'If she wanted to let Pam know about Stew's passing, she's probably heard through the old Leeds-to-Nottingham grapevine. It's well established. Branches everywhere.'

There was a hint of mischief in her voice. Despite myself, I immediately warmed to her.

'It was actually my dad who wanted to speak to Pam. Ian Kane.'

Chrissy bent to tickle the dog's ears. She stayed with her head down for several moments. 'I'm sure someone up north will be able to put him in touch, if he tries hard enough.' She looked up. 'Matt mentioned he'd had a visitor acting on Pilar's behalf, said you were asking about a painting. What's that got to do with Ian? Or Pam for that matter.'

Spits of rain were in the air. The wind was whipping my hair around my face. I brushed it out of the way.

'Stewie was conned into buying a forged painting. He lost a lot of money on it. Pilar wants to find out who conned him. Dad offered to help her.'

'And they say chivalry is dead.' Chrissy held up her palm to feel the rain. 'Do you want to come inside? I think we might get wet if we stand here gossiping.'

Chrissy had so far offered very little in the way of gossip, but I smiled a thank you.

I followed her to the rear of the house where I could see the extent of the land. The cottage was surrounded by paddocks. Nearer the house was an unkempt grassy area complete with a pond, home to several ducks and geese, while chickens roamed free in the yard. There were outbuildings too, one of which I assumed was her studio.

She stopped at the door to remove her boots but assured me I didn't need to do the same. I followed her into a compact farmhouse kitchen with pine units very similar to the ones I'd ripped out of Goldstone Villa. A tabby cat was curled on a chair by a range.

'Sit down. Would you like tea, coffee?'

'Tea please, thank you.'

I was conscious of her scrutiny as she waited for the kettle to boil.

'We've met before,' she said. 'You won't remember. You were a toddler. I met you and your sister at the golf club.'

'At Clifftops?'

'Yes. We were on holiday. Stew looked Ian up, we called in.'

'Really?'

'Stew bought his first restaurant on the island not long after that. I think he liked what he saw here, the potential.'

Dad had never mentioned socialising with the Beeches on the Isle of Wight. I had no recollection of mingling with Chrissy and Stewie and their family as a child, but perhaps that was why Matthew had seemed so familiar. We had met before.

'My dad implied he lost touch with Stewie years ago and didn't hear from him again until he bumped into him in York fairly recently. I didn't know he and Stewie worked on the island at the same time.'

Chrissy gave a small shrug. 'Memory loss. It affects us all.'

It was more than a case of memory loss, it was total amnesia. I was caught off balance by the unexpected turn of the conversation. Why hadn't Dad said anything? First the row Debs had mentioned, and now these cosy family get-togethers.

Chrissy put her head on one side. 'It's a long time since I've seen Ian. How is he?'

'He's okay,' I replied cautiously. 'He's currently got a broken ankle. He came over for Stewie's funeral and he fell over, and that's why he's stuck with me for a bit. Or I'm stuck with him.'

'I see.'

'I was only six when he and Mum split up. I've not seen much of him over the years. I suppose you could say we're doing a bit of bonding while we try and track down these forgers.'

'Right, well good luck with that.' Chrissy placed a mug of tea in front of me and removed a pile of clothes from a chair to sit down. 'So where does Pam Pacey fit in? I wouldn't have had her down as a forger.'

'We don't think she is, but Stewie has been paying her regular sums of money, starting from around the time Pilar reckoned he acquired this painting. We wondered if he persuaded her to lend him the cash to make the initial purchase, an amount he is, *was*, repaying in instalments. We hoped she might know something or could tell us a bit more.'

Chrissy put an elbow on the table and a hand under her chin. 'Stew had a habit of asking his friends for money. Your dad could have told you that.'

'He did mention Stew had offered him an opportunity to invest in *Absinthe* at one point.'

'*An opportunity to invest.* That sounds like Stew.'

Chrissy was the wronged woman, the woman thrown out of her house, the woman who had been replaced with a younger model. I'd anticipated bitterness, but Chrissy didn't sound bitter. She sounded amused.

'You wouldn't have any idea who'd want to con Stewie? Someone with a grudge against him perhaps?' I asked. I found her gaze unnerving.

She sat back and took a sip of her tea. 'I hope you're not suggesting this has anything to do with me?' The tone in her voice was teasing, as opposed to indignant.

'No, of course not…it's just you have connections with the art world.'

'Do I?'

'You took classes here on the island. You may know someone who has the necessary talent, the means to create a fake Birdie Adams.' It sounded very lame.

'Birdie Adams? Matt didn't mention this was about Birdie Adams.' Her eyes twinkled with delight. 'Are you saying Stewie bought a fake Birdie Adams and thought it was real? Don't tell me, a male nude?'

I felt myself flushing. 'Dad thinks Stewie presumed it was the piece he sat for all those years ago when you were on your holiday with the Mintrums at Waverley House. So, you see, there might be a connection.'

'You really have got me down as a prime suspect, haven't you?'

'No...' My conviction that Chrissy was our forger was evaporating with every minute. In fact, I wasn't sure of anything anymore.

She raised her eyebrows and studied me over the rim of her teacup. 'I mostly paint landscapes, love, not nudes, although I am quite flattered at the assumption I could master a Birdie. Was this your dad's idea?'

'No, no definitely not. I'm just following up all possible leads.'

'Would you like a tour of my studio?'

'Really, there's no need.'

'Come on. Then you can cross me off your list.' She put down her cup and stood up with a stretch. 'Is everyone who stayed with Sasha Mintrum's family that summer a suspect?'

'We can't dismiss the idea.'

'You're taking your role of art detective very

seriously. Do you do this for a living?'

'No. I'm a–'

'Have you looked into other cases of art forgery on the island? Seen whether they are any similarities?' Christine Beech was enjoying my discomfort.

'We haven't found any other cases, which is why we think this might be something personal.'

'A sensible deduction,' she agreed. 'Who else have you quizzed?'

'Dad can't recall the names of anyone else who was present that summer, apart from you and the Paceys.'

'He really does have a serious case of memory loss.' Chrissy's laughter bubbled forth in an uncontrolled gush. She paused by the back door to recover, hand on the doorjamb. 'Do you want me to give you a rundown? There's Sasha Mintrum, of course, she was the ringleader, we revolved around her like puppets, and Rachel, my old school friend. She went into wallpaper design. It's a lucrative career, or so she tells me. Can't see her rustling up forgeries simply to fool Stew. And I mean Pam, well Pam was a painting by numbers sort of girl. Neat and precise if you know what I mean and content to follow the rules. I don't think she'd have the imagination.'

Chrissy had revealed more about the guests that summer in thirty seconds than Dad had in several days. I was struggling to keep up. 'What about Sasha's family?'

'There was an older brother, Roly, he was pissed off we'd taken over his house, but he wasn't arty, he worked in finance I think, like the dad. Did you know Mr Mintrum ran off with his secretary? They had to sell the house and everything, or so Rachel told me.'

'Are you and Rachel still in touch?'

'I hear from her a couple of times a year. Roly had his boyfriend Jason with him, who was in the music business. It was the first time I'd met a gay couple. Can you believe that? I had a very sheltered upbringing in Nottingham.'

'Would they have a grudge against Stewie?' I remembered what Josh had said about his dad's attitude to Matthew. Had Stewie antagonised the gay couple so much they'd sought revenge forty years later?

'He might have made a derogatory comment or two, but not to their faces, plus I don't think they'd have taken offence. At least not that much offence. There was a younger brother too, he was a menace, and twin sisters, but they took no notice of us.'

Chrissy continued to talk as she strode across the yard, throwing her words over her shoulder into the wind. 'Apart from Dennis, and another lad who was camping with Stew and Ian, the others were all at Brighton School of Art with Rachel and Sasha. They had a band, The Future. Great name that, isn't it? End every performance with a shout of *we are The Future*. Couple of good lookers amongst them but not my type. They played this electronic stuff, saw themselves as the next Kraftwerk, or the Human League. You're far too young to know what I'm talking about, but Gideon, he was the lead singer, had the Phil Oakey haircut, all one-sided. Personally, I thought he was a bit of a prat. I can't even remember the other lads' names because they didn't have a lot to do with me and Pam. I know from Rachel that Gideon and Sasha ended up together, but he never made it as a rockstar. Apparently he and Sasha revolve around the festival circuit selling second-hand clothes, weird and wonderful antiquities, curios, that type of thing.' She slowed down for a moment. 'Sometimes I think I see her, Sasha, here on the island, or a younger version of her, but then perhaps she and Gideon are still here plying their wares. Plenty of festivals on the island in the summer.'

She unlocked the door of the studio and swung it open wide. 'Here you are then, this is me, Christine Noble, amateur artist. No royal academy accreditations to my name, I'm afraid, and definitely no forgeries. Changed my name by deed poll, went back to my maiden name, in case you're wondering. I make a few sales each year at struggling artist festivals and art shows. I paint because I love it. It relaxes me.'

Chrissy's vibrant depictions of the island's coastal and rural landscapes relaxed me too. A half-finished scene of sunset over the familiar red and white striped Needles lighthouse was propped on an easel. Brightly coloured artwork covered three walls of the brick shed, canvasses in all shapes and sizes. The fourth wall was made entirely of glass and overlooked one of the paddocks and a pair of grazing alpacas.

'Bert and Mary,' she said, nodding at the animals. 'After Mary Poppins. It was Matty's favourite film as a child.'

'How funny, it's one of mine too.'

'Stew and me splitting up was the catalyst I needed to reclaim my life.' She came to a halt beside a large paint splattered square table in the centre of the room. 'Our marriage was a mistake from day one. I stuck with him because I thought he'd change, or maybe because I thought my feelings towards him would alter. Whatever. Stew was always chasing a dream, and his dream was to be better than anyone else. We moved constantly. He changed jobs like other people change their underwear. Every step he took was a calculated step up the ladder. It was exhausting.

'When we split up, I realised I could slow down. Make my life all about me, not all about Stew. I was forty-eight and on my own for the first time. I didn't look back and I've never been happier.'

I felt foolish. Kurt and Dad had been right and I had been wrong. I owed her an apology.

'You have a wonderful eye for colour,' I said, admiring a large canvas of a rolling meadow dotted with cowslips and poppies. I wondered if it was for sale. It would look perfect on the wall above my bed in Goldstone Villa.

'Thank you.' She appeared to have finally run out of breath. 'Stew's the sort of man, *was the sort of man*, who could rub people up the wrong way very easily. He was quite good at making enemies.'

'He was uncompromising,' I said, recalling my neighbour Jenny's complaints about *Absinthe's* lack of wheelchair accessibility.

'That's a very polite way of putting it.' Chrissy hesitated slightly. 'You know what was odd though, about Stew's death, getting caught out like that on the tides. He's been fishing in Newtown Creek for years.'

'He wasn't caught out on the tide. His boat was tied to a buoy in the channel.'

'Was it? I thought the newspaper reports said he was stranded on the mudflats. Why didn't he call for help?'

'Pilar said he didn't have his phone.'

'He'd have the VHF radio on the boat. He could have used that.'

'Maybe he didn't have time. You must be relieved none of the boys have inherited his heart condition. Josh told me Stewie had them all tested.'

There was another slight hesitation. 'You've met Josh too?' Chrissy picked up a paintbrush from the table and ran the bristles of the brush against her hand. 'You are being thorough.'

'It's my middle name.'

'You must have inherited your tenacity from your mother.' She looked up. 'If, when, you find out what happened about this painting, perhaps you could let me know? Stew must have been furious when he discovered someone had got the better of him.'

'I believe he was.'

'Could it really be connected to what happened at Waverley House?'

What happened. What did that mean? 'Did *something* happen at Waverley House?' I asked. 'Something that might have repercussions forty years later?'

'Well, no, nothing serious, not that I can think of, but there were pranks and stuff.' She gave a slight shrug. 'And the fact that it was a Birdie. Someone must have known he sat for her. No wonder I was your prime suspect.'

'You weren't, you're not,' I assured her.

Her smile suggested she didn't believe me. She lowered her eyes again. 'Your dad, Ian, did he ever marry again after he and your mum split up?'

'No. Various girlfriends have come and gone, but he's still single.'

'Oh.' She continued to fidget with the brush.

'Tell him I send my regards.'

I had no intention of telling him anything. The last thing I wanted was another triumphant *I told you so* smirk when I announced Christine Beech had been well and truly ticked off the suspect list. I didn't want Dad to know I'd even been here. I liked Chrissy and I liked her paintings. I'd wasted valuable time pinning my hopes on her being our forger. It was time to start looking elsewhere.

CHAPTER THIRTY-ONE

STEWIE HADN'T TREKKED cross country from Shalfleet quay to confront his ex-wife, so where had he gone? Could Dad's theories about Albie Whittaker and/or William Mintrum be correct after all? Albie had committed fraud sixty years ago. There was the dubious story of the cleaning woman with the same name as the dead student. The Lemmings and their picture had disappeared. It could be construed as suspicious. On the other hand, it could all be coincidence. And why would a successful businessman like William Mintrum feel the need to con Stewie Beech?

If only I could find something that connected either of them to Stewie. Before returning to the apartment, I headed down to the marina in Cowes in search of Brian Riggs.

I'd grown up in Ventnor where the small yacht haven was a working fishing harbour. The marina in Cowes was very different. This was where millionaires kept their yachts, their trans-Atlantic catamarans and luxury motor-cruisers. Hundreds of vessels berthed here, all different shapes and sizes. I asked for directions to *Absinthe* from a nautical looking man in waterproofs and was told the yacht was on its usual mooring. When I looked blank, he waved vaguely to his right, but then told me the gate to that particular pontoon was locked with a keycode.

'Which means no-one's on board,' the sailor explained. 'You'll catch Brian there most mornings.'

The skipper had told me afternoons. A deliberate ploy to avoid an interrogation?

'What time does he usually roll up?' I asked.

'Sometime between nine and ten.'

'I'll be back tomorrow.'

BACK AT THE apartment, Dad was glued to the laptop.

'Had a good day, love?' he called from the sofa without looking up. 'How was the shop?'

'Busy,' I lied. He looked far too cosy nestled in my cushions, and I felt a fleeting moment of resentment. My forays to Cranmore and the marina had been futile. I was wet and windswept.

'Did you know an avid fan has made a compilation of Treasure Trove on Tour's greatest finds on YouTube?' he said, patting the spot on the sofa beside him. 'Take a look at this.'

I wanted to ask why he hadn't been honest

with me about his on-off relationship with the Beeches, but that would mean revealing where I'd been. 'How long is it?' I asked. 'I need a shower and we have to be at Charlie's for six. My Golf Sparks feature is going to be broadcast tonight on local TV. We'll watch it at Charlie's before we go out for dinner.'

'I can whizz it on to the Lemmings' slot,' Dad assured me.

I sat down. I'd quiz him later when I'd had time to assemble my thoughts.

The clip of the Lemmings was midway through a series of reeling Treasure Trove guests shocked into speechlessness at receiving the news their long-forgotten treasures could now buy them holidays, new cars, and increased insurance premiums.

'There are twenty cases in this video,' Dad said, pausing the footage as the camera panned away from a shocked Mrs Lemming clutching her husband's arm for support. 'Only four of the regular eight Treasure Trove experts feature. Guess what percentage of these wonderful finds were discovered by our friend Albie?'

'A quarter?'

'Fifty percent. Half of these clips feature Albie Whittaker. I've watched this thing three times just to make sure.'

'You have had an exciting day.'

'Interesting statistic about Albie though, isn't it?' Dad stretched. 'He definitely needs further scrutiny.'

'Perhaps he likes grabbing the headlines. These are his valuations only. We've no way of knowing if any of these objects or paintings are later sold for anywhere near the value he puts on them.'

'Exactly Eliza,' Dad said with an emphatic nod. 'Just as I suspected. The man's a con artist.'

UNLIKE ALBIE WHITTAKER, my moment of glory took up very little time at all. My feature had been reduced to less than three-minutes. Charlie and Dad were quick to assure me I was a TV natural.

Over pizzas in a nearby restaurant, Lucas was full of his trip to Greece and only fell quiet when I inadvertently mentioned something about school.

'I hated school,' Dad confessed.

'What made you become a chef?' Charlie asked.

'Just sort of fell into it. I had a pot-washing job in a pub as a teenager. Gradually I started doing more food prep. I didn't have a clue what I wanted to do when I left school, but the chef at the pub told me how good the local catering college was and suggested I give it a go. I wasn't academic and back in those days you didn't need too many qualifications to get into catering. Any ideas what you fancy doing, Luc, when you finish school?'

'I want to work in marine conservation.'

'That's fantastic,' Dad said with great enthusiasm.

Charlie and I exchanged glances. It was the first

I'd heard of Lucas' ambitions in marine conservation, although I agreed with Dad, it was fantastic career choice.

After dinner we walked the short distance to Charlie's house for coffees.

Lucas wanted to show Dad his new games console and took him off to the back room. Charlie and I remained in the kitchen.

'Those two seem to be getting on like a house on fire,' Charlie remarked as we made coffee in the kitchen. 'He seems to prefer Ian's company to mine right now.'

'Don't worry, it won't last.' I sidled up to Charlie for a hug. It had been a frustrating and exhausting day. 'And it's good that the trip to Greece worked out okay.'

'I suspect it was Rowena who put that idea into his head about marine conservation.'

'That's not a bad thing, is it?' I was surprised at Charlie's attitude. 'It's good to have ambition. In any case, you know what teenagers are like. They're very fickle. After listening to Dad earlier on Lucas will probably declare he wants to be a chef tomorrow.'

Charlie heaved a sigh. 'You're right. It's just that there was part of me that was hoping he wouldn't enjoy himself in Greece.' He gulped and ran his fingers through his hair. 'Isn't that an awful thing to say? I didn't want him having so much fun in case he didn't want to come home. He's already asked me to look at flights for Easter.'

'Oh Charlie.' I hugged him tighter. 'It's important he spends time with both his parents.'

'But the roles have reversed, don't you see? Now I'm the bad guy chasing him up to do his homework, and Rowena's the one doing the fun stuff, like getting him interested in marine conservation. I didn't think it would be this hard.'

'Lucas is adjusting to a lot of changes, we all are. Give him time. It'll be fine. He loves you, you're a great dad, and if his relationship with his mum has improved, that's a good thing too, isn't it?'

'I suppose. Oh Lizzie, what would I do with without you?' Charlie's heartfelt plea took me by surprise. He stroked my cheek. 'Helping out with the shop, making me see sense about Lucas, everything really. I couldn't do it without you.'

'Don't be daft.'

'I'm not being daft. I'm being serious.'

'We're a team.' I slipped out of his grasp. Being in such close proximity to Charlie tended to send certain parts of my body into overdrive and I wanted to keep control of my thoughts. 'I want Making Waves to be a success for you, but as the summer approaches my work with Golf Sparks will increase. I'm going to be travelling a bit more.'

'I know and I think what you're doing with Golf Sparks is great.'

'I won't be around so much to help you out in

the shop. I know I let you down today by shooting off at lunchtime.'

'We were quiet. It was okay. How did you get on by the way?'

'I'll tell you later. The thing is, Charlie, the shop won't always be quiet. You don't want it to be quiet. The season's about to kick off.'

'Dexter says Amelie will happily put in some hours.'

'That's great, but you need a proper plan. Will Amelie want to work full-time? What if Pilar returns and decides to re-open *Absinthe*?'

'I'll worry about that when I have to.'

'You should be worrying now. Make a strategy, Charlie.'

One of the things that had attracted me to Charlie was his laid-back attitude to life, but he was so laid-back he was almost sleepwalking. His responsibilities had changed since we'd first got together last year.

'You know me, Lizzie, I prefer to go with the flow.' His arms were back around me.

Debs had said something very similar about Dad. I'd fallen for a man who was just like my father. A psychologist would have a field day.

'Sometimes you need to control the flow, Charlie.' I eased out of his arms on the pretence of locating the coffee cups. Now that I'd started I had to say my piece. 'Make it work for you, be proactive.'

'That's what Rowena used to say.'

I didn't want Rowena hijacking our conversation, but she had a point. Whenever I'd had the misfortune to run into Lucas' mother, she had a habit of belittling Charlie's capabilities. I'd always put down it to spite. I didn't want to agree with her.

Charlie sighed. 'I know you're right. It's just hard breaking the habits of a lifetime.'

It was on the tip of my tongue to remind him that at thirty-eight, perhaps it was time to break the habits of a lifetime. However, I suspected he'd had enough of those lectures from Rowena.

Almost as if he could read my thoughts, he straightened his shoulders. 'You're right. I'll speak to Amelie tomorrow, see if she'll agree to work full-time. She's good with the customers and knowledgeable about the gear. I ought to grab her before she finds something else.'

'That's exactly what you should do, although not literally grab her. That wouldn't be good.'

'No. There's only one girl in Cowes I literally want to grab right now.' He gave me one of his special smiles before drawing me to him again. I gave in. We'd had a semi-serious conversation. We'd discuss our future relationship when Dad was out of our hair. His lips were on mine.

'Ugh you two, go get a room, will you.' Lucas dashed into the kitchen, poured a glass of water and dashed straight out again.

'You need to talk to him about us,' I whispered. 'I'm pretty sure he can take it.'

'Yeh. Let's be pro-active. You're right as always, Eliza Kane.'

CHAPTER THIRTY-TWO

Faye rang first thing the following morning. She suggested we meet in Seaview later that day so that she could give me an update, not just on progress at Goldstone Villa, which was romping along, but on her successful undercover work in tracking down a Birdie Adams. 'Lots to tell you,' she said.

'Is Lilian's sting about to pay off?' Dad remarked when I came off the phone.

'I don't know. But if Faye has been successful in sourcing us a second forgery, we'll never hear the end of it.'

'I was talking to young Lucas about the case last night,' he said. 'He was intrigued. I heard all about his trip with the Scouts to Newtown. Apparently one of the boys got chased by an enraged farmer for trespassing on his fields. Threatened them with a shot gun.'

'You know what country folk are like. I didn't get a chance to tell you last night but the landlord at the New Inn gave me a call yesterday too. One of his customers saw Stewie land at Shalfleet on the Tuesday afternoon. He's even got a picture to prove it. Stewie was stuck there for several hours because of the tide. He must have gone there to meet someone. I'm going to see Brian Riggs this morning before I meet Faye in Seaview to ask about Stewie's phone. What about Albie Whittaker? Did Lucas have an opinion on his involvement in your criminal gang?'

'No need to be sarcastic. Leave that to your sister. Lucas has never watched Treasure Trove on Tour, so he hadn't heard of him. I still reckon it's too good to be true, this knack Albie has of sniffing out those valuable heirlooms. I'm going to try and catch some more episodes.'

'I believe it runs to ten series so you'll have your work cut out.'

Dad seemed determined to pin the case on Albie Whittaker and I was happy to leave him to it. There was part of me that would like to find the art expert guilty of something, if only in vindication for his treatment of Kurt. But could we connect him to Stewie Beech?

I KNEW NOTHING about yachts, but even I could appreciate *Absinthe* was a thing of vintage beauty with her sleek white hull and polished wood trimmings. Tied up next to her was a small motorboat, the *Little Lady*. The gate to the pontoon was open and a man in his late sixties was on deck, rubbing at the brass handrail with a cloth.

'Brian Riggs?' I called.

He touched his Breton cap in a greeting. 'That's me, how can I help?'

I put one foot on the wooden gangplank. 'Have you got a few minutes? I'd like to ask you some questions about Stewart Beech.'

'Not a reporter are you?'

I shook my head. It was a ruse I'd adopted in the past but the skipper's attitude seemed to suggest it wouldn't work on this occasion. 'We spoke on the phone. My name's Eliza. My dad is an old friend of Stewie's. You might have met him at the funeral. Ian Kane. He was wearing a red velvet jacket, grey hair, beard.'

'You've described half the mourners.'

'My dad has concerns about the circumstances surrounding Stewie's death. I was hoping you might be able to provide some answers.'

He paused. 'You look trustworthy enough. I can spare a few minutes.'

He beckoned me on board. I'd seen pictures of *Absinthe's* interior on the restaurant's website, but nothing had prepared me for the opulence on display. The boat had been beautifully restored, using materials and techniques of the original period. The centre piece of the panelled dining room with its shiny parquet floor was a magnificent glass chandelier. Tables were set for dinner, although there had been no diners since Stewie's death. It really was quite breath taking, a step back in time.

'I understand it was you and Anton who found Stewie that day in Newtown Creek,' I began, taking the offered seat on a high stool at the bijou bar, discretely tucked into a corner. 'Would you mind telling me a bit more about it?'

'What exactly do you want to know?'

'Did you think it was odd, Stewie going off like that?'

Brian Riggs pursed his lips together. He didn't seem ready to speak.

'I know Stewie had a heart condition,' I pressed on. 'I know there's nothing suspicious about his actual death, but his behaviour, his actions, beforehand, just seem a bit puzzling, don't you think?'

'I don't want to get caught up in any funny business,' Brian said after a few moments.

'Funny business?' I leapt on his words. 'You knew about this painting?'

'Painting?' He shook his head. 'I don't know anything about any paintings. What's this got to do with a painting?'

'I don't know, that's what I'm trying to find out. But go on, you sound like you know something wasn't right.' I gave him what I hoped was my sincerest trustworthy look. 'Anything you tell me will be treated in the strictest confidence.' I lowered my voice to prove my point. 'You were aware of this other woman Stewie was seeing?'

He almost fell off his bar stool. 'Woman? What woman? Stew wasn't seeing another woman. Goodness me, what claptrap. Are you sure you're not one of those scumbag journalists?'

'I am definitely not a journalist.' All those times I'd tried to convince people I was and no-one believed me. Now I was trying my hardest not to sound like a journalist and I appeared to be pulling it off effortlessly. My online course was paying unwanted dividends. I brought out my phone.

'Look, this is me. My name is Eliza Kane. I'm a professional golfer. If you watched the local news last night, you'll have seen me on it.'

He took my phone for a closer look. 'Could be you I s'pose.'

'It is me.' I assured him. 'Have you had trouble with reporters sniffing around?'

'Not recently, no.' He handed my phone back. 'But you'll know Stew had a run in with a restaurant critic a couple of years ago? That all blew up out of hand. You've got to be careful.'

'You have,' I agreed. 'I'm not here to dish up any dirt, I just want to know what happened in the hours before Stewie's death.'

'But you mentioned another woman?'

'There is a rumour.'

He narrowed his eyes. 'I've worked with Stewie Beech for the best part of six years now. I considered him a good friend. He was devoted, besotted even, with Pilar. He wasn't seeing another woman. How could he? He couldn't go anywhere without Pilar, he didn't drive.'

'He had a boat,' I pointed out.

'You think he went off to Newtown Creek to see a woman? Who put that idea in your head?'

No good detective ever revealed their sources. 'What was he doing there?' I asked. 'He wasn't fishing, was he?'

Brian dithered, rubbing his fingers, before letting out a long sigh. 'He told me was going to see a man about a dog. I was here that Tuesday when he went off in the *Little Lady*. The forecast was good for the coming weekend, and I was running some maintenance checks. *Absinthe* had been stuck in the marina for weeks – nobody wants to eat their dinner in a force eight.'

'I can see that might spoil the experience.'

'I was getting her ready to take out, then I see Stew roll up and jump into the *Little Lady*. Next thing I spot him motoring out into the Solent. That's a bit odd, I think. I give him a quick call, but his phone goes to voicemail. I try the radio, you can't ignore that. Sure enough he answers. Where you going mate, I say. Just round the coast to Newtown, he replies. What for, I ask. Going to see a man about a dog was his answer.'

A man about a dog encompassed all manner of possibilities, most with dubious connotations. 'You didn't hear anything else from him after that?' I asked.

'No. I finished what I was doing on the engine, then headed to the yacht club for a pint. After that I went home. It wasn't until Anton called me the next morning that I realised anything was wrong.'

'Is that when you alerted the coastguard?'

He shook his head. 'Anton said we should make our own search first, no point panicking. I agreed with him. Me and Stew often went fishing together, but this time, Stew clearly didn't want me tagging along. That usually meant he was up to something dodgy, and I was worried about him.'

'What exactly do you mean by dodgy?'

Brian took off his cap and placed it in his lap. 'This is strictly between you and me, right?'

I nodded.

He cleared his throat. 'There's a man called Bellingham, runs a wholesale business in Southampton. He's a keen fisherman too. Stew would sometimes meet up with him in Newtown Bay. They'd been doing a few deals on the side for a number of years.' He paused. 'When you're in the catering business, it's tempting to find ways to cut costs. He and Stew had an arrangement.'

'What sort of arrangement?' I asked.

Brian Riggs winced, as if he found our whole conversation extremely unpleasant. 'When local suppliers couldn't deliver exactly what Stew wanted, Bellingham helped him source alternatives, at a lower price. It was only once or twice, like. To start with.'

The whole ethos of *Absinthe* was using seasonal, local produce, and Stew wasn't playing by his own rules. He was sourcing ingredients elsewhere.

'Are you saying Stew was buying cheaper produce and pretending it was from the island?'

Brian nodded.

'Was Pilar aware of this?'

'Pilar's a simple girl, it wouldn't be that difficult for Stew to substitute produce without her knowledge.'

'But you knew. What about the other staff?'

'I couldn't say. When the waiting crew bring the food to the tables, part of their job is to tell diners where the ingredients have been sourced, down to the last lettuce leaf. They would rely on Stew to provide that information.'

I immediately thought of Amelie. She worked on *Absinthe* and for Pilar's private catering business. Was she party to Stew's deception? Had I just told Charlie to offer a job to someone who was dishonest?

I took a deep breath. 'When Stew went off in the *Little Lady*, you thought he was meeting up with Bellingham?'

'Yes.' Brian fidgeted with his cap. 'And I wasn't happy about it. I'd told him this racket had to stop.'

'Did Anton know this too?'

Brian Riggs nodded again. 'That's why we wanted to find Stew first. Obviously, I tried calling him on the radio, nothing, so I borrowed a rib from a mate and we headed round to Newtown. The *Little Lady* was tied up near the estuary. We pulled alongside and saw Stew slumped on the deck. It was quite obvious he was dead. That was when we called for help.'

'You didn't get on board the *Little Lady*?'

'No.'

'Did Anton?'

'No.'

'You don't recall seeing Stewie's phone on the boat with him?'

'No. I told you, we didn't board. We kept a vigil alongside until the coastguard arrived.'

'We know Stew went ashore at Shalfleet that Tuesday afternoon. A witness saw him. Could he have gone to meet this man Bellingham there?'

Riggs shook his head. 'I wouldn't have thought so. Bellingham had a motor cruiser. He'd stay out in the deeper water.'

'Have you spoken to Bellingham since Stewie's death?'

'No I haven't. You won't mention this thing about switching produce to anyone, will you? If Pilar wants to continue running the restaurant, things'll change, I'm sure they will. I don't think Pilar would willingly deceive her customers like that. I don't think she's capable.'

I didn't think she was capable either. However, Anton was. Had he fabricated the story of Stewie's mystery woman to put us off the scent of the substitution racket? No doubt he would claim it was to protect Pilar, but he was protecting himself. If news of this food scam came to light, the Beeches' reputations would be ruined and by association, Anton's credibility. His future job prospects would be in serious jeopardy.

Brian cleared his throat. 'When did this witness see Stew at Shalfleet? Are you sure it was that Tuesday afternoon?'

'I've not spoken to him personally, but he keeps a boat on the quay. He recognised the *Little Lady*.'

'That is odd. You can only land on the quay three hours each side of high tide. When Stew left the marina the tide was already on its way out. He'd have just made it to Shalfleet in time, but he wouldn't have been able to linger. He'd have had to move the boat back out into the main channel fairly swiftly.'

'This witness says the *Little Lady* was moored up all afternoon.'

'Really? So how did she get back out into the river?'

'Presumably Stewie returned at high tide.'

'But that wouldn't have been until...what nine, ten o'clock at night?'

'Yes, so Stewie must have set off for Cowes around then. I imagine he started to feel ill and moored up because he didn't want to risk the journey home.'

Brian shook his head and twisted his cap between his fingers. 'Your witness must be mistaken. They reckoned Stew had been dead for about twenty hours when we found him, and that was around midday on the Wednesday. That would imply he had his fatal heart attack around four o'clock on the Tuesday afternoon, long before the return of the tide.'

CHAPTER THIRTY-THREE

AS I WALKED away from *Absinthe,* I took out my phone and studied the picture the landlord at the New Inn had forwarded to me. A small motorboat was clearly visible resting on the mudflats behind a freshly painted dinghy. To my untrained eye it was identical to the boat now moored beside *Absinthe.* The photo had been taken in the fading light of a January afternoon.

I needed to stay calm and think rationally. The guesstimated time of death by the coastguard, paramedic or whoever had spoken to Brian Riggs, could be wrong. Brian had looked confused and upset. I didn't want to give the impression I was questioning his honesty or his memory by challenging him about the timings.

The urge was to go straight home and relay this new information to Dad. Who was right? The witness at Shalfleet, or *Absinthe's* captain? Or was there some other explanation? In my entire thirty-six years I'd never wanted to talk to my dad like I did at this moment. *I needed him.* He was the Dr Watson to my Sherlock Holmes. Or was it the other way round? Then another thought struck me, even more bizarre than the first. Was I actually going to miss him when he headed back north?

No, surely not? I was succumbing to another dose of mawkish sentimentality. Dad was fixated with Albie Whittaker and would want to shoehorn him into the equation. It would be much better to seek out the facts about the timings first. Either Josh or Matthew Beech had said something about Stewie being dead for nearly twenty-four hours before he'd been found. I should have picked up on this. There would be a record somewhere documenting Stewie's time of death. *Facts, Eliza, not heresay and supposition.*

Faye was expecting me. She wouldn't appreciate being kept waiting. In any case, she had positive news and right now, very aware of my own failings, I needed something positive to hold onto. I hurried on down to Seaview.

Resplendent in a pastel pink jumpsuit, high-vis jacket and hard hat, Faye was pacing out my extension, the walls of which were now complete.

I was delighted with the size of the enlarged kitchen and family room which ran the entire width of the house.

'Still a long way to go, obvs,' Faye said, 'but I just wanted to give you options on the positioning of the Velux windows.'

I wasn't aware I was having Velux windows. We spent several minutes studying the architects' initial drawings and flicking through window brochures. I selected my options before Faye suggested going for a coffee. I bit back my impatience.

'I'd love a coffee but I'm on a schedule.' Whatever valuable information Faye had to tell me could easily be imparted in the shell of my extension.

'We won't be long, and I'm sure you'll be very pleased with my progress.' The real reason for our excursion became apparent when Faye introduced me to her new car, a white Porsche which had been parked out of sight at the end of the lane to avoid contamination with any dust from my building work. We took the two-minute trip to Lily's Tearooms at top speed.

'This search for your painting is proving very interesting,' Faye said as we sat down with our Lattes. 'As I told you, I've been putting feelers out. Most of my regular contacts seemed to think it would be impossible to obtain a piece of Birdie Adams' artwork on the open market, but one of the smaller galleries I deal with put me in touch with a specialist consultancy. *Et voila*, I think I can obtain the genuine article for you.'

'I don't want the genuine article,' I reminded her. 'I'm on the lookout for a forgery.' The last thing I wanted was Faye promising a large sum of money from my hard-won winnings, just minutes earlier further depleted by the purchase of the latest must have anti-glare Velux windows, in exchange for the most hideous painting imaginable.

'I know you are, and this is why it's all so exciting. As soon as I spoke to the owner of the consultancy, I was able to set up a meeting here on the island. That immediately aroused my suspicion. I've been in this business a long time and some of my clients have requested unusual objects. It's never this easy.'

'What is this consultancy?'

'It's called Blak, based in Battersea. The proprietor's name is Tiffany Snow.'

'You've set up a meeting here?'

'Yes. These people are inevitably "unavailable" because they want to give the impression of being so much in demand.' Faye could have been describing herself. 'But, the mere mention of a Birdie, and here she is at the drop of a hat, not just available but available here on the Isle of Wight, where she just happens to be visiting family this coming weekend.

'Unfortunately,' Faye gushed on, 'she did want to know all about you. A mystery client didn't wash, I'm afraid. She wanted a name to ensure my approach was genuine. I played you up of course, world championship golfer, bags of money, refurbishing your island home to the highest spec, keen to purchase an investment piece from a local artist. I had to assure her you had real cash to spend.'

'Thank you.' I wasn't sure whether I was grateful or not, but Faye had a point. It was all starting to sound very convenient.

'Three o'clock at the Seaview Hotel on Saturday.' Faye held out her phone. 'Here's Blak's website. Tiffany looks like a bit of a vamp from her profile pic, so dress to impress Eliza, and act like you've got money to burn.'

Tifffany Snow did indeed look vampish. She also looked familiar, although I couldn't place where I might have seen her before. The photo on her website showed a young woman of perhaps thirty, dark hair severely pulled off her pale face, dressed in a business suit. My social circle was limited and I rarely ventured to London, but I couldn't shake off that feeling of déjà vu.

I EXPECTED TO find Dad asleep over the laptop when I arrived home. Instead the flat was empty. I was just checking my phone to see if he'd left a message when one of the neighbours knocked on the door.

'This came while you were out,' he said, handing me a parcel.

The package was addressed to Dad, and judging by its size and weight, I suspected Debs had found his photo album. As I debated the ethics of opening the parcel myself, I heard the familiar ping of the lift doors opening, followed by the tap of Dad's air boot along the corridor.

He exchanged a few words with the neighbour, before entering the apartment.

'Just went out for a walk,' he announced. The fact that he volunteered this information without me having to ask immediately suggested he was lying. Plus, it must have been a long walk. Our post usually arrived first thing, which meant he must have set off early. He was carrying some sort of document wallet which set off alarm bells, and beneath his blazer he was dressed in a smart check shirt I hadn't seen before and his blue chinos. Without a doubt he'd been on a property search. 'What have you got there?' he asked with a nod at the parcel, still clutched in my hands. I put it down on a side table.

'Your photo album I hope, from Debs.'

'I didn't ask for any photo albums.'

'I know, but I did, to jog your memory.'

'My memory doesn't need jogging, not now. We know this is connected to Will Mintrum, Albie Whittaker, and the Lemmings.'

'We don't know, you just suppose. I found something out about Stewie Beech today. He's been running his own scam. He's been substituting cheaper produce, making false claims about using only local food.'

Dad sank onto the sofa. 'Who told you that?'

'Brian Riggs.'

'Surely he couldn't get away with that?'

'How would the customers know the difference?'

'Taste, for a start.'

'Not everyone knows what an Isle of Wight tomato tastes like. If a top chef tells you you're eating an Isle of Wight tomato, you'd believe him, wouldn't you?'

Dad looked doubtful. No doubt he had a very refined palate. 'What about this missing phone?' he asked.

'No sign of it. Riggs says neither he nor Anton put a foot on the *Little Lady*. There's no mystery woman either. That was a lie invented by Anton to throw us off the scent. Stewie used to meet up with a wholesaler called Bellingham in Newtown Bay and do a few dodgy deals. Riggs assumed that was where he was going when he went off that Tuesday.

'In addition, Riggs is under the impression Stewie's death occurred sometime on the Tuesday afternoon, so even if he did land at Shalfleet, he couldn't have stayed there until the tide came back in.'

'But I thought you had photographic evidence? This witness from the pub?'

'I've a picture of a boat that looks like the *Little Lady* tied up alongside the quay, high and dry on the mud, yes, but you can't see its name.

There's quite a few of those little motorboats about. I'll have to ring landlord back to ask how reliable this witness is.'

'Didn't they do a post-mortem? That would confirm the time of death. I'll give Pilar a call to see what's on the death certificate.'

That's exactly what I should have done. 'Thanks Dad. Either way it seems this whole fishing trip is one big red herring. I should have quizzed Riggs earlier.'

'Don't be so hard on yourself. How did you get on with your friend Faye?'

'Some progress at least.' I flopped onto the sofa next to him and opened my laptop. 'She has arranged a meeting with an art specialist called Tiffany Snow. Faye thinks she's too good to be true.'

I showed him Tiffany's website. He leaned in for a closer view.

'She looks familiar.'

It was odd that both of us should have the same sense of recognition. Dad and I moved in very different social circles at opposite ends of the country. It would be a major coincidence if we'd both met Tiffany Snow somewhere else before.

'I thought that too. Does she look like someone famous, an actress perhaps?' I studied Tiffany's perfectly poised photograph.

'I don't watch an awful lot of films,' Dad confessed. 'I prefer a good book. Perhaps it'll come to us later. Maybe she looks like a celebrity, one of those Love Islanders or something.'

Tiffany Snow didn't have enough eye lashes to be on Love Island, or the requisite spray tan. However, Dad did have a point. There was a haughtiness about her which suggested she was well used to posing. A model perhaps.

'Umm. I'll have a Google,' he said. 'See what I can find out. Maybe we can find a link between her and Albie Whittaker, Will Mintrum and the Lemmings.'

He wasn't going to give up. I took a deep breath. 'I don't understand why Will Mintrum or Albie Whittaker would target Stewie Beech.'

'Maybe Albie was a disgruntled customer, getting his own back. Perhaps it takes a forger to recognise a like mind. It does open up a motive.'

'A very tenuous one. Stewie could have pissed off hundreds of customers over the years, and not just because of his underhand dealings. If you're using that as a motive our fraudster could be anyone.' Including Jenny's sister Ruth.

'A restaurant like *Absinthe* would appeal to people like Albie Whittaker,' Dad insisted. 'I wonder if we can find out if he ever dined there? I said all along this thing about Stewie sitting for Birdie Adams could be coincidental, but it would have worked to Albie's advantage.'

'What is Will Mintrum's motive? Is he a disgruntled diner too?' My frustration bubbled over.

'Or did he remember Stewie from your holiday? Perhaps he was seeking revenge for you and Stewie pushing him in the pool.'

'How do you know we pushed him in the pool?'

'I don't.' Although Chrissy had mentioned pranks. I had to keep quiet about that. 'It was a joke.' So much for Holmes and Watson. We were more like a pair of sparring boxers.

I left the sofa and picked up the package containing the photo album from the side table. 'Let's have a look at your album. It will be fun to see some pictures of you when you were young. Mum didn't keep any.'

'I don't think it would be fun at all.' Dad struggled to his feet and snatched the parcel from my hands. 'You shouldn't have gone behind my back with Debs like that. I don't know why you don't believe me about Albie Whittaker and the Mintrums. You just don't like the fact that I've solved this case before you.'

Before I could point out we hadn't solved anything, he disappeared off into his bedroom, slamming the door behind him.

CHAPTER THIRTY-FOUR

DAD EMERGED FROM his sulk after an hour. I turned down the sound on the re-run of the old detective drama I was watching on TV. By the bounce in his step his mood had changed.

'Now you're going to have to believe me,' he announced. 'Tiffany Snow.' He sat down and opened his photo album with relish. He placed his phone on top of the first page. Tiffany's website mugshot was displayed on the screen. 'Look at this. Can you see you the similarity?'

The plastic sheets covering the photographs he'd taken forty years ago were browned and no longer sticky. There were six photos on the double spread page, with none of the clarity of today's sharp images.

The first photo was of four girls in varying shapes and sizes, sat on the edge of a pool. The girl at the end of the quartet sat slightly apart from the other three, cigarette held in her hand. She had a severe black bob and her eyes were heavily kohled like Cleopatra.

'That's Sasha Mintrum,' Dad said. 'She and Tiffany Snow could be sisters.'

There was no denying there were similarities between Sasha Mintrum and Tiffany Snow. They shared the same haughty demeanour, pale colouring and slender build. I knew what Dad meant, but that wouldn't explain why I felt I'd seen her before.

The second photo on the page was of three young men standing proudly beside two tents.

'The lads from Leeds?' I asked.

'Yep, this is Stewie, that's Mick, and then there's Den.'

Mick with his long hair and wispy beard wore a leather waistcoat over a checked shirt and jeans. The other two, clean cut in comparison, were dressed in what I assumed had to be the youth fashion of the day, football shorts with open denim shirts over their T-shirts.

I studied the other photos on the page. In one, the girls had been joined by the three boys from the tents, in another they were splashing in the pool, although Sasha Mintrum remained aloof on the edge with her ubiquitous cigarette.

'I want to see a picture of you,' I said, reaching across to turn the page.

'I was the one taking the pictures. I think I'd just got a new camera.'

Two of the girls wore identical polka-dot bikinis, one in red and one in yellow. The third was in a halter-neck swimsuit.

'Which one of these girls is Pam and which is Chrissy?' I asked, although it was easy to identify the woman I'd met the previous day. I recognised the elfin features and mischievous grin.

'This one is Pam,' Dad said, pointing to the girl in red with a mass of blonde curls. His finger lingered over the photograph. 'And this is Chrissy.' He paused. 'Rachel, that was their other friend's name. I can remember now.'

'See it is coming back to you,' I said.

Another photo showed Dennis entwined with Pam on a deckchair, while Stewie and Mick made a rude hand gesture behind them, to the ignorant bliss of the happy couple. Another showed Stewie wrapped in a bathrobe, while Sasha, wide grin on her face, the only picture I'd seen of her smiling if that's what the gloat could be called, tugged at his arm.

'That was when he was going off to sit for Birdie,' Dad grunted. One picture showed a group of boys sat on the grass with Rachel and Sasha, although the focus appeared to be on Chrissy, sat by herself on her sun lounger. Dad shifted position. 'What do you think, Tiffany Snow and Sasha Mintrum? They have to be related.'

'They certainly look alike,' I agreed, 'but not sisters. She's too young. A daughter, niece even. But I thought I recognised her too and I had no idea what Sasha Mintrum looked like until today.'

'You've travelled all over the world. They say we all have a doppelganger somewhere.'

I thought about this for a few moments. Chrissy had said she thought she'd seen Sasha here on the island – or a younger version of her. Perhaps she'd seen Tiffany Snow.

'We're not to tell Lilian she was right all along about the Mintrums being behind this,' Dad said with a yawn. 'She'll never let us forget it.'

'We still don't know the Mintrums are behind this,' I pointed out.

'But it's looking very likely, isn't it?'

'We don't know Tiffany Snow is any relation to the Mintrums. We don't know she was the one who sold Stewie his forgery. We need proof.' I tugged at the corner of the page. 'Can we see some more?'

'There are no more pictures of Sasha.' He kept his hand firmly on the page to prevent me turning it over.

'What about the art students? Can you remember anything more about them?' Chrissy had already told me one of them had hooked up with Sasha Mintrum. Another thing I couldn't let on to Dad about. I wanted him to be open and honest with me, but I wasn't being open and honest with him.

'They were all posh kids. The girls seemed to think that one,' he pointed to a youth in leather trousers with a very bad haircut on the grass beside Sasha, 'was the best thing since sliced bread. He had an odd name, Gideon, that's it. He was a bit of a jerk. Lost his cool a couple of times with me and Stewie.'

I squinted at the picture of Gideon. 'Why? What did you do to him?'

'Nothing.' Dad put his hands up in the air. 'We wound him up, that's all. They were in a band, insisted on putting on a performance every night. One evening Stewie and Den whipped the fuse out of the box in the main house, pretended we had a power cut. That kept them quiet for a bit.'

'Are you sure there aren't any pictures of you in here?' I willed him to turn to the next page. There were several more sheets in the album. 'I want to know what you looked like as a young man.'

'Did your mum really not keep any photos?'

'No, at least not that she ever showed us. It seems a bit mean considering she was the one who had the affair and went off with Alistair. You were the innocent party.'

'Umm.' He sighed. 'Things aren't always black and white, Eliza. Me and your mum were mismatched from the start.'

He leaned back on the sofa and concentrated on the TV for a while, his hands firmly resting on his photo album. Within minutes his eyelids started to droop. I found this particular detective had the same soporific effect on me.

'I worked there for a bit,' Dad murmured with a nod to the screen as the murderer was forced into a waiting police car. By a string of amazing coincidences our TV detective had cracked the case without a shred of solid evidence. 'Whitley Bay. Nice place but that North Sea wind whipping across the bay would freeze the balls off a brass monkey.'

I waited until his breathing deepened before gently easing the photograph album from his knee.

Could a peeved art student be behind our forgery campaign? Presumably he'd have the artistic talent and knowledge to recreate a Birdie Adams. If Sasha Mintrum and Gideon had a child together, there was a strong possibility she might resemble Tiffany Snow. They were a distinguished looking couple, even at twenty. I should have asked Chrissy for Gideon's surname, although if Tiffany dealt in forged art, she'd hardly be using her real name.

I flipped to the page after the one Dad had shown me. There were some scenic shots of the island, the lads from Leeds at Blackgang Chine with the girls from Nottingham, there were panoramas of the beach at Ventnor, the Needles and Alum Bay. There was a candid snap of Chrissy, tucking into a candyfloss, and another where she sat by herself on a towel on the sand, looking directly at the camera, a sultry pout on her face. On a second towel beside her was a can of coke, a Dick Francis novel and a Leeds United football shirt.

For the last two pictures in the album Dad had entrusted someone else with his camera. In one, all eight of them stood together, Den and Pam, arm in arm, Mick and Stewie with Rachel and Sasha squashed between them, and Dad with his arm around Chrissy's waist, cuddling her close. The second shot was of him and Chrissy; a bare-chested young man sporting in a pork pie hat and a pair of cut-off denim shorts, kissing a laughing girl with chocolate coloured hair in a yellow polka-dot bikini.

Now I knew why he hadn't wanted me to see the rest of his album. I'd thought this was the holiday where Stewie Beech and Chrissy had got together, but I'd got that wrong. Christine Noble might well have gone on to marry Stewie Beech, but that summer she'd been Ian Kane's girl. And that changed things.

It would explain the row Debs had mentioned. It would explain his refusal to consider Chrissy a suspect. But what I didn't understand, was why he hadn't he told me himself. Didn't he trust me? Or was it something else?

CHAPTER THIRTY-FIVE

Chrissy August 1981

IT WAS THE morning after the black-out. Chrissy had returned to the house at first light to use the loo and crept up to her bunk for another few hours' sleep.

Stew had been full of bravado, keeping them awake until the small hours, relaying the events of the evening. He was very proud of his ingenuity.

'I lifted Den up onto my shoulders and we whipped out the wire. Easy peasy.'

Sasha waltzed into the kitchen, immaculately made up as usual, not a hair of her sleek blue-black bob out of place. Why did she never look hungover? Chrissy couldn't understand it.

'Want to hear some gossip?' She slid onto the bench next to Chrissy.

'Not especially.' Pam gave a mock yawn.

'Guess what Tweedle Dum just told me? His friend Tweedle Dee has a girlfriend, a fiancé no less, back in Leeds.' Sasha reached for the butter dish as she spoke and ran her finger across the block. 'Sexy *lad* like that, I suppose it's not so surprising is it, really?'

Pam made a little 'o' with her mouth.

Sasha licked her finger. 'I thought you might like to know. Or has he already told you?' She looked directly at Chrissy and raised an eyebrow. 'After all, some people enjoy being the bit on the side. Makes things more spicey.'

Chrissy tried to think of something to say, some clever retort, but no words came. She crushed the urge to reach across the table and slap the smirk off Sasha's face. She also recognised Sasha was not the only one who deserved slapping.

Sasha beamed. 'What are the plans for today, girls? Shall we beach it again? One more oggle at that wonderful six pack while we can, 'eh?'

OF COURSE HE'D have a girlfriend. He'd been toying with her. She was the distraction. Sweet, innocent little Christine. Hopes all dashed. To not have the balls to tell her himself. To have to hear it from somebody else.

Let's go away somewhere together, he'd said. *We'd be free spirits, just you and me, going wherever the mood took us. Where do you fancy? France, Spain, Italy? Crushing grapes with our bare feet? Swimming in the ocean? Sight-seeing, Pisa, Rome, Naples...*

She'd relished the thought of not returning to Nottingham, of telling the team at work she wouldn't be coming back. *Ever.* Of sticking two fingers up at Alan Wickstead. Of living in a gite, or a chalet, or even a tent, it didn't really matter what. Of looking out over a vista of lavender fields, sunflowers, vineyards. Of sitting at an easel and painting.

She avoided him all day. Her last day. She and Pam gave the trip to the beach a miss and instead went to Newport to do some shopping. Chinese whispers must have made it back to base because he tried to talk to her when she returned to Waverley House, but she brushed him away with a brusque 'don't'.

She changed into her favourite candy-striped mini dress with the wide plastic belt, the one he said he liked best, the one that accentuated her breasts and showed off her legs, the one she'd been wearing on the day they first met over chicken in a basket at the pub. As The Future played she drank too much vodka and sang along with Angus and Rachel, but the band's performance was as lacklustre as she felt. Jason Ross had left that afternoon for London.

'Den says you should let him explain,' Pam whispered through the darkness of the attic room in the early hours, as an owl hooted in the trees outside. 'He's not engaged, and this girl, well they've been together since school and Ian's not really into her anymore…he's been looking for an excuse to break up with her.'

Did that make it any better or worse? Just a fling so he could go back to Leeds and tell his long-term girlfriend it was over? *No thank you.*

Stew had told her the opposite. He'd cornered her earlier at the makeshift bar in the barn as she topped up her vodka, and told her Ian and Lisa, that was the girl's name, were childhood sweethearts, dating since they were fifteen and all set for marriage, mortgages and babies.

'I thought he must have told you,' Stew said, 'and you were just having a bit of fun.'

She had had fun. She'd had loads of fun; she and Ian had clicked from the very first moment they met. They liked the same music, they shared a sense of humour, she'd given herself to Ian as she'd never given herself to anyone before and she thought he'd given himself back. Clearly not.

When she crept down into the kitchen first thing in the morning, she saw Auntie Birdie out of the window, going for her customary dip, and there was Sasha, wearing nothing but a Leeds United football shirt, crisscrossing the lawn, coming from the direction of the lad's camp. That shirt smelt of Ian. Chrissy had wrapped herself in it several times, asked if she could keep it. He said no – at least not until the end of the holiday and now he'd given it away, just like that. What was the opposite to icing on the cake? The straw on the camel's back.

The journey home to Nottingham was miserable. Pam buried herself in a book and kept quiet. Chrissy stared out of the train window, watching the countryside flash by through her tears; suburban gardens merging into a patchwork quilt of lawns, flowerbeds, shrubs, swings, and gaudy plastic slides.

WHEN DENNIS CAME to Nottingham two weeks' later to meet up with Pam, he said he was bringing a friend with him. She dared to hope, but the hope died. Stew could be charming, funny and attentive, but he wasn't Ian Kane. It was a month later, on Stew's second visit, he told her Ian had left Leeds.

'He's jacked in his job and gone off to Europe on his motorbike with Mick Levine.'

At least he hadn't gone with Lisa. It wasn't a great deal of consolation.

Stew's courtship was calculated and consistent. He said none of them had heard from Ian for months, although Mick was now back in Leeds. Accept it, she told herself, and move on. Life at home was unbearable. Alan was laying down his house rules. There were curfews. He was a light sleeper. Didn't she realise how much noise she made sneaking up the stairs after a night out, coming home on the last bus? She was selfish and ungrateful. Alan had a responsible job with the local council. He needed a routine, meals on the table, a full eight hours' sleep.

I'll go mad if I stay here, she thought.

'I've got a new job,' Stew told her. 'Four-star hotel in Oxfordshire. Comes with accommodation. Do you fancy coming with me, moving down there together?'

It wasn't Naples, it wasn't Provence, but those dreams had long gone. *Did she fancy it?* She didn't hesitate.

She maintained a secret hope that Ian might come to the wedding. She wanted him to see her, glorious in her bridal dress. The other half of her wanted him to storm up the aisle, scoop her into his arms and whisk her off on his white charger. Neither scenario materialised. He didn't attend Pam and Dennis' wedding either, just six months' later, although Dennis had done his proposing first.

'We can beat them to the altar, can't we,' said Stew. It was the story of their life. She'd not seen it, the competitiveness, but now that they were married, living together, Stew had nowhere to hide his warts. He always had to be one better than everyone else. Success meant everything to him, and if he couldn't be the best, he did his utmost to create that illusion. Desperate and compliant, she was just part of his grand plan.

CHAPTER THIRTY-SIX

Eliza

I SAT FOR some time staring at those photographs as a jumble of thoughts tumbled around in my head. Right from the very start of this investigation instinct had told me this case was personal. We were looking for someone with a grudge. Was I delving into the realms of fantasy to think Dad had the biggest grudge of all?

The bitterness had been there all along in his voice. I knew he'd been hiding something. That convenient "memory loss", the sparsity of details he'd provided from that all important holiday.

Treasure Trove on Tour aired on national TV. What if he'd watched that episode with the Lemmings all those years later and seen the opportunity to get his own back on his former friend for stealing his girl? Had he paid somebody to recreate Stewie's portrait and then managed to bring the picture to Stewie's attention? Had he attended the funeral with the sole intention of retrieving his fraudulent piece of art before anyone discovered the truth? Had Tess been instructed to abscond with it back to Harrogate when Dad realised he couldn't leave the Isle of Wight? Had this whole investigation been a ruse, instigated by Dad, not Pilar? *Was he that devious?*

Dad's over-enthusiasm to take on a starring role in solving the mystery was the double bluff. I'd seen it played out in plenty of police procedurals on TV, read enough crime novels. The prime witness, eager to be of assistance, deflecting attention elsewhere. How many times did those individuals end up being revealed as the perpetrators of the crime? Dad had drip-fed me information. He had a motive – revenge. What about opportunity and means? I could picture him and Stewie on a late night drinking session after hours in Turpin's, sipping their whiskies, Dad slipping in a word or two about a certain picture that he'd seen for sale in some exclusive gallery in York...

He twitched beside me. His body shook with a snore, jolting me back into sense. *Seriously?* Did I really believe this soft, cuddly bear of a man capable of such subterfuge? There was a huge chunk of Dad's life I knew nothing about, but he couldn't possibly have masterminded such a complicated plot, *could he?* He did like his crime novels...

Stop it, Eliza!

Dad was like Christine Beech. He wasn't malicious. He was generous, warm-hearted, loyal, demonstrative, *tactile*. He'd forgiven Stewie for stealing Chrissy away from him long ago. He'd met and married Mum. After he'd had his own family, his friendship with Stewie had resumed. When my parents had separated, Dad had headed back to Yorkshire while the Beeches remained on the Isle of Wight. Dad lived the life of a feckless bachelor. Stewie was a family man.

I knew Dad carried a burden of guilt at his failed marriage, parenthood, or whatever, but he didn't harbour grudges. I'd only met Chrissy once, and I'd immediately liked her. Kurt had been charmed. It was easy to see why Dad had jumped to her defence. There was nothing sinister about it.

But I couldn't dismiss my hurt. If only he'd have been honest with me from the start. I closed the photo album and slid it back onto his knee. I didn't want Dad to know I'd sneaked a peep and discovered his secrets, nor must he ever know I had fleetingly considered him a suspect. Unlike Chrissy, I doubted Dad would find the idea amusing.

I picked up my laptop. Just as I was about to type IS TV ANTIQUES EXPERT ALBIE WHITTAKER A DISHONEST ROGUE? into the search bar, my phone rang. It was Charlie. What a relief. I needed a diversion before I caused any more trouble.

'I thought you'd be pleased to know Amelie has accepted my job offer and can start immediately.'

'That's great,' I replied in a whisper, although I wasn't entirely convinced that it was now that I knew about Stewie's food scam and her possible collusion in it. Dad stirred beside me. 'Will she be able to work this Saturday?' I asked. 'I can cover the morning but I'll need the afternoon off.'

'No problem,' Charlie assured me. 'Let's all have dinner together again on Sunday.'

'Good idea. Come here. Dad will do the cooking.'

'What am I cooking?' Dad opened one eye. He checked the photo album was still within his grasp. 'I thought you were doing dinner tonight?'

'I am, this is Sunday with Charlie and Lucas.'

While I carried on talking to Charlie, Dad took the photo album into his room. I decided to leave Albie Whittaker alone and work on some Golf Sparks admin. An email had arrived reminding me to submit my travel expenses.

I heard Dad on the phone, probably calling up his estate agent. It was another hour before he returned to the living room.

'I've spoken to Ryan Bellingham,' he announced. 'His business card was in Stewie's wallet. We took pictures, remember.'

'Oh yes, that's good. And?'

'He says he was on holiday the week Stewie died. He didn't have any plans to meet him in Newtown Bay. Offered to send me a copy of his ski pass.'

'How did you get that information out of him?'

'Said I worked for one of the catering industry magazines, doing a bit of investigative work. I looked at those spreadsheets we downloaded from the flash-drives, the ones I assumed were lists of suppliers. There are some genuine ones on there, it all looks very plausible, but others are totally fictitious. Stewie invented local companies; *Loveday Leaves* for his salads, *Pennydown Poultry* his free-range eggs, *Molehill Farm* for his finest pork. I've looked them up online and none of them exist. I reckon those spreadsheets are crib sheets, reminders, so he could tell his waiting staff where each element of a dish was sourced. They probably had no idea what was going on.'

Hopefully that got Amelie off the hook.

'It does bring us back to the question of why Stewie ended up in Shalfleet,' Dad continued with a frown. 'If he wasn't there to meet his mistress, he wasn't there to meet Ryan Bellingham, and he wasn't there to fish, what was he doing there?'

'Meeting his forgers?' I suggested hopefully. 'Not that we know how long he was there for, or whether he had time to do anything.' We were right back at square one with absolutely nothing to go on.

'Umm.' Dad scratched his head. 'I've left a message for Pilar. I've got Josh's number so I might try him, see if he's got access to the death certificate. Meanwhile we need to talk about our strategy for Saturday.'

'Saturday?'

'Our meeting with Tiffany Snow.'

'*Our* meeting? You have to let me deal with this.'

'Of course, but you're going to need back-up. Can you give your friend Grace a call?'

CHAPTER THIRTY-SEVEN

FAYE SUGGESTED I arrive deliberately late for my meeting with Tiffany, like a "proper diva". I'd never behaved like a diva in my life. In my book being late was the height of rudeness, the arrogant *my time is more important than yours* mentally, although I knew plenty of golfers who would turn up late for a match deliberately to spook their opponent. My old adversary Aggie MacDonald was one of them. I still couldn't quite believe we were both going to be Golf Sparks ambassadors. How was that ever going to work out?

I kept my lateness to five minutes, only to discover when I walked into the lounge bar of the Seaview Hotel that Faye was sat on her own with a bottle of Prosecco.

'Where is she?' I asked, sliding onto a chair.

'Heaven knows,' Faye huffed. 'Go powder your nose or something and come back in ten minutes.'

Dad and Grace were a short distance away on a table for two. Grace had jumped at the chance for a spot of undercover surveillance, although there was nothing undercover about either of them. Dad had insisted on wearing his red velvet smoking jacket because he felt it was appropriate for the elegant surroundings, while Grace was in one of her favourite flowery frocks. Blend into the background they did not, but fortunately, they were well-matched. They kept to the script and neither of them acknowledged my arrival.

It seemed Tiffany Snow was the expert diva, not me. She arrived after another twenty minutes, full of apologies. She was dressed in a bottle green trouser suit with her black hair scooped into a chignon. She carried a tan briefcase.

'So sorry ladies,' she said, as we stood to greet her. 'My morning meeting over ran. Good of you to wait and not give up on me.'

Faye gave a giggle as she shook Tiffany's hand. 'Oh, we were tempted. Only joking. This is a wonderful opportunity. We're so glad you're willing to help us.'

'Ah yes, the Birdie Adams.' Tiffany retrieved a leatherbound notebook from her briefcase as she sat down. 'It's lovely to meet you Miss Kane, Eliza, but I confess I am a little intrigued. Why are you so interested in acquiring a Birdie?'

'A friend of mine had one,' I said. 'I've always admired it. There's the local connection. I'm a native islander.'

I hoped the mention of a friend might lead Tiffany to enquire who my friend was, but it didn't.

'I've been reading up about you,' she said, shaking her fountain pen. 'I've never taken an awful lot of interest in sport I'm afraid, but I see you've had an illustrious career. I'd be delighted to help source the perfect picture for your new house.' She had a home counties accent, clipped tones so reminiscent of Amelie they could have been to the same school. And there it was. In that instant I knew exactly where I'd seen her before and I knew we'd found our forger – or at least the tip of the forgery iceberg. Who knew how many people were involved in this scam.

'Thank you.' My voice faltered as the realisation sank in. Tiffany Snow was none other than Tufty, the former waitress whose scribbled name and phone number had been retained in Stewie Beech's wallet. 'Thank you for coming over to the island to meet with us.'

If I recognised her, there was every chance she would recognise me, although I had taken Faye's advice and smartened myself up considerably. I was just very glad Grace had been a willing participant in our plan because if she'd been unavailable, Amelie had been the next candidate on our list. That would have been a disaster.

Tiffany gave no indication of being aware I'd seen her before. 'Not a problem, as I said I had other business here this week. My parents have a place on the island.'

Parents. Had we stumbled upon that link back to the summer of 1981? It was getting better by the minute.

Faye had already placed the order for the hotel's afternoon tea, which finally arrived now that Tiffany had deigned to join us. The distraction gave me a welcome moment to compose myself. A three-tiered cake-stand and a large pot of tea were placed on the table.

'Would you like me to pour?' the waitress asked.

'Oh, I'd rather have a cappuccino if that's not too much trouble.' Tiffany placed a hand over her teacup. A tattoo of a snake was just visible on the underside of her wrist, extending past the cuff of her blouse. It was quite apt as there was a serpent-like quality about her.

For the next ten minutes conversation revolved around the food, delicate crustless cucumber and salmon sandwiches, lemon curd tarts and cherry scones. I stole a glimpse at Dad and Grace, their slices of Victoria sponge had long gone. Grace was showing Dad pictures on her phone.

Faye sat back in her chair, half a scone and the remnants of a sandwich remained unfinished on her plate. 'Let's talk about the painting,' she said. 'How feasible is it that you will be able to source a piece of Birdie Adams' work for Eliza here?'

'They do occasionally come onto the market.' Tiffany dabbed at her mouth with a napkin. 'It may take me a while.' She turned to me. 'I take it you are fully aware of the costs involved? Birdies don't come cheap. Fifty thousand plus at least.'

I tried not to blanch. The Treasure Trove piece had been valued at between twenty and thirty. 'I'm aware I'm buying an exclusive piece of art. I see it as an investment.'

'Which period of Birdie's work are you interested in? If you're looking at this as a long-term investment, I highly recommend her later work.'

'You mean her life sketches?'

'Absolutely.' Tiffany gave an emphatic nod. 'Glad to hear you've done your research. Not to everyone's taste but definitely the most valuable. I do have friends in Birdie's world, so to speak, private collectors. I can certainly make enquiries. Would you prefer a male or female nude?'

I tried to keep my face impassive. 'I'm open to either.'

Faye, who had just helped herself to another glass of Prosecco, choked on her bubbles.

Tiffany returned her notebook to the briefcase at her feet. 'I've got all the information I need. I'll be in touch.'

I cleared my throat. 'Before you leave, I know this is rather indelicate, but I would need some reassurance that my piece of work was genuine. I know forgeries have appeared on the market in the past.'

Tiffany raised a perfectly plucked eyebrow.

'Oh? Where did you hear that? I'm not aware of any forgeries involving Birdie's work.'

'It is paramount that any work my client purchases should come with a certificate of authenticity,' Faye said.

Tiffany busied herself in her briefcase. 'Any painting which passes through my consultancy undergoes a rigorous examination and will be authenticated by our specialist valuer Albert Whittaker. You may have heard of him.'

It was as if every box had been ticked. 'Albert Whittaker? The TV expert? That's very reassuring,' I said.

Out of the corner of my eye I could see Dad paying his bill. He briefly glanced in my direction. There was no sign of Grace. Hopefully she was already in her car outside in the street. She'd been instructed to go the minute she saw Tiffany drawing our meeting to a close.

'Has Albert Whittaker worked with you for long?' I asked. Albie Whitaker's appreciation of genuine art matched Stewie Beech's advocacy of Isle of Wight lettuce leaves. Part of me felt they deserved each other.

'Four or five years.'

'And how did you and Mr Whittaker end up working together?'

Tiffany frowned. 'It's a small world. Everyone knows everyone in this business.' She stood up. 'Very good to meet you, Eliza.' She turned to Faye and gave her a brief nod. 'You too.'

Faye and I rose in unison. Tiffany Snow turned to leave but was forced to pause at the lounge entrance to make way for a party of arriving diners. To my horror I recognised those diners as Phil Flowers and Jenny Murphy. Even worse, they had to wait for a chair to be removed from a corner table to make space for Jenny's wheelchair. There was no avoiding them.

My horror wasn't so much that they would recognise me, I'd made no pretence about who I was, and in fact, being recognised would only add credence to my claim to fame. It was who I was with. Dad in his crimson impossible-to-ignore jacket, was right behind me. It would be perfectly natural for Phil to assume we were together.

'Eliza, Ian,' he said before I could stop him. 'What a surprise, lovely to see you again.' His eyes travelled to Faye and Tiffany Snow. 'Are you all out celebrating something?'

'Afternoon tea,' I answered, not knowing quite where to look.

There was an awkward pause. 'Jenny, have you met Eliza's Dad?' Phil was clearly puzzled I had not made the introduction.

Tiffany Snow's hands gripped the handle of her briefcase. 'What's going on?' she hissed at Faye.

After an initial hesitation, Faye put her arm through Tiffany's. 'Poor Eliza,' she murmured, guiding Tiffany past a bewildered Jenny. 'Her Dad is so over-protective, borders on the obsessive. He hates letting her out of his sight, follows her everywhere. I don't know how she copes, he's a complete Svengali. Do you know all the time she was competing, he never missed one of her games…'

CHAPTER THIRTY-EIGHT

'I'M SO SORRY,' Dad said, as we headed out of the hotel a few minutes later. We'd explained the situation to Jenny and Phil, who were both mortified they'd interrupted our amateur hustle, despite repeated assurances it wasn't their fault. In any case, the afternoon wasn't entirely ruined because hopefully Grace was now trailing Tiffany in her car to see where she went next.

'Don't keep apologising,' I told him. 'We got what we needed. I'm pretty sure we've found our forgers. Tiffany Snow is Tufty the waitress, which is presumably how she first made contact with Stewie Beech. We know she's in cahoots with Albie Whittaker. Let's hope she's heading back to this so-called family of hers now, with Grace on her tail. If we find out where they live, we should be able to work out if she is connected to your old friend Sasha Mintrum. It would certainly tie up a lot of loose ends.'

Dad gave a grunt but didn't comment.

'We'll have to wait for her to deliver the actual painting before we confront her, unless Tess comes clean and returns hers, or rather yours,' I continued. 'We'll use Kurt's story to prove we know Albie is untrustworthy. Once Tiffany realises we've cottoned on to her scam, hopefully she'll confess. We can round them all up in one go. Think how good it will be for Kurt to know Albie has finally got his comeuppance.'

Dad didn't look anywhere near as cheerful as he ought and remained silent on the journey back to Cowes. When we reached the apartment, he retreated straight into his bedroom.

I wasn't sure how long it would be before we heard from Grace. I still had to do the grocery shopping for the meal Dad was planning for our Sunday dinner with Charlie and Lucas. I left him alone for an hour before giving a tentative knock on his door.

'You can come in,' he called.

'I need a list of ingredients for tomorrow.' I pushed the door ajar. He sat propped up on the bed, pillows behind him, photo album on lap. It was open on the page with the picture of him and Chrissy together. His eyes were red. On the bedside table was a pile of scrunched up tissues.

'Oh Dad,' I sighed. 'What's up?'

'I overheard what Faye said as she steered Tiffany Snow out of the way. She called me obsessive. It was a good diversion tactic, but I've been the complete opposite, haven't I? I was never there for you. I've never seen a single one of your games apart from clips on the TV.'

'You and Mum split up when I was six. I didn't pick up a golf club until I was in my teens.'

'I wasn't part of your life. Alistair Stonehouse did it all, didn't he? He took you on, taught you to play golf, made you the person you are.'

'You and Mum made me the person I am.'

'No we didn't. There's more to a person than genes. I walked out on you and Meg when you were just kids. It was unforgiveable.'

'It's not unforgiveable. It happens.' I sat down on the bed next to him and gave his arm a squeeze. 'You've got to stop dwelling on this, it's not good for you.'

I had my own memories of that horrible afternoon when Dad had taken me and Meg to the local playpark, and as we walked together, a rare treat, he'd told us he was moving out because he and Mum were making each other unhappy. He'd promised he would see us as much as he could, he'd stay close by, find another job locally. We'd meet up after school, he'd see us at weekends.

At first his absence from the house had brought relief from the icy silences, the slamming doors, the shouting matches. Mum was happier. Dad, when we saw him after school one evening each week, positively cheerful. But the second crushing blow had come just months later when he'd told us he would be heading north.

'I'm going to stay with your other grandparents in Leeds for a bit. I'll probably look for a job up there.'

At six years old the only thing I knew about Leeds was that it was a long way from the Isle of Wight. Leeds was a car journey we took as a family once a year, to stay in a house with grandparents we hardly knew. And I was always sick. Always car sick.

Children are notoriously resilient. Had I missed him? It would be cruel to tell him the truth. Thirty years later, I snuggled into his side, my head on his shoulder. 'You and Mum were miserable. Marriages break up all the time. By the time I reached high school nearly all my friends had parents who'd divorced.' That wasn't quite true, but I wanted the wallowing to stop. 'Regret is a negative emotion. We all have to make choices in life. We do what seems right at the time and we learn to make the most of those decisions. We can't go back and change things.' Meg would be very proud of me for the pep talk.

'But what if we make those choices for the wrong reasons?' Dad heaved a big sigh. 'I just wish...I just wish I'd put more effort in. I wish I'd seen more of you. I should have stayed closer.'

Was this a prelude to preparing the way for a move back to the Isle of Wight after all these years, to make amends? I'd got used to having him around, but I didn't necessarily want him living on my doorstep. He'd want us to do things together. *He'd be a commitment...*

I put those thoughts aside. Charlie was the one with commitment issues, not me. I gave him a friendly prod. 'Come on, what are you going to cook for us tomorrow? Come shopping with me.'

He gave a weak smile. 'Just give me ten minutes and I'll get myself ready.' He seemed reluctant to put his photo album to one side.

'You and Chrissy were together on that holiday, weren't you?' I said.

He hesitated. 'Yes, yes we were. She was lovely. Warm, funny, bubbly. I'd never met anyone quite like her before. They didn't make 'em like that in Leeds.'

'I wish you'd told me.'

'Why? It didn't have any bearing on solving this forgery business, did it?'

Didn't it? It had implications for our relationship. I wasn't sure I had the energy for an emotional debate right now. 'Why did she end up married to Stewie Beech?' I asked instead.

'Because I was a fool.'

'Wasn't it awkward when you met up together afterwards? When you were all living here on the Isle of Wight, mixing socially as families?'

'We didn't mix socially.'

Chrissy had said they had. Why did I believe her over Dad?

I took one last look at the photo of the two of them together. Maybe I was wrong, maybe Mum had kept some pictures because I was sure I'd seen that handsome young man who looked like Dad but not quite like Dad somewhere before. Perhaps Nanna had held onto some family snapshots, and I'd seen them at Clifftops. As I considered this improbability, my phone rang.

'Grace!' I jumped. 'Where are you? I was getting worried about you.'

'I was getting worried about me too. That's the last time I ever tell you I'm free on a Saturday afternoon. I followed her all the way across the flippin' island before I lost her.'

'Oh no. Where did you end up?'

'She turned off into a farm track, in the middle of nowhere, not too far from Shalfleet village. I couldn't follow her up there, it would be too obvious.'

Stewie Beech had told Brian Riggs he was off to see a man about a dog in Newtown Creek. We'd been right all along. We'd solved the mystery of why Stewie Beech had sped off on that Tuesday afternoon. We'd found the people who'd defrauded him.

I thanked Grace for her help and sat back down on the bed.

'Do you think he actually confronted those con merchants?' Dad asked. 'Or did he die before he got the chance? Have you double checked with the pub landlord about the boat sighting?'

'I'll do it now. You've not heard from Pilar?'

'No but I've left a message for Josh.'

The landlord at the New Inn, sounding irritated at being disturbed during a busy Saturday early evening service, informed me Robert Hedges was an ex-SAS officer who had fought against the insurgence in Iraq. If I wanted to ask Major Hedges if he was one hundred percent sure he'd seen Stewie Beech's boat moored up for the entire afternoon, that was up to me, but the landlord wasn't going to risk incurring the veteran's wrath.

'Anyway, I thought I sent you the photographs? Didn't you receive them?' he said.

'Yes, but one boat looks very much like another to me.'

'Rob Hedges has twenty-twenty vision and a photographic memory. He's Shalfleet's equivalent of James Bond. If he says that was Stewie Beech's boat, it was Stewie Beech's boat. Trust me.'

'So that's it,' Dad said. 'He had plenty of time to seek out and confront his swindlers. Do we go to the police?'

'What with?' I asked. 'Any criminal case against Tiffany Snow and her gang will have to be based entirely on the evidence she presents to us. There's nothing more we can do but sit tight and wait.'

I shared his frustration, but there was no point doing anything rash. I didn't want to point out yet again that having the original forgery would help our case considerably. I'd broach the prickly subject of his return to Yorkshire after the weekend. We had no idea how long it would take for Tiffany Snow to get back to me. He couldn't expect to hang out in my apartment indefinitely.

CHAPTER THIRTY-NINE

DAD WAS UP early on Sunday morning, baking.
'It is only Charlie and Lucas,' I reminded him.

'I gave Meg a ring,' he replied, 'invited her and Frank.'

I hadn't seen Meg since the disastrous tapas night out, so was happy for the catch up, although a little put out he hadn't run the idea by me first. This was my flat, after all, although my kitchen was currently unrecognisable. There was also another major flaw in Dad's plan to play happy families again.

'In case you hadn't noticed, I've only got four dining chairs.'

'Not a problem. I told Meg to bring a couple with her.'

Charlie and Lucas arrived first, Charlie bearing two bottles of wine and something fizzy for Lucas.

'I wasn't sure you stocked child friendly beverages,' he whispered, brushing my cheek with a kiss.

I made a mental note to ensure I was fully prepared in future.

When Meg and Frank rolled up, Dad ushered us all out of the kitchen apart from Lucas who had volunteered to be sous chef and waiter for the day.

'At least there's a more pleasant atmosphere than when we last met up for a meal,' Meg remarked. 'Have we heard from Tess again?'

I shook my head and put my finger to my lips. 'Best not to mention her name.'

The fragrant aromas of Thailand soon wafted out of the kitchen and Lucas told us to take our seats. Dad had done something wonderful with butternut squash and sweet potatoes. Frank and Charlie who would never normally touch anything that didn't contain meat, declared it was one of the tastiest dishes they'd ever eaten. Dad's curry was followed by a sticky toffee pudding because it was apparently Lucas' favourite.

'How he did he know?' Charlie looked bewildered. 'You've never told me that, Luc.'

'He messaged me yesterday to ask.'

'You've exchanged numbers?'

'Only so we can keep tabs on each other's gaming scores,' Dad said with a wink. 'You don't mind, Charlie? It's not inappropriate?'

'No, not at all, I didn't mean it like that.'

'You're right to ask for Charlie's approval,' Meg said with a nod to Dad. 'I wish more parents kept a closer eye on their kids' social media accounts.'

I forestalled one of Meg's lectures with a suggestion Charlie and I clear up.

Frank leapt from his chair. 'Me and Meg have contributed nothing to this meal so far. Let us do it.'

When we moved to the lounge, Lucas asked if he could borrow my laptop.

'I want to show Ian something,' he said, a huge grin on his face. 'You know you were talking about that programme Treasure Trove on Tour. Well, guess what?'

'What?' Dad asked.

'I watched that YouTube clip you told me about. I've noticed something.'

'Oh?' I was intrigued. We bunched up on the sofa for a closer look.

'This woman,' Lucas said, pointing to Donna Lemming, 'and this woman…' he fast-forwarded the video for a few seconds, 'are wearing the same necklace.'

A guest in another best bits clip, the same age and build as Donna Lemming but dressed in an orange bolero over a yellow shift dress, was indeed wearing the same set of chunky multi-coloured beads. A watercolour of Oxford which had hung at the top of her stairs for the last twenty years had just been valued by Albie Whittaker for fifteen thousand pounds.

'Ace detective,' Dad said, putting his hand up for a high-five. 'I told you the Lemmings were professionals. That's why they looked so innocuous. Nobody looks that boring in real life.'

'This woman is hardly innocuous,' I pointed out. 'She's pretty memorable in that outfit.'

'Exactly, that's all you're focussing on,' he said. 'You're not looking at her face at all. This is it, we've got Albie now, whatever. We need to write to the programme's producers and get the crooked old codger taken off air. Kurt will be vindicated. That's fantastic. Well done, Lucas.' He ruffled Lucas' hair. Lucas glowed with pride.

'Don't write to the TV company yet,' I said. 'We need Albie to validate our forgery first. Then we'll go after him.'

As Meg distributed teas and coffees, Dad and Lucas remained buried in the laptop, mulling over Google Maps.

'Now what are you doing?' Meg asked. 'Are you still talking about Stewie Beech's painting? I wish his widow would let Bizzikids know what's happening with their funding.'

Dad looked up briefly. 'We believe he went ashore at Shalfleet quay to confront the people who conned him.'

'And then he was never seen alive again,' Lucas added.

'I thought he died of a heart attack?' Meg said. 'There's nothing sinister about that, is there?'

'We're looking for the forgers' lair,' Dad explained.

'Then we can catch them in the act,' Lucas put in.

Meg rolled her eyes while I glared at Dad. 'We're going to do no such thing,' I said.

Charlie shook his head and smiled at me. 'Not too much longer, Lucas. You've got school in the morning and I'm sailing over to Poole with Dave and Fiona. We've got an early start.'

Dad declared the case closed for now and somewhat reluctantly Lucas and Charlie went home, closely followed by Meg and Frank.

'Wasn't that a lovely evening,' Dad reflected when we were finally on our own. 'We should do it more often. I'll set up a family WhatsApp group, include the boys too. It'll make things easier in the future. We can all be in the same loop.'

I'd had a lovely evening too, but exactly how many dinner parties was Dad planning on hosting in my flat? 'It's not going to be quite so easy when you're back up north,' I pointed out.

'Umm. I thought I might stay on…for a bit. That's if you don't mind?'

'It could be weeks before Tiffany Snow gets back to me.'

'I know but I'd still like to know exactly what happened with Stewie that afternoon.'

I sighed. 'We've gone over this. Whether he confronted these forgers or not, all we know is that eventually he must have gone back to the quay, set off for Cowes and presumably didn't feel well enough to continue the journey. If, when, we hear back from Tiffany and we have the evidence to make our own accusations, we might get the truth. But only then.'

'Stewie deserves justice.' Dad reached behind a cushion for his Jo Nesbo book. 'I'm tired, love. I'm turning in for the night. Let's talk about it in the morning.'

I was covering for Charlie at Making Waves in the morning. At this rate, I'd be the one moving out before him.

Just as he reached the bedroom door, his phone rang. It was very late in the day for an estate agent's call, especially on a Sunday. I picked up the scattered coffee cups and realised Meg and Frank had forgotten to take their chairs. I was about to message her when Dad returned to the lounge, phone clutched in hand, his face ashen.

'We've got a problem,' he announced. 'That was Josh Beech. Brian Riggs was right after all.'

'What do you mean Brian Riggs was right? He can't be.'

Dad plonked himself onto one of Meg's chairs. 'Josh has a copy of the death certificate. The pathologist narrowed Stewie's heart attack down to a three-hour window between four and seven o'clock on the Tuesday afternoon.'

I sat down too. 'But that's impossible. Stewie couldn't move his boat until at least eight o'clock. Does that mean Shalfleet's answer to 007 got it wrong after all? The boat in those pictures isn't the *Little Lady*?'

'It's the *Little Lady* all right. It wasn't Stewie who moved her.'

CHAPTER FORTY

THERE WAS NO sign of Amelie when I arrived at Making Waves at nine the following morning. Dexter explained she wouldn't be in until later.

'It's not as if we're busy first thing on a Monday is it?' he said. 'Most of Cowes doesn't get out of bed until gone ten, Amelie included.'

I had forced Charlie into giving a job to someone with abysmal time-keeping skills as well as questionable honesty.

'What about Alfonso?' I enquired. 'Isn't she looking after him anymore?'

'No, her friend Stephanie is doing it for her. She's always up early. Steph wears the cap and the sweatshirt just like you did. Pilar will never know.'

Charlie would be better off employing Stephanie.

'What do you know about Amelie's friend Tufty?' I asked.

'Not a lot,' he confessed. 'Apart from the fact that she was once ginger and now her hair's jet black. Up until the other week I hadn't seen her since she left *Absinthe* three years ago.'

No doubt she left straight after persuading Stewie to buy her painting.

'But she does have family on the island?' I persisted. Family who had potentially witnessed a man's heart attack and rather than call the emergency services, they'd left him to die and subsequently transported his body out to sea in a fishing boat. Dad and I had stayed up until the small hours running through every possible scenario. So much for getting an early night.

Dexter shrugged. 'You'll have to wait for Amelie.'

At ten the shop phone rang with a curt female caller who demanded to speak to Mr Harper as a matter of urgency. I explained Charlie was unavailable.

'That's simply not good enough,' the woman replied. 'It's Mrs Copythorne here, from the school. We have three numbers for Mr Harper on our records and I can't get hold of him on any of them.'

'Can I help at all?' I asked, bracing myself. If Lucas was sick or had injured himself, I could rise to the challenge and dash to the school to collect him. He hadn't been ailing last night, in fact he'd been in very high spirits.

'Who are you?' the caller demanded.

'I'm Mr Harper's partner.' It felt strange, but

rather pleasant, declaring those words out loud.

'Do you have a name?'

'Eliza, Eliza Kane.'

There was a short pause. 'You're not on our contact list.'

'Is there a problem? I may be able to get a message to Mr Harper.' I wasn't quite sure how as he would be halfway across the Solent, but it was important to sound intelligent and concerned.

'Yes, you can tell him we've not received a notification for Lucas' absence this morning. That's the fourth time since Christmas. We make our policy on unauthorised absences perfectly clear to all parents. We are aware of the change in family circumstances. We have tried to show leniency. After the last incident Mr Harper assured us it would not happen again and this is extremely disappointing. If a child is ill or has a medical appointment we expect a call by nine thirty in the morning at the latest. It's just a question of leaving a recorded message. That's not too difficult, is it? Even for Mr Harper.'

'I understand, Mrs Copthorne. I will ensure Mr Harper is made fully aware of the situation.'

'It's Copythorne.' She then proceeded to spell her name as if talking to one of her most junior pupils.

I put the phone down and took a deep breath. Now what did I do? I called Dad and explained the situation.

'You said you had Lucas' phone number? You couldn't give him a ring could you, find out where he is for me? Then at least I can phone Mrs Copythorne back and let her know. Charlie must have forgotten.'

Dad promised to get onto the task without delay. He called me back within minutes.

'Goes straight to voicemail. His phone must be off. Charlie wouldn't have taken him sailing, would he?'

'I wouldn't have thought so. I better pop round to Charlie's and check up on him.'

Dexter assured me he could manage the shop single-handedly. I suggested he give Amelie a call to see if she could chivvy herself along to arrive before lunchtime.

There was no reply to my knock on Charlie's front door. I peered through the letterbox. My shout of 'Lucas, are you home?' was met with silence.

I turned away from the house and was surprised to see Dad hobbling towards me at the end of the street.

'Any luck?' he panted. Drizzle was in the air and he hadn't even stopped to put on a jacket.

'He's not answering.'

I fumbled through my bag in search of Charlie's door key. Once inside another shout up the stairs elicited no response.

Lucas' bedroom door was open. This room was

usually out of my domain and I was surprised how tidy it was compared to the rest of the house. The duvet had been pulled across the mattress, which was more than could be said for Charlie's bed across the corridor. Lucas' school rucksack sat on a chair.

'He's out somewhere,' Dad said.

'He's bunked off school?' I'd assumed Mrs Copythorne had been berating Charlie for failing to adhere to the procedure for phoning in sick. This was far more serious. Lucas had an issue which needed addressing. Charlie couldn't go on burying his head in the sand. 'Has he mentioned problems to you?'

Dad shook his head. 'Nothing.'

'Where will he be?'

'Hanging out in town somewhere I expect. That's what I used to do. I'd pretend I was catching the bus to school, wait for my mam to go off to work and then sneak home again.'

Charlie would have been setting off early with Dave and Fiona and had probably trusted Lucas to sort himself out for school. He wouldn't even have had to pretend to catch the bus.

'There's nothing we can do about it,' Dad said. 'No doubt he'll be back by the time Charlie gets home tonight.'

We traipsed back downstairs. The door to Charlie's study, usually shut to hide the mess, was ajar. The large coastal map Charlie kept pinned on the wall had been taken down. It covered the desk like a tablecloth, folded in half to display the northwest corner of the island, weighted down with a stapler, an old mug and a book of tide tables. It could be that Charlie had been plotting the route to Poole, but I doubted it. Dave and Fiona's sailing boat was kitted out with the latest navigation equipment. With increasing dread, I noticed pencil marks on the map around the nature reserve at Newtown, lines drawn inland. Lucas had been very excited by his Treasure Trove discoveries. He had started the day as sous chef and ended up amateur detective. Dad had a lot to answer for.

'You were talking about this, weren't you?' I hissed. 'The forgers' lair. What if he's gone looking for it?'

Dad was immediately defensive. 'We identified a couple of possible farm buildings in the vicinity of where Grace lost track of Tiffany, but–'

'You shouldn't have got Lucas involved. These people aren't just forgers. They're psychopaths.'

'Now don't exaggerate. We don't know that–'

'*Exaggerate?* You think some random passer-by came across Stewie slumped under a hedge and thought, oh look, there's Stewie Beech, the famous restauranteur. Let's just see if there's a boat with his name on it up at the quay, then we'll bundle him in it and take it back out to sea without telling anyone?

'We went over this last night. Whoever put

Stewie back into the *Little Lady* knew exactly who he was. They knew he'd arrived by boat, and they had access to their own vessel in order to get back to the shore after they'd taken him up the river. They tied him to a buoy. They did it all in the dark. They're locals, they're used to being on the water. The point is they went to a lot of trouble to hide the fact Stewie was either on his way to see them or had been to see them. That's not the behaviour of rational ordinary people. When rational ordinary people come across someone having a heart attack they call an ambulance, administer CPR, and they're happy to hang around afterwards to deal with questions such as who was your visitor and why was he with you? Questions which might be quite awkward for a gang of serial fraudsters to answer.'

'Okay, okay. There's no need to shout. I had no idea the boy would be so interested and go off like this. It's not just because of me, he wants to impress you too. He looks up to you. He was telling me all about his golf lessons last summer–'

I put up my hand to stop him. 'Funnily enough, that doesn't make it any better. I'm going to run home and get my car. You stay here and grab yourself a waterproof from the boot room out the back. Who knows what these people will do if they catch Lucas sniffing around. We've got to find him.'

CHAPTER FORTY-ONE

THE ONLY WAY Lucas could get to Newtown Creek was on the bus, and that involved a change in Newport and a walk. At least we had time on our side. We decided to start our search on Shalfleet quay itself, an area used for the storage of small boats and dinghies. We arrived at low tide. On a dank, dismal day like this the creek was deserted and desolate, a flat wilderness with nothing to see but a pair of swans out in the channel and half a dozen seagulls pecking at the rank seaweed on the mudflats.

'It's not just seagulls,' Dad pointed out as I made my complaint. 'I think that's a sanderling, and there's an egret over there. We should have brought binoculars.'

We probably should have brought binoculars, although not to look at the birds. Dad had located a couple of farm buildings on the map accessible cross country from the quay. A farm building would make a suitable base; a light airy converted barn would be the perfect studio for an artist. In hindsight Grace's Union Jack mini was probably not the most suitable vehicle for surveillance work. My bright blue BMW was equally as conspicuous and the last thing I wanted to do was alert the forgery gang we were on to them. We set off on foot.

'Are you sure you can manage walking across these fields?' I asked Dad, half wishing he wasn't with me due to his lack of speed but knowing it would be foolish to tackle the forgers on my own.

'You're not going without me,' he replied.

The sky was dark. The rain, a drizzle back in Cowes, was now quite persistent. We followed a muddy path inland towards a clump of trees, hoping we might stumble across Lucas en route.

'There's a building on the other side of that spinney,' Dad said, 'half a mile or so away. He could be heading there.'

What exactly a twelve-year-old boy was going to say when he encountered a gang of hardened criminals, I had no idea. More worrying was what they were going to say or do to him. I would never forgive myself if anything happened to Lucas. Charlie's reaction was too awful to contemplate.

We continued along the edge of the field, keeping as close as we could to the hedgerow. As we drew nearer, I realised the building Dad had spotted was a wooden cladded chalet bungalow. It was the perfect hideaway, sheltered by a coppice.

Approaching from the rear, we were able to remain out of sight of the house.

A light was on inside.

'Someone's home, at least,' I whispered to Dad.

The chalet was surrounded by a low rustic fence. To the side was a large area of gravel. A white transit van was parked up with its rear doors wide open, next to it, a red hatchback. I should have asked Grace for a description of Tiffany's car.

'Do we just knock on the front door?' Dad hissed. 'Say we're looking for a lost boy?'

'Let's have a scout round first.'

Dad was not an ideal scouter. He was large and laborious.

A car approached, possibly using the farm track that led from the main road. I pulled Dad in towards the nearest holly thicket. Crouching amongst the prickles, we were unable to see the car come to a halt. Doors opened and slammed. Then all was quiet again. I stood up with a stretch. A blue Mercedes saloon had now joined the others outside the chalet. The visitor, or visitors, had gone inside.

'Quite a gathering.' Dad winced, struggling to creep out of our uncomfortable hiding spot. The rain had turned heavier. I pulled my hood tightly over my head.

'If Tiffany Snow is here,' I told Dad, 'there's a good chance she'll recognise me but she only caught a glimpse of you at the Seaview Hotel.

Knock on the door and tell them you've lost your grandson.' Hopefully Tiffany had been blinded by Dad's red smoking jacket and not taken much notice of his face. Before he could move, there was a scrunch in the leaves behind us.

'You're trespassing. Didn't you see the sign? This is private property.'

I turned. A tall gaunt man stood a few metres away wielding a shotgun. He wore a leather bush hat and a full-length waxed coat. A grey lurcher wagged its tail beside him.

Lucas had mentioned a man with a shotgun when he'd stayed at Newtown with the Scouts. Was this the same man? Did he regularly pace these fields and woods threatening strangers? The dog, now sniffing around Dad, seemed friendly enough. A raving psychopath would own a pit bull. Our assailant was most probably hunting pigeons and rabbits.

I tried to remain calm. 'I am sorry, we didn't see the sign. We're looking for a boy–'

'My grandson,' Dad interrupted. 'Twelve, blonde hair. He's run away and we're very worried about him.'

I spotted another figure strolling through the coppice and my heart sank. She was dressed in a yellow waterproof and a black cockapoo danced at her heels. She came to a halt beside the figure with the gun.

Tiffany Snow stood on tiptoe and whispered

something in the man's ear.

He lifted the gun slightly. 'Follow me.'

I glanced at Dad. He made no attempt to move. 'We're not about to cause any trouble,' I called, turning sideways in an attempt to conceal my face beneath my tightly drawn hood.

'I know exactly who you are,' Tiffany Snow called. 'Don't try and pretend otherwise.'

The man with the gun marched towards us. 'This way.'

My mouth was dry and my heart raced. We had no choice but to fall into step. As we approached the chalet, the front door opened. Two women emerged, carrying a large cardboard box between them. One was thin and dark haired, wearing a padded jacket and hunting boots, while the other was blonde and dumpy in comparison, with a see-through plastic cape over a floral dress. She immediately dropped her end of the box as she caught sight of Dad.

'Good grief. It's Malcolm. What are you doing here?'

For a moment I was flummoxed. *Malcolm?* Then I realised. This had to be Dad's art teacher Bethan Edwards. So they were all connected. Tiffany Snow, Albie Whittaker and William Mintrum. The second woman, who I now suspected was Sasha Mintrum, swore loudly. The box slipped from her grasp and tumbled to the ground, splitting open to reveal framed prints and canvasses of various shapes and sizes.

'Malcolm? Who the hell is Malcolm?'

'They were snooping in the woods,' Tiffany said as the cockapoo ran in excited circles. 'I recognised them immediately.' She pointed to Dad's leg. 'He was at the hotel. I told you she was on to us. The minute you mentioned that other commission, Bethan, I told you it was too much of a coincidence.'

Dad stared at me. 'What other commission?' he mouthed.

I knew that drunken phone conversation with Bethan had been a bad idea.

'I was looking for a genuine Birdie. Not one of Gideon's twopenny fakes,' Bethan snapped at the younger girl.

'We haven't got time to deal with them now,' Sasha said. 'Let's get this lot into the van before they're ruined. Lock those two in the shed.' She began to retrieve the pieces of art from the ground and shove them back into the box.

'You can't lock us in a shed,' I cried, although anywhere dry would actually be preferable to standing in the pouring rain. Poor Dad was in a state. The waterproof coat he'd snatched from Charlie's boot room was far too small and his air boot was caked in mud. The one good thing, however, was that there was no sign of Lucas – unless he was already locked in the shed.

Bethan Edwards shook her head, struggling to

control her voice. 'I'm not happy about this.'

'I'm not happy about it either, Beth,' Sasha replied. 'But we can be gone in twenty minutes. The house is clear. They'll have a hard job proving anything.'

'We can prove absolutely everything,' I called. 'We've got the picture you sold Stewart Beech. We know you defrauded him, and then when he came here to confront you, he had a heart attack. Rather than call an ambulance, you left him to die to avoid discovery. It's despicable.'

'We didn't leave him to die,' Sasha said. 'There was nothing we could do. Gideon found him by the gate when he took the dog out. The kindest thing to do seemed to be to send him off in his boat.'

'Kindest thing? Are you nuts?' Dad had trouble controlling his voice.

'There was no point calling an ambulance.' Sasha remained chillingly calm. 'He was well and truly dead. The boat idea seemed quite fitting. Would you have rather we left him in a ditch?'

'Stewie Beech was my friend,' Dad snarled. 'I'd known him since we were kids. Have you absolutely no compunction? No compassion?'

Bethan looked appalled. She swayed slightly before reaching out and clutching onto one of the wooden posts supporting the canopy over the front door.

Tiffany helped Sasha lift the box into the van.

A second man, in cords and tweeds, now appeared in the chalet doorway. 'Bethan? What's going on?'

'We've been rumbled, Uncle Will,' Tiffany chirped. 'It's these two, here. That golfer I told you about, Eliza Kane and her mad dad.'

'I'm not the one who's mad,' Dad retorted. 'You lot are. That's it, I've had enough. I'm calling the police.' He reached for his phone, despite the gun still pointing in our direction.

'You won't get a signal out here, Malcolm.' Bethan's voice quivered.

'Malcolm?' Sasha's eyes narrowed. She came closer. Her face was heavily lined and wiry white roots showed through her badly dyed hair, now plastered to her head. 'You're not from here, are you? You've got an accent. Have we met before?'

'His name's Ian, not Malcolm,' Tiffany said. 'Just lock them in the shed and let's get out of here.'

'Oh Ian, yes,' Sasha said. 'That's it. I remember you. You were at Waverley that summer, weren't you? You and little Christina. All loved up, and then Stewart Beech comes along and spoils it for you. Drops you right in it. Tells sweet Christina all about your fiancé back in Leeds. Some friend he turned out to be. Still, he got his just desserts in the end, didn't he?'

I knew Dad had a temper. I'd witnessed it first-hand. I'd lived through the arguments he'd had with my mother. I knew he'd once been cautioned by the police after a fight in York. He'd mellowed, but not entirely. He was a big bloke, and our gunman, presumably failed rockstar Gideon, was tall but built like a beanpole.

With one swing of his arm, Dad knocked the gun out of Gideon's hands.

'Grab that, Eliza,' he shouted, lunging forwards and pinning Gideon to the bonnet of the Mercedes.

I'd never held a gun in my life and I didn't want to. *What if it went off?* I kicked it away from Gideon and reluctantly picked it up. It was much heavier than I'd anticipated. Struggling to keep it aloft, I aimed it at the two women. There was a shout of approval from behind me.

Lucas jumped to his feet from behind the fence, and not just Lucas, but another boy who could possibly have been his school friend Bailey, the one with the attractive mother and the fancy camera, which he was putting to very good use, although right now the most incriminating evidence would be against me and Dad.

'Get them all into the house,' Dad ordered. 'There'll be a landline there and we can call the police. Lucas, Bailey, pictures please. The stuff in the boxes, that van.'

'Don't worry Ian,' Lucas yelled. 'Bailey's caught everything on video.'

CHAPTER FORTY-TWO

THE FIGHT HAD long left Bethan Edwards. Once inside, she offered to make us all a cup of tea, although we declined.

'Can't fraternise with the enemy I'm afraid, Bethan,' Dad said far too politely. He grimaced as he spoke. He was doing a bad job of disguising the fact he was in a lot of pain.

We assembled in the open plan kitchen-cum-lounge. The Mintrums lined up on a threadbare plaid sofa, the dogs moping at their feet, sensing the fun was over. The heavy dark furnishings inside the bungalow were at odds with its modern exterior.

'How long are you planning on keeping us here?' Tiffany asked with a scowl.

'The police won't be interested,' Will Mintrum muttered. 'They've got better things to do.'

'Who's idea was it originally to con Stewart Beech?' I wanted answers before the police arrived and began their own questioning. 'Was he a one-off, or do you have a string of victims?'

'We know all about Albie Whittaker, by the way,' Dad added.

'Albie Whittaker is an old fool.' Tiffany yawned. 'Should have been pensioned off long ago. He wouldn't know a piece of Ming from a piece of Wedgwood.'

'I don't think he's that stupid, darling,' Sasha chuckled. 'Would you know a piece of Ming from a piece of Wedgwood, Ian?'

Dad clenched his fists but said nothing.

'What made you do it?' I asked. 'What was your motive?'

'The opportunity was simply too good to miss.' Sasha stroked the lurcher on the head. 'The value of Auntie Birdie's work had risen–'

'Thanks to your friend Albie.'

Sasha continued to tickle the dog. 'Partly, I suppose. Tufty was staying with Will and Bethan here a few summers back. She got the job on *Absinthe* and as soon as she started talking about her new boss, we realised who he was. He was easily persuaded. Naturally, he believed our Birdie was genuine. He'd sat for the picture himself. You do know it was his fault Giddy never made it. You've heard of Jason Ross, I take it? Big name in the music business. Giddy and his band would have got a record deal if it wasn't for your friend Stewart pulling the plug on their performance.'

'Don't be daft,' Dad quipped. 'I'm sure there

were other opportunities. You can't hold Stewie responsible for all the things that have gone wrong in your life.'

'He was ripping his customers off,' Tiffany put in with a pout. 'Swapping so-called local delicacies with cheaper produce. He wasn't exactly honest, you know. We thought it would be fun to trick him with a piece of fake produce of our own.'

'Swapping a Lidl spud for an Isle of Wight new potato isn't the same thing as passing off a piece of your own artwork for a Birdie Adams,' Dad snarled.

'How much did he pay you for it?' I asked.

'He got a bargain. Twenty thousand.'

Dad let out a whistle of breath.

'How many other people have you conned?' I asked. 'Is it always something personal?'

'The world is full of fools.' Gideon had taken off his hat to a reveal a shiny shaven head. He was a striking looking man with unusual green eyes. It was easy to picture him as a rockstar, but equally as easy to picture him peddling his wares at festivals and fayres like a mystical Wizard of Oz.

'Do you do this all over the country?' I asked. 'Following the footsteps of Treasure Trove on Tour?'

He gave a shrug. 'What if we do?' He had a mesmeric, melodic voice now that he was no longer growling orders.

'Presumably Mr and Mrs Lemming of Ryde are

friends of yours?'

'My sister Immi and her husband, actually.' Sasha giggled again. 'They were good, weren't they? We used Immi in our negotiations with Stewart. Obviously, we couldn't deal with him directly, although he immediately recognised us when he came here.'

'I thought you said you found him slumped in the garden?'

In the kitchen Bethan swore. A trickle of water had pooled on the floor from her plastic mac. 'What did you do?' She glared at Will and Gideon in turn. 'What exactly did you two do?'

'I didn't do anything.' Will shuddered. He'd already physically distanced himself as far away from his sister and her partner on the sofa as he could. 'This has nothing to do with me.'

'This has everything to do with you. You let them stay here in our house.' As Bethan's voice rose her Welsh accent became more prominent. 'You're complicit, you idiot. You know who they are, what they do.' She turned to face Dad. 'I'm so sorry Mal, Malcolm, Ian, whoever you are. I had every intention of finding a genuine Birdie Adams for your birthday. Truly, I wanted to. I misled you when I said my partner was a great painter. He isn't. Will doesn't paint at all. Will was desperate to play a part in the consortium's plans at Waverley House. It was his childhood home.'

'Those pictures you showed me at Waverley?'

Dad looked baffled, and not just about the lack of Will's artistic ability. The mention of a genuine Birdie Adams for his birthday had come as a great surprise. 'They weren't Will's?'

'They'd be mine.' Gideon smiled at him. 'You see I am very good, aren't I?'

'Giddy, you're wonderful.' Sasha grabbed his arm and gave him hug. 'I've always said what a talent you have.'

Dad had underestimated her. She wasn't just nuts, she was totally toasted, roasted and sticky caramelised nuts.

Bethan began to pace the room, head down. 'What happened? What did you do to that man Beech?'

Gideon shrugged. 'He collapsed, Bethan. We answered a knock at the door and there he stood, ranting and raving.'

'The next moment his face turned blue, he clutched his chest and crumpled to the floor. It was just like you see in the movies.' Sasha beamed at us.

'He must have kept my number,' Tiffany piped up. 'I left *Absinthe* as soon as he'd bought the painting. He must have remembered me mentioning my family had a house here. He phoned and demanded his money back. I was in London but I was able to warn Ma and Pa he was on the war path.'

'We always over-winter on the island,' Sasha

continued. 'Will and Bethan's place here is perfect for us. Giddy works on his pieces ready for the next festival season. Then we can load up with supplies and hit the road.'

It was as if she was seeking praise for her ingenious scheme. Dad ignored her. 'I suppose you took his phone? Just to ensure nobody could trace where he'd been.'

Gideon gave another infuriating shrug.

'And then what did you do?' Dad pressed on. 'I suppose Tiffany here must have told you he'd come by boat–'

'The key fell out of his pocket when he collapsed,' Sasha said. 'We didn't really know what to do at first, to be honest. But obviously, if we called for an ambulance, things could have got quite awkward. We'd no idea who else he might have told about the painting, about us, and as he was well and truly dead, well, it seemed sensible just to pretend he'd never been here.'

'Sensible?' Dad fumed. 'There's nothing sensible about any of it.'

'It's not like we cut him adrift. We knew he'd be found sooner or later.' She flashed Dad a smile. 'If I remember rightly, Malcolm, didn't we console each other that evening at Waverley House after poor little Christina had stormed off?'

Dad didn't answer. He was struggling to contain his temper. Sasha turned back to me. 'We tied the boat to a buoy, we're not totally heartless. Will keeps a dinghy up on the quay so we took that with us and Giddy rowed us back. It was quite an adventure.'

'You used Will's dinghy?' Bethan collapsed against the kitchen worktop, babbling incoherently in Welsh.

It was a relief when Lucas and Bailey, who had been left to stand guard in the front porch, banged on the window as instructed to alert us to the imminent arrival of the police. One car and two constables. I'd hoped for the entire flying squad, but perhaps Will Mintrum was right, the police probably did have better things to do with their time. I didn't relish the task of having to explain everything all over again, and Dad's expression fluctuated between fury, pain and exhaustion.

'Bethan,' I said, approaching the sobbing heap in the kitchen. 'Now might be a good time to make that cup of tea.'

CHAPTER FORTY-THREE

DAD AND I had lots to discuss, but all I wanted to do was get him home. He looked ill. The two young constables listened with great patience to our story. They examined the contents of the boxes in Gideon's van and assured us a colleague in Yorkshire would to be despatched to Tess' pub in Harrogate to see if the original offending piece of artwork could be obtained. For once, I seemed to be believed.

Perhaps it was the Mintrums' attitude that swayed them. Sasha relished in relaying the gory details of the transportation of Stewie's body from the house to the boat, and then out into the channel as if the event had been one of the highlights of her sad little life. She didn't appear to have an ounce of remorse.

Gideon was less forthcoming, but Bethan, wishing to exonerate herself as much as possible, happily filled the police in with a list of his various convictions for fraudulent activities stretching back many years. Even Tiffany, real name Winter, realised the show was over. She admitted her consultancy, Blak, was a figment of her imagination. She'd been raised by a pair of fantasists and had proved equally adept at convincing the elite of the London art world of the exclusivity of her imaginary dealership. Albie Whittaker had been co-opted into the set-up after he'd crossed paths with the Winters at an antiques fayre. Fantastic finds made good viewing and Albie had found a way for his specially selected guests to avoid too much scrutiny from the production team at Treasure Trove on Tour.

'Once we'd raised the value of a piece, it was easy money to sell it on,' Sasha concluded. 'We had to give Albie a cut of course, but he basked in the glory of the good news story.'

A second squad car arrived and evidence was removed, including the gun – a very good replica we were reliably informed by the police. No doubt Gideon had picked it up at a Treasure Trove roadshow. The Winters and the Mintrums were lead away for further questioning. Dad and I promised to make formal statements at Newport Central Police Station first thing the following morning.

Lucas and Bailey, still bubbling with excitement squeezed into the rear of my car along with the two dogs, who had befriended the boys during the lengthy police interrogation.

'Why are we taking the dogs?' Dad muttered.

'We can't leave Spliff and Moby here on their own,' Lucas argued.

'Who the hell names a dog Spliff?'

'Someone who's lost too many brain cells smoking them,' I suggested. 'Bethan Edwards won't be detained. Her only crime was letting Sasha and Gideon stay in her house. Oh and forging Will's CV. Another rookie mistake. We should have checked where Will Mintrum lived.'

'I assumed he was still in St Lawrence because of his connection to Waverley,' Dad said.

'Me too. We slipped up. Bethan's got my number. She'll collect the dogs as soon as she's released.'

'I can't believe you asked her to find a Birdie Adams for my birthday.'

'Neither can I to be honest.'

'Poor Stewie.' Dad sighed, shaking his head for the umpteenth time. 'To discover he'd been swindled by that bunch of degenerates must have been mortifying. It's no wonder he had his heart attack. What a horrible way to go.'

My personal feelings about Stewie remained ambivalent, but I could only agree.

Bailey was deposited on his doorstep. I wasn't sure how the head of the Friends Committee would react to the knowledge he'd skipped off school for the day, but apparently Bailey had perfected the art of leaving messages on the school's automated answerphone authorising his absence.

'I pre-recorded Mum's voice on my phone,' he said. 'I just call up the number and put it on replay. She's no idea.'

'That's brilliant,' Lucas said. 'I wish I'd thought of that.'

So did I. It would save Charlie getting into trouble, although I wasn't sure how many times Bailey thought he could get away with excruciating headaches on the same day as double French. Mrs Copythorne would eventually cotton on.

Lucas wanted to go straight home but I didn't think he should be left on his own, so he collected up some dry clothes and came back to the apartment. I had the impression he was hoping to keep his escapade a secret from Charlie, who wasn't due back from his day's sailing until after five.

'That's going to be impossible,' I said. 'You were wrong to skip school, and whilst I'm very grateful for your help, you put yourself in a dangerous situation.'

'Do you think Dad will be angry?' he asked as I sent Charlie a text to let him know Lucas was with me.

I'd never witnessed Charlie in angry parent mode, but I suspected I was about to.

'I'm sure he'll just be pleased to hear you are safe,' I assured Lucas.

'You were never in any real danger,' Dad said. 'That gun, like everything else, was a fake.'

I didn't have the energy to point out that none of us knew that at the time Gideon was aiming it at us.

I double dosed Dad with bourbon and painkillers, and he retreated to his bedroom. I changed into a pair of baggy sweatpants and made hot chocolates for me and Lucas. We settled onto the sofa. Within minutes Lucas nodded off, with Moby the cockapoo snuggled on his lap.

Charlie texted at five thirty to say he was on his way over. I told him to let himself in quietly.

He responded with ??, but fifteen minutes later the door to the apartment opened and I heard him slip off his shoes and tiptoe along the hallway. Neither Lucas nor the cockapoo stirred, although Spliff raised an ear and trotted over to greet him.

'What the...'

I put a finger to my lips and wriggled off the sofa.

'We've had a bit of a day,' I said, giving him a kiss.

'Is Lucas all right? Did he get sent home from school or something? I suppose they couldn't get hold of me–'

'Shush. Let him sleep. I need to explain.'

In hushed tones I filled Charlie in on our excursion to Newtown Creek. A muscle in his cheek flinched as he listened. I left out the bit about Gideon's gun and just hoped Bailey would have the good sense to erase those shots from his camera when it was returned to him from the police station. The air remained tense as I finished my recap. The fact that none of this was Lucas' fault did not appear to lighten Charlie's mood. If anything, it made it worse. His body was taut, his fists balled at his side. Charlie didn't often swear, but he swore now. He was furious.

Lucas began to stir on the sofa. He blinked a couple of times before wrinkling up his face. 'Oh Dad, you're here.'

'Yes I am. Eliza's told me what happened.'

Lucas made no attempt to get up off the sofa. He gave Moby a tight squeeze.

'You're not cross?'

'You're safe, that's all that matters.' Charlie's body language told a different story.

'The swindlers will go to prison. That's good isn't it?' Lucas said.

'It's in the hands of the police,' I explained. 'They'll have to decide whether there is enough evidence to take the case to court. There may be other offences to consider.'

'We need to go.' Charlie held out his hand. Reluctantly Lucas removed the dog from his lap. Moby gave a whimper.

'Dad, can we have a dog?' Lucas asked.

'It's not really practical, is it?' Charlie replied. 'With me being at work and you at school. Who's going to walk it?'

'We could manage it between us, I'm sure we

could, especially with Eliza. You don't both work the same hours. And there's Ian too.'

'I'm not sure either Eliza or Ian are responsible enough to be left in charge of a dog,' Charlie muttered. He refused to look me in the eye as I handed over the bag of wet clothes. 'Probably best you give us a bit of space for a few days. Amelie can cover your shifts at the shop.'

I opened my mouth to protest but no words came out. Was Charlie giving me the sack? *Or worse?*

Lucas' bottom lip wobbled. Charlie put a firm arm around his shoulders. 'C'mon, let's get you home.' They left the apartment without another word.

CHAPTER FORTY-FOUR

I MADE MYSELF another hot chocolate and drifted off watching my go-to Scandi Noir on Netflix, only to be jolted awake by my vibrating phone. Hoping for Charlie in a conciliatory mood already, I snatched it out of my pocket.

'Hello?'

It was Debs. 'How's things? How's my brother?'

'He's asleep. Have you been trying to call him? He must have turned his phone off.'

'Asleep? It's only half eight.'

'We've had a bit of a day.'

'Oh right, but no, I haven't been trying to call him. It's you I wanted to talk to. You remember I told you I was meeting up with my old work colleague who knew the Paceys? I've got Pam Pacey's contact details for you.'

It hardly seemed relevant now. I made a note of the address and phone number.

'We had a great catch up,' Debs continued. 'I

hadn't seen my colleague for a few years. She's one of those friends you can pick up with exactly where you left off. She knew the Beech family too. Had a bit of interesting gossip about Stewie and his wife.'

'Oh? Pilar?' I braced myself for a second helping of the food scam.

'No, the first one. Apparently when Stewie had a heart attack twelve years ago, he got some tests done on the boys. Turns out he discovered one of them wasn't his.'

IT WAS ANOTHER hour before Bethan Edwards called to collect the dogs. She was bedraggled, grovelling and full of apologies. William was waiting outside in the car. She couldn't stop, which was a relief. I didn't want her to. I had something far more important on my mind.

She pleaded for my discretion, gabbling on about the importance of Will's job, of how his father had left him penniless, left all the Mintrums penniless, as if that absolved their crimes. If the scandal emerged, she and Will could be ruined.

'You understand we had no part in these forgery schemes,' she insisted.

'But you knew about them,' I pointed out.

'Not the full extent. We felt sorry for Tufty. We looked after her as a child. Sasha and Gideon gadded about all over the country to festivals and fayres. It was no life for a young girl. She was this lively little thing, masses of red hair, hence the nickname. She was our little squirrel. You have a family, Malcolm and that young boy. You must recognise how easy it is to overlook flaws, to forgive weaknesses. You'll know how strong that instinct is to protect and watch out for each other, to care. It's what families do.'

Being part of a family was a new concept for me. Living with Dad had taught me a lot, and not just about my levels of tolerance. Yes, I did know what it was like to care. That panic, the horror and fear, *the guilt*, that Lucas might have come to some harm because of me, was a feeling I never wanted to experience ever again. Being part of a family came with responsibilities as Charlie had rightly pointed out, and in future I would be much more aware of the consequences of my actions.

It was a relief to bustle Bethan and the dogs out of the door.

DAD WAS STILL snoring softly on his bed, fully clothed. I took one of the throws from the sofa and tucked it over him. I retrieved the photo album from the bedside table and took it to the lounge. I turned to the final page and the photograph of Dad with Chrissy. I knew now why I thought I'd seen pictures of that tall, slim young man with blue-grey eyes and light brown hair before. The resemblance wasn't strong, but it was enough.

In the hour or so since Debs' phone call I'd

found out everything there was to find out about Matthew Beech online and I'd studied every photograph. I knew exactly when he was born thanks to Ancestry.com. I knew his favourite beer, courtesy of Instagram.

Why do I know that name? I'd overheard Nanna whisper to Dad.

You don't, he'd replied.

But Nanna did. She knew the name Christine Beech. When I'd suggested contacting Mum for news of the Mintrums, Dad had been adamant it was bad idea. *Because Mum knew.* Mum knew about Dad and Chrissy and so did Nanna. Mum wouldn't have confided in Nanna about a holiday fling that had happened before she and Dad had even met. This was something else, something that happened later when the Kanes and the Beeches were all living on the island. Chrissy had said she'd met me before, she intimated our families had socialised. I'd misunderstood. I suspected it was just her and Dad doing the socialising.

My instincts had been wrong before, but it would certainly explain why Dad had been so unforthcoming. The burden of guilt he carried, that load that weighed him down, wasn't just about me and Meg, it was about an affair. The sweet passion of a first love had been rekindled.

I made a decision. I'd got to know Ian Kane pretty well over the last couple of weeks. I recognised we couldn't all be movers and shakers and that some people were perfectly happy to go with the flow. But sometimes the go-with-the-flow-ers needed a prod in the right direction, and not just a prod, but a kick and shove in Dad's case. I'd promised to do what I could to help him out when he returned to Yorkshire, but Dad wasn't going anywhere near Yorkshire anytime soon. I couldn't stand back and let him waste another thirty years.

First thing tomorrow we had to go to Newport Police Station to make our statements. After that I was going to suggest he made a social call.

CHAPTER FORTY-FIVE

Chrissy – present day

IT WAS MILD for the beginning of March. The door to the studio was open. She liked working like this, with the scent of fresh country air, the sounds from the yard. She thought she heard a car stop in the lane, and Frida the retriever, the useless guard dog that she was, pricked up her ears, strolled across to the doorway and gave a short bark. Chrissy carried on painting. She was working on a new, larger canvas. There was something liberating about the act of creating those loose open strokes. Frida's bark was seconded by the cackle of geese, a far more effective early warning system.

She didn't keep the gate locked when she was working. Not that she received a great number of visitors, Matt mostly, but it made it easier than having to stop everything and answer a ring on the front door. That's if visitors knew the procedure, of course. Sometimes they stood on the front doorstep, persistently ringing. Not today's visitor.

The hens joined in the chorus. Chrissy put down her paintbrush. Frida trotted to the door again. Chrissy followed her.

A heavy man with receding grey hair, one foot encased in an air boot, walked hesitantly across the yard. It took a few moments for her to realise. And then he spoke.

'Hello Chrissy, my love.'

She'd spent a lot of time imagining how it would feel to see Ian Kane again. At first she'd scripted potential scenarios. As the years had drifted by, she realised he wasn't going to seek her out. He'd gone, just as she'd told him to. Off the island. Out of her life.

She wiped her hands on her grubby denim dungarees. If only she had known he was coming she would have...what? Tidied herself up a bit? Found a fancy frock to wear? Put on some make-up? She couldn't recall how long it was since she'd last worn lipstick. Anything lingering in her drawers upstairs would be long past its best by date and probably crawling with bacteria.

Take me how you find me. He wasn't exactly looking glamorous himself. Definitely not her knight in shining armour.

'Hello Ian.' She surprised herself with how nonchalant she sounded as her heart thumped against her ribcage. 'I thought I heard a car, although the animals always let me know when I have visitors.'

'You have a lot of them.'

'Visitors?' She shook her head, puzzled. 'No.'

'Animals I mean.'

He'd kept his accent. Over the years Stew had done his best to hide his roots. Inner city Leeds became classy Yorkshire Dales. When Mr Beech senior had died of a heart attack at the tender age of fifty, a stash of money had been discovered in the canny Yorkshireman's numerous bank accounts. Stew was an only child and his mother's needs were minimal. Stew's accent diminished with his newfound wealth.

Ian didn't seem to know what to do with himself.

'Come in,' she beckoned. 'Would you like me to fetch you a chair?'

'You've got a fabulous place here,' he said, not answering her question. Once inside the studio, his gaze turned to the walls adorned with her art. 'These pictures are great, Chrissy. Beautiful.'

'Thank you.'

Ian would have never stopped her painting. He wouldn't have derided her hobby. Or insulted her.

'The colours are all inspired by the island,' she explained.

'I can see.' He turned his gaze back to her. His eyes had lost their brilliance. 'Eliza thought you had something to tell me.' They stood a couple of metres apart.

'Do I?' Chrissy shook her head. She and Eliza

had wrapped up their conversation with no unanswered questions. It was Eliza who had left with a promise to be in touch. 'No. I don't think so.'

He took a step closer. He had a clean smell about him, as if every part of him had been scrubbed and groomed. His aftershave was an expensive one. Probably Eliza's influence, a gift or present perhaps. Chrissy had googled Eliza Kane. She'd had quite a career.

'Something about Matthew?'

Her painting table acted as a safety barrier between them. She gripped the edge for support. She needed to stall for time. To think. He didn't give her a chance.

'Come here.'

She hesitated for a second, and then she thought, what the heck. He held out his arms and she allowed herself to be enveloped in his hug.

STEW AND CHRISSY had just celebrated their third wedding anniversary when they took a holiday on the Isle of Wight. On the ferry to Cowes, she wondered if the Mintrums still had their house in St Lawrence and whether old Auntie Birdie sat at her easel in the old barn, turning out those ugly, unsettling pictures.

Stew suggested they go for a drink at a golf club.

'A golf club? Do you want to have lessons?'

'No, I've heard it has a great bar.'

It was a hotel, as well as a golf club. They ordered burgers for lunch. After they'd eaten, Stew asked the barman if he could have a word with the chef.

'Was something wrong with your meal?'

'No, he's an old mate of mine.'

'He'll clock off at three if you want to wait,' the barman said.

They waited. Stew could have warned her. He should have said. At least she was wearing a pretty sundress, bought for the holiday. For all his faults, Stew liked her to look her best.

Twenty minutes later Ian Kane appeared in his chef's whites. Unchanged, or perhaps not. Older, suntanned, spikey haired. Broader, more rugged.

His greeting was cautious. His eyes flicked over the pair of them. 'Stewie, Chrissy. This is a surprise.'

'How's it going mate?' Stew jumped up and whacked Ian on the back. 'We're on holiday. I heard you were working here.'

Stew pulled up a chair. Ordered another beer from the barman.

'I don't drink lunchtimes,' Ian said. The beer sat untouched on the table.

Stew was half-way through a resume of the recipes on offer at the country house hotel where he now worked as head chef, when the little family arrived. The mother was a slender brunette in denim shorts and a cotton blouse, pushing a toddler in a pram. A curly haired blonde girl, maybe three or four, walked by her side, holding her hand, until she caught sight of Ian.

Stew's brag of 'no burgers at my place' became lost in a shrill shriek.

'Dadeeee.' The little girl let go of her mother's hand and ran towards their table. Ian's face broke into a smile which shattered Chrissy's heart all over again.

Stew had always claimed they weren't ready to start a family. That night, back in their caravan on the holiday park, he suggested she came off the pill. Callum was conceived within months.

Things were never the same after that. Their life had changed because they now had Callum, but for Chrissy an undefinable sense of dissatisfaction wormed its way into her heart. It was nothing to do with the baby blues. Chrissy loved Callum to pieces, and Stew was made up with his son. *His son.* 'At least I've got a boy.' What was that supposed to mean? *Who was it for?*

She lay awake at night, thoughts churning in her head. *He hadn't married Lisa in Leeds. He'd called that off, but then he'd met and married someone else.* And had children, instantly. He didn't carry a torch for her like she did for him. *And yet…*

When Callum was eight months old Stew announced he'd been offered a job in Yarmouth on the island's west coast. She wasn't aware he'd been applying for other things. He'd only just got a promotion to a bigger hotel in Gloucestershire.

'Won't it be great,' he said. 'We'll be able to meet up with Kaney again.'

Chrissy didn't want to meet up with Kaney again. She knew exactly how it would end. One ear would always be open for the sound of that white charger.

'It would be great if the children got to know each other,' Stew insisted, 'especially as we're living so close.'

Callum wasn't a year yet, and Ian's girls were older. They wouldn't get on, and they weren't living close. The Kanes were in Ventnor on the opposite side of the island. The invitation was issued. Thankfully excuses were made.

Stew took up golf. Good for business he said. There were courses other than Clifftops he could have played, but he didn't.

One day when Stew was out playing golf, the restaurant phone rang. Chrissy was alone, setting the tables ready for evening service. There was the slightest pause from the caller after she picked up the receiver and said hello.

'Can we meet?'

'You mean all together, with the children?'

'No,' he said. 'On our own.'

SHE MET HIM in Totland Bay. She took Callum

with her in the pram for protection and they walked along the sea wall.

'I tried to tell you that night at Waverley House that Lisa meant nothing to me,' Ian said, 'not compared to how I felt about you. Afterwards, I called you in Nottingham a few times. You didn't return my calls.'

'You rang me?'

'Yes. A man used to answer. He always said you were out.'

'I was out. I went out a lot because I didn't like being at home with Alan and Mum. He never told me.'

'I took it that meant what you said, that you never wanted to see me again. I went abroad with Mick.'

'How long did you stay away?'

'A year, eighteen months. When I went back to Leeds, Mick told me you and Stewie were together. I didn't want to stay in Leeds, run the risk of bumping into the pair of you. I wanted to get as far away as possible.'

'You took the job here on the island?'

'The island had happy memories for me.' But instead of remembering her, he'd met and married Jackie. 'Her parents run the hotel,' he said. 'It just sort of happened.'

She wondered if he'd got Jackie pregnant. She was a few years younger than Ian, and very attractive.

'Are you happy with Stewie?' he asked. He put his hand over hers on the pram handle to force her to a halt. 'Does *he make you happy?*'

'Yes of course.' She jerked her hand away.

She said it would be best if they didn't meet up again. He said he had the afternoon off on Tuesday week. She said she didn't know where Stew would be.

'He'll be playing golf.'

'I won't be able to get a babysitter.'

'You won't know until you ask.'

How LONG HAD it lasted? A couple of months and then Jackie had found out and there had been a scene. He'd promised to try and make things work for the sake of the girls. Chrissy understood. She wasn't cut out for having affairs, of lying, going behind Stew's back. Stew wanted to try for another baby now that he was settled in his new job. She was running out of excuses. She accepted circumstances, human nature, their own stupidity, whatever, had forced her and Ian apart. She'd had her fling and got him out of her system. Her role in life now was to be a good mother and wife. Callum would have his little brother or sister and she and Stew would live happily ever after.

'You'll never guess what I heard today,' Stew said, arriving home from his golf lesson with uncharacteristic exuberance. Golfing usually made him cross because by his own admission, he wasn't good at it. Stew hated not being good at things. 'Kaney and his wife have split up. She's been having an affair with the golf pro at Clifftops. He's moved out to caravan in Sandown.'

She digested this piece of news, attempted to control her emotions to display an appropriate reaction.

'Is he still working at the hotel?' she asked when she found her voice.

'Seems so for now. Can't see that lasting though. Maybe I should offer him a job here.'

She called the hotel from the phone box on the edge of Yarmouth.

'Are you okay?' she asked when she finally got put through to Ian. 'I heard about you and Jackie. I just wanted to say how sorry I was, wanted to check how you are.'

He gave her the name of the caravan park. This wasn't her doing, she told herself. This was Jackie's fault. Jackie was the one who had cheated – after Ian had cheated on her. Tit for tat. She imagined if Stew found out he would have done the same. Or probably worse.

The caravan park was less salubrious than the one where she and Stew had stayed a few years earlier when they'd come for their holiday. She left Callum with a new friend she'd made at toddler group. A routine medical appointment at the hospital, she said. Nothing serious, but she wasn't sure how long she would be.

'Take your time,' her new friend insisted.

They took their time. Slowly, tenderly, caring, generous. That was how Ian made love. She couldn't apply any of those terms to Stew.

'What will you do?' she asked afterwards, huddled beneath the threadbare sheet on the uncomfortable bed. 'Will you stay on the island?' She didn't dare mention Stew's job offer. Ian wouldn't take it even if she did.

'I don't know,' he confessed. 'I want to be close to the girls. I don't want to miss them growing up.'

'Is it definitely over? Could you and Jackie get back together, do you think?'

He shook his head. 'I don't want to. In any case, Alistair Stonehouse is a far better catch than me.'

The next time they met he asked her to leave Stew. 'If I moved away, to the mainland perhaps, not far, found a job in Southampton or Portsmouth, would you come with me?' he asked.

The last time he'd suggested they run away together he'd offered her Italy. Now it was Portsmouth. 'You once said you'd take me to Rome,' she reminded him.

'We could still go.'

With his two girls and a toddler in tow? It wasn't just impractical, it would be impossible. Stew would never let her take Callum, especially not to be with Ian. Reality set in.

When she realised she was pregnant, she had to

make a decision and she chose to stay with Stewart Beech. She allowed her head to overrule her heart. Ian Kane kissed his daughters goodbye and went back to Yorkshire.

'I can't stay here and watch you do this,' he told her.

She didn't tell him about the baby – there was no point, it could as easily have been Stew's as his, but the minute Matthew made his calm, easy way into the world, she knew exactly who his father was. Stew must have always had his suspicions, but he waited twenty years before he pounced.

When he told her to get out, he let her take just one bag and the clothes she stood in. When she dared to suggest the tests he'd insisted all three boys take might have been misinterpreted or inconclusive, he grabbed her arm, twisted it behind her back and frog marched her to the door.

His finances were trussed up like a Christmas turkey to ensure she wouldn't get a penny. It was only when she inherited her mother's house in Nottingham she had the means to finance her return to the island and purchase Merryvale. Over the years she'd imagined this scenario many times; the scenario where Ian Kane came back to find her. He would come to the restaurant, he would turn up at the house. They'd bump into each other casually one afternoon in Totland Bay. Funnily enough Merryvale was the one place she'd never pictured him. And yet here she was, in his arms.

She'd split up his family. He'd missed being part of his daughters' lives – because of her. She'd denied him the opportunity to get to know his son. The harm she had done to this poor man and yet all he said as he stroked her coarse grey hair was that he was sorry it had taken him so long.

CHAPTER FORTY-SIX

Eliza

I FOUND THEM together in the hen coop collecting eggs.

'Look at these.' Dad opened his palms to display the harvest. 'Breakfast.'

'I'll fetch you a box from the house,' Chrissy said.

In the two hours since I'd dropped him off, Dad's whole demeanour had changed. The greyness had left his face. His step was lighter as we walked together across the yard. Chrissy's eyes were red and swollen. She brushed her hand against mine, squeezed my fingers.

'Thank you,' she whispered.

The eggs were placed in a box. Dad fussed around the retriever before giving Chrissy a hug.

'I'll see you Friday,' he said.

'Eleven thirty,' she replied. 'I'll book a table at the pub.'

'I'm going to meet Matthew,' he explained as we got into the car. 'Chrissy's going to collect me and then we're going for lunch. Another time you and Meg must come too.'

'I'd like that,' I assured him, 'but it's important you have time with Matt on your own first. You'll like him, I know you will.'

Dad waved at Chrissy as we pulled away. 'Did you really never know?' I asked.

He shook his head. 'She told me she didn't want to see me again. I couldn't bear the thought of her staying with Stewie. I had to get away. I'm sorry.'

'I can't believe Stewie never said anything to you, all those pally catch ups you had in York.'

'Neither can I. I assumed he didn't know about me and Chrissy. I suppose he kept it like an ace up his sleeve, enjoyed the power of knowing it was his bombshell to drop whenever he wanted.'

'But Matt knew you were his father.' That reaction in the workshop when I'd said my name now made sense.

Dad nodded. 'According to Chrissy Stewie told him in a moment of spite.'

'Did it not click when you saw him at the funeral?'

'Why would it? There were so many people there. I had a quick chat with Josh, but I don't even remember meeting Matthew. Chrissy showed me pictures, he takes after her, not me.'

'He has your nose. That little bump in the middle.'

'Really?' Dad rubbed his nose.

'Did you come back for Stewie's funeral because you hoped Chrissy would be there?'

He hesitated for just a second too long. 'No...I came because Stewie was my old mate.'

'A mate you didn't even like.'

'Umm. It's complicated. I slept with his wife, remember.'

Maybe that's what this whole hunt for Stewie's swindlers had been about. A chance for Dad to assuage his guilt.

'Why didn't you and Chrissy get back together when she and Stew split up after his first heart attack?'

Dad sighed. 'I didn't know they had split up, not until he turned up in York with Pilar. Looking back, he was there to rub my nose in it, showing off. That's what Stewie did best. Look at me Kaney, I've got my fancy yacht and a pretty young girl on my arm. I only gleaned the briefest of details from him about Chrissy. She'd taken off, he said, was living Cornwall. To be honest she could probably have found me if she wanted to. I was on Facebook. There were a few mutual friends, relatives in Leeds who could probably put us in touch. I decided to leave things be. You know me, love, I've not been lonely. I've been happy enough. It's just now that I've found her again, and now that I know about Matthew, it's as if this will make me complete.'

Complete. Was that how Charlie and Lucas made me feel? Could I imagine a life without the pair of them in it? I would never have willingly put Lucas in danger. Surely Charlie knew that? The boy had spirit. I didn't doubt twelve-year-old Charlie possessed the same sense of adventure, and probably shared his son's dislike of school. Dad and I were not the most responsible adults in the world, but then we'd never needed to be – until now. We were adjusting.

He was quiet on the journey back to Cowes, but not the brooding moodiness of the previous few days, a contented calm.

When we pulled up in the parking lot underneath the apartment he reached across and clenched my hand.

'Now we've just got to get your love life sorted,' he said.

'Don't worry about me.' I'd briefly explained about the Charlie situation before we'd set out for the police station earlier that morning. 'I'm going to let him stew for a few days.'

'Don't leave it too long,' he said. 'It's not wise to let things fester.'

That was rum advice from a man who'd waited thirty years to sort out his own romantic affairs, and even then I'd had to do it for him. I wasn't like my father. I loved Charlie and I would fight to save our relationship and make things right. I was tenacious and competitive. That was how I'd won tournaments and why I enjoyed solving mysteries. I didn't like being defeated. I would win back my man.

The following morning we visited Marsh House and broke the good news to Nanna that she had been right all along about the Mintrums.

'They were running a forgery scam,' Dad explained, 'dealing in all sorts of fake paintings and antiquities. The whole family were involved, apart from the oldest brother, who's dead, otherwise I'm sure he would have been up to his neck in it too, and one of the twins. She's something high up in the prison service.'

This information had been gleaned during a long telephone conversation between Dad and Bethan Edwards after our return from Merryvale. Bethan had used the same family loyalty card on him as she had on me. Dad was far more susceptible. She'd even convinced him to sign up for another workshop. He had, however, been able to elicit a promise out of Bethan that Meg's Bizzikids' group could use the grounds of Waverley House for their Easter nature camp, at no charge.

Nanna sat with a smug grin on her face while he also explained that Albie Whittaker was likely to disappear off our TV screens very soon.

'About time too,' Kurt said with a nod. 'Thank you, Ian.'

'What made them do it?' Nanna asked.

'In Albie's case it was probably pure greed,' Kurt huffed.

'It probably was. As for the rest of them, I'm not sure. Some perverse idea they'd been hard done by when the father ran off and left them destitute,' I said. 'As for picking their victims, it was totally random, whoever they could con at festivals and county shows, until they came across Stewie Beech, purely by coincidence. Then Sasha and Gideon set their heart on a spot of revenge for some stupid prank he'd played on them forty years ago, with devastating consequences.'

'Actions always have consequences.' Kurt mused. 'Albie's prank caused years of heartache for me and dear Madeleine.'

Dad stood up to leave. He shook Kurt's hand and held out his arms to Nanna.

'I suppose you'll be heading home now Eliza's solved the mystery for you,' Nanna said, accepting Dad's conciliatory embrace somewhat reluctantly.

'Actually, I'm sticking around for a bit,' Dad told her. 'I've got a bit of catching up to do. I want to enjoy some family time.'

'Better late than never,' Nanna muttered. Dad winked at me over the top of her head and gave her an extra tight squeeze.

AFTER I'D WAVED Dad off and wished him luck for his meeting with Chrissy and Matthew on Friday, I received a text from Charlie.

I knew Charlie's weaknesses and I intended to ask Dad to keep Lucas company at the weekend while we had a heart to heart, amongst other things. My planned seductive first move had been pre-empted with anything but seduction.

'We need to talk. I'm sorting out stuff for my folks in Ventnor today. Can you meet me at the rotunda at 1.00 pm?'

We did need to talk but I'd have quite liked a please or thank you to go with it. I wanted Charlie to become more assertive, but his message was far too terse. It didn't exactly shout 'let's kiss and make-up'. And why Ventnor, on the other side of the island? Why couldn't we meet after he'd finished doing whatever it was he was doing for his parents?

I could be awkward. I could reply with a sorry that's not convenient, but being awkward was hardly going to put me back into Charlie's good books. *Act responsibly, Eliza.*

I mooched around the apartment until twelve thirty and then sped across the island to Ventnor.

I found a parking spot a short walk away on the esplanade. Charlie had chosen a sunny spot and was waiting for me on one of the benches inside the bandstand.

'You're late.' He jumped up but didn't attempt to kiss me.

My heart sank a little further towards my stomach. 'I'm sorry, traffic.' It was a lame excuse. 'How's Lucas?'

'He's recovered.'

'That's good. What were you doing for your parents?'

'Hanging wallpaper.' Charlie shoved his hands deep into his coat pockets. 'Shall we go for a walk along the beach?'

That sounded ominous. 'Sure. Charlie, I just wanted to let you know that I would never have willingly put Lucas in dang–'

'I know,' Charlie interrupted. He took the steps down onto the sand two at a time. 'Me and Lucas have had a big chat. All the usual son and dad stuff. He was trying to help you and Ian. I'd have probably done the same. He hates school, but so did I at twelve.'

Now was not the time to mention I'd suspected as much. 'Is it anything in particular at school?' I asked Charlie's back view.

He paused to wait for me. 'A multitude of things. The curriculum is very academic, Lucas isn't. He's sporty like me. There's another Lucas in his year so one teacher came up with a clever way to distinguish them by referring to our Lucas as Lucas H-P.'

'Harper-Pallet. I see.' *Our Lucas.* It gave me hope.

'He's since become known as HP Sauce. Or brown sauce. Or just brown stuff. You can probably get the gist. Anyway, the outcome is we're going to look at moving schools.'

'What about Lucas' grandmother? I thought she paid the fees?'

'I'm working on a strategy.' He caught my eye.

'I've made a plan. You should be pleased.'

I was pleased, especially with the look in the Charlie's eyes. He might not be quite so cross with me as I thought. There was something bubbling under the surface.

'I'm going to suggest the money set aside for school fees go into a university fund,' Charlie said. 'Luc may not ever go to university but that doesn't matter. It sounds impressive and hopefully will keep Rowena's mother happy.'

'I'm sure Lucas will go to university. Most kids do these days.'

'No. He wants to join your detective agency.'

'Oh well…I mean, you know with Golf Sparks about to take off, there may not be much more detecting. I'm not sure I'm that good at it.'

'You're very good at it, Eliza. You're good at everything you do, and you know it. That's why…well, I may have been a bit harsh on you and your dad. I'm sorry.' He came to a halt. The tide was out. The sand was smooth and compacted here, easier to walk on.

I tried not to show how relieved I was at his words. 'You were upset. It was perfectly understandable.'

'You're right, I was upset. Worried. Guilty, too. Guilty that I'd gone off for the day enjoying myself when Lucas was in trouble.' He ran his fingers through his hair. 'That's why I lashed out at you. My own failings. It's bloody tough being a parent.'

'We're in this together, Charlie. You know how I feel about Lucas. He's a great kid. You and him come as a pair, inseparable, and I accept that if I want to be with you, then Lucas is part of the set-up. I cannot apologise enough for what happened on Monday.'

Charlie smiled. 'You don't have to apologise, Eliza. All is forgiven.'

'All is forgiven.' It was what families did, although I wasn't sure if he was forgiving me or I was forgiving him. Either way it was irrelevant.

Charlie's shoulders relaxed. 'Anyway, I'm glad you feel that we're in this together. Lucas told me I'm much more fun when I'm with you and it's a shame I'm not with you more often.'

'So we're okay?' I tried not to show how relieved I was.

'Oh I think we're more than okay, Eliza.' He put his hands firmly back in his pockets, which was odd, as this seemed the right moment for some sort of reunion kiss. 'Shall we walk along to the Spyglass Inn and have some lunch?'

The Spyglass Inn was a tourist pub at the far end of the beach, complete with a pirate ship playground. It would never have been my first choice of venue, but out of season many of the town's hostelries were closed. Perhaps the Spyglass was the only place open, and at least Charlie was inviting me for lunch, with food, although I would have been quite happy with lunch of the other variety. Perhaps I could suggest it for dessert.

He seemed in a hurry. I slipped my hand through the crook of his arm. Ahead of us there was something written in the sand, the waves already encroaching into the message, about to wash it away.

'Oh look Charlie,' I said, pausing to read the words. I could just about make out *ill you arry me* and some sort of squiggle, which could be a question mark. 'Someone's written a proposal.' I looked around, expecting to spot a happy couple celebrating further along the beach, or kids mucking about, but apart from an elderly gent with a dog way ahead of us, there was no-one else in sight.

'Yes,' Charlie said. 'It was me.'

'You?' Why was Charlie writing proposals in the sand?

As the realisation dawned, he dropped down onto one knee, his hands finally coming out of his pockets to hold up a small square box. 'You were late, but you can get the gist of it, can't you? Will you marry me, Lizzie?'

After everything that had happened on Monday, he was proposing? *To me?*

He opened the box to reveal a single sapphire on a band of white gold. The stone was the colour of the sea in summer, of Charlie's eyes, of brilliant blue skies above the island on the clearest days of winter.

'I haven't thought things totally through,' he continued, 'and I'm not sure how it's going to work out or where we're going to live, because I know you won't want to stay in Cowes, and I'm not sure Lucas will be keen on Seaview, but you probably won't want to sell Goldstone Villa, not after having all that work done–'

'Yes.'

'I just know I'm so much better with you, than without you. I know I'm not perfect, but you don't put me down, you lift me up, and it's important that when you find someone who makes such a positive difference to your life, you hold onto them–'

'I said yes, Charlie.' Emphatically. Heart, head, everything, I really did like this new assertive Charlie. He just needed to stop talking, get to his feet and kiss me. 'Yes, yes, yes. More than anything I want to marry you, Charlie.' I could hardly believe the words spilling out of my mouth. New, soppy, Eliza Kane, who'd have thought. Years of being on my own and now this, less than twelve months after my return to the Isle of Wight saying yes to becoming Charlie Harper's wife, my teenage crush Charlie Harper's wife, my best friend Charlie Harper's wife…

He rose to his feet and I flung my arms around him. His mouth pressed down onto mine. I'd been lucky enough to have lots of highs in my life. I'd won tournaments, I'd been a national champion,

I'd represented my country, but this moment, here on the beach with Charlie, surpassed it all.

'This is why you made me come to Ventnor?' I said when we finally came up for air.

'Yes, I wanted to do it here because this is where it started, isn't it? You and me all those years ago, up there on the fairways at Clifftops.'

'You're not really here to hang wallpaper?'

'Trust me, I'm the last person my dad would ask to help with DIY.'

'You could have just said, let's go and have lunch in Ventnor.'

'Ah but we couldn't arrive together. I had to get here first to make my big romantic gesture.' Charlie's big romantic gesture had been taken by the tide, but it would be forever etched in my heart. To think, another five minutes and I might have missed it altogether. That's why punctuality was important. 'And I needed to grab a ring from Andrew, who owns the jewellers in town,' Charlie continued. 'If you don't like it, he says you can change it for something else.'

'It's perfect,' I said. 'Just what I would have chosen. What made you decide to ask me now?'

'You think it's too soon?'

'I've said yes, Charlie. Don't try and talk me out of it. No, I meant, after what happened on Monday? It's a bit of turnaround.'

'Monday was me being a prick. I've been thinking about it ever since we got together to be honest, but with opening up the shop and everything, I just kept pushing it back.

'I had forty-eight hours of Lucas not talking to me. I realised I'd upset the two people I care about most in the world. I'm stubborn, I can be stupid. I don't want to mess this relationship up like I messed up my last one. I've known you for over twenty years, Lizzie. I love you. I don't want to carry on seeing you part-time. I want to wake up next to you every morning. I want everyone else to know how much I love you. Why wait? Although we can wait for the wedding, if you want. There's no rush, and I don't know what sort of wedding you want, big, small…I'm just happy to go along with whatever you choose. It was just important for me to make that commit–'

I kissed him to stop him talking. 'A small wedding will do,' I said, eventually. 'But there is one thing. I won't change my name. I like Eliza Kane too much, but I would appreciate it if next time I meet your parents you introduce me as your girlfriend, or fiancé, and eventually wife, as opposed to Lucas' golfing instructor.'

'We could go and tell them now if you like,' he replied.

I turned to face the bandstand and linked my arm through his. 'No, let's save it for another time.' I wanted Charlie all to myself for the rest of the afternoon. 'Let's forget the Spyglass Inn. Dad's out. I'll race you home.'

CHAPTER FORTY-SEVEN

Five Months Later

WORK AT GOLDSTONE Villa was complete. I'd spent the last two days moving back in. Joel and Faye had done a fantastic job; my house had undergone a complete transformation. No longer the faded dame but fully restored to the elegant Edwardian duchess she had once been. There were concessions to the 21st century such as a fabulous new kitchen and those fantastic power showers, but other period features had been beautifully enhanced and restored. Faye had carried out the necessary styling she needed for her social media accounts. Furnishings had been moved in and moved out, but now the house was mine. And not just mine. Charlie and Lucas were moving in too.

Convincing Lucas to move to Seaview had been easier than anticipated. He'd been won over by lure of his own bathroom and the knowledge he would no longer have to tidy up after his dad. The house in Cowes had been sold. Once the money came through Charlie would pay off a large chunk of his business loan allowing him to employ another full-time member of staff in the shop. This would free us up to spend more time together as a family. My work with Golf Sparks continued and I enjoyed being part of the team, but I always looked forward to coming home.

We were getting married in October; a quiet affair at Newport Registry Office, followed by a meal at the Dressed Crab in Ventnor. Faye and her PR Guru Katy Pimm were adamant I was missing a social media opportunity by not indulging in some flamboyant affair, but I disagreed. We just wanted to share the day with a few close friends and our families. The important people.

Charlie and Lucas had helped with the transportation of my boxes. Their belongings would arrive in a few days' time before the start of the new school term. Lucas came running in from exploring the garden, waving his phone.

'It's started!' he cried. 'Come on you two, we've got to go to Merryvale.'

Dad had moved in with Chrissy just two weeks after their meeting. 'That cottage of hers needs fixing up,' he'd said when he made his announcement. 'It'll be a lot easier if I just stay there to help her out.' He didn't need to make excuses. After thirty years no one could accuse him of being too hasty. Dad and Chrissy deserved their happy ever after. I liked the idea of living close to them –

although not too close. We were going to be part of their lives and of Matthew's life too. Having been brought up in a household of testosterone, Matt had been delighted to discover he had two sisters, and I was equally delighted with my new brother. He'd inherited the Kane family nose, but he'd acquired his warmth and wit from his mother. He was great company to be with.

The Dad who lived at Merryvale was very different to the Dad I'd bumped into back in February. He'd lost weight and gained a suntan. He'd decorated every room in Chrissy's house and he mucked out alpacas and sold strawberries and homemade jams and chutneys from a stall he'd made out of old pallets from his son's workshop. He maintained his special relationship with Lucas who was a regular visitor to the smallholding.

Numerous charges had been brought against Gideon and Sasha Winter. I had acquired a useful contact at Newport Central Police Station who kept me updated, a young officer called Eve Horan who had taken our initial statements. She told me she'd been part of the original team called in at the time Stewie's body had been found. She'd always felt the circumstances surrounding his death had been suspicious, but when his heart attack had been confirmed by the island's top pathologist, with no question of foul play, a further investigation had been deemed unnecessary.

'If his wife had voiced her concerns to us, we

might have taken it further,' she said. The only person Pilar had voiced her concerns to was my dad and despite his denials I remained convinced the only reason he'd attended Stewie's funeral and offered to help Pilar out was because he hoped to run into Chrissy. I was so glad Charlie had seen the advantages in being pro-active. No longer a man going with the flow, but totally in charge of his own destiny.

The original fake Birdie Adams had never materialised, despite several searches. Dad and I both suspected it was doing the rounds of Yorkshire flea markets.

Pilar had been given all the facts about Stewie's painting, and his final hours. On her return to Cowes she put *Absinthe* straight up for sale.

'There are debts to pay off,' she told us, having invited me and Dad to Sandpipers for coffee. 'I had no idea. Stewart kept a lot of things from me but I want to honour the pledges he made to local charities. It is important to carry on his good name.'

There seemed little point mentioning the food scam.

'What about your grandmother's nursing home fees?' I asked.

'If I sell the house there will be enough. Me and Alfonso will move somewhere smaller.'

I wondered how Alfonso would react to downsizing to a bijou hutch. Pilar and Anton now ran their private catering business from a lock-up unit on a retail park. Pam Pacey had confirmed our theory about her money being used to fund Stewie's rash purchase. Pam, Chrissy and Dad had reconnected, and their friendship renewed.

As for Albie Whitaker, he had been quietly removed from Treasure Trove on Tour. Eve told me evidence was still being collated for his prosecution, going back many years.

'Come on,' Lucas urged again. 'We don't want to miss anything.' He grabbed Charlie's car keys from the countertop and threw them at his dad. 'Hurry up. Chrissy reckons there's at least six of them.'

Charlie caught the keys deftly with one hand. 'Are you sure you want to witness this Luc? I've heard it can be a bit messy.'

'If I'm going to be a vet I've got to get used to it.' Lucas jutted out his chin and looked just like his father in one of his stubborn moods.

Charlie threw the keys back. 'Go on, get in the car. We're just coming. Eliza needs to grab a pair of rubber gloves.'

'You're so mean, Charlie Harper,' I said, watching Lucas run on ahead. 'Get a move on. Don't you want to see Frida's puppies being born?'

'Of course I do.'

'I still can't believe you haven't told him he's having first pick of the litter.'

'We agreed. Ian is going to be the one to tell

him. It has been hard not caving in, trust me.'

Charlie was going to let my dad take all the glory. The man who'd missed out so much with his own kids was going to be the coolest step-granddad in town. Charlie was anything but mean. I couldn't love him any more than I did in that moment.

'You do know Lucas probably won't be able to choose and we'll end up having two?' I said.

Charlie gave me a kiss. 'Or maybe all six…'

Charlie had changed a lot too. *Six puppies.* We were going to be more than complete.

The End

ACKNOWLEDGEMENTS

FIRSTLY I WOULD like to thank you, dear reader, for your continuing support. To all the friends who've told their friends and shared my social media posts and to the reviewers and bloggers, thank you. I would have given up writing, or at least publishing, long ago if it wasn't for the totally supportive community of readers and authors who have encouraged and inspired me. I'd particularly like to mention fellow authors Isabella May and Kiltie Jackson, plus the following Facebook Groups – Anita Faulkner and Chick Lit and Prosecco, Helen Pryke Domi and Meet the Authors, and the amazing double act of Sue Baker and Fiona Jenkins from the Heidi Swain and Friends Book Club, plus all the group members!

As always I'd like to thank my family, my husband Neil, a man of great patience and brilliant dad to our daughters Ellen and Zoe, my sister Carrie, and dear friends Tracey, Pauline and Cliff who continue to champion my writing journey.

Writing can be a lonely process and I want to thank my Hampshire writing buddies, particularly Sally Russell and Anne Wan, plus Ant, Grethe,

Gill, Linda, Avril, Tania and Julie from the Harem. Also to the Hythe Writing Group who listened to some early chapters of this book, and the Scribblers of Bursledon – especially Eve, Maggie N and Dave, who have been unwavering in their support.

Finally, once again I'd like to thank Anna Britton for her editorial advice and Berni Stevens for creating another wonderful cover, and also thanks to Jane Usher for scrutinising the final copy of the manuscript.

ABOUT THE AUTHOR

Rosie Travers grew up in Southampton on the south coast of England. She loved escaping into a good book at a very early age and after landing her dream Saturday job as a teenager in WH Smith, she scribbled many stories and novels, none of which she was never brave enough to show anyone. After many years juggling motherhood and a variety of jobs in local government, Rosie's big break came when she moved to Southern California after her husband took an overseas work assignment. With time on her hands she started a blog about ex-pat life which rekindled her teenage desire to become a writer. On her return to the UK she took a creative writing course and the rest, as they say, is history.

Trouble on the Tide is Rosie's fifth novel and the third in a series of cosy mysteries featuring professional golfer turned amateur sleuth, Eliza Kane.

You can find out more about Rosie and her writing at www.rosietravers.com.

ALSO BY ROSIE TRAVERS

A Crisis at Clifftops
(Eliza Kane Investigates Book One)

The Puzzle of Pine Bay
(Eliza Kane Investigates Book Two

The Theatre of Dreams

Your Secret's Safe With Me

Printed in Great Britain
by Amazon